A WOLF ON THE FOLD

A WOLF ON THE FOLD

DONAL GREAVES

authorHOUSE®

AuthorHouse™
1663 Liberty Drive
Bloomington, IN 47403
www.authorhouse.com
Phone: 1-800-839-8640

This is a novel in which all the characters are fictitious and there is no intention to criticise anyone extant or any state or country. True events are already well documented in history.

Published by AuthorHouse   09/24/2012

ISBN: 978-1-4772-3155-5 (sc)
ISBN: 978-1-4772-3156-2 (e)

TABLE OF CONTENTS

§ SYNOPSIS

Captain Miles Scholland of the Royal Marine Commando Force takes leave from his duties as an Assistant Liaison Officer with the British contingent of the U.N. in Lebanon to spend time with his wife Candida. The couple's daughter Patricia being resident in a private boarding school.

Towards the end of a happy and loving reunion while touring the Northern part of Israel, The couple become innocently caught up in the repulse, by the Israeli Defence Force, of a group of terrorists who have breached the security of the northern border.

In the melee, the wounded Captain's wife dies of her injuries after being removed from the blazing vehicle they had hired. After hospitalisation for his wounds, the broken hearted Officer resigns his commission and tries to find solace and peace of mind roaming the

Scottish Highlands. However, another bad experience completes the deterioration of his mental state and he turns to crime.

He abandons his daughter to the care of her Aunt and over the years gains a reputation for being a hard man and a fixer. Also, where the remuneration for a deed is enticing enough, an executioner. He jumps at the chance of what he terms 'vengeance' for his wife's death when offered a large sum by a member of a quartet of illegal arms dealers to assassinate members of the Jewish Parliament and if possible the Prime Minister of Israel.

The story deals with the journey of Scholland alias 'Candor', through France by road and air and from there to Israel. The attempts made by the police of Britain and France to apprehend him and the Mossad's surveillance of him. The deaths of the various men and women who have the misfortune to come into conflict with him and his eventual failure to carry out his task.

Having lost contact with his daughter over the years, he is unaware that she has married a Jew she met while they were both at the same college. The young man subsequently becomes an agent of the Mossad and is unaware of the true identity of Candor.

Together with another Mossad agent, Aaron Plaistot, the young man Hiram Woolley, is responsible for the discovery of Candor in Jerusalem after the tracking of him across Southern France by Plaistot and another man, a double agent in the French Police. The double agent, Hassan Mradmoor, of Algerian extraction, is murdered by Candor while assisting in the surveillance of him. Hiram, meanwhile, makes a grave error and is trapped in the same aircraft as Candor when he boards the plane to leave France and narrowly avoids discovery by the assassin.

In the final chapter Candor and an accomplice, Hussein Muhkram, are pursued through Jerusalem by the two Mossad agents, Plaistot and Woolley. Plaistot is wounded by Muhkram, leaving the pursuit of Candor to Hiram alone.

However, unknown to Hiram, the action and chase has been followed by his wife, she having witnessed Plaistot and Hiram's odd behaviour before the pursuit, from a table in a café.

She sees the shooting of Plaistot and aquiring the fallen agent's pistol, catches up with Hiram in time to see his life threatened by Candor. So many years have passed since, as a schoolgirl, she last saw Candor and not recognising him as her Father, her only concern being for her husband's safety, she shoots the assassin with Plaistot's weapon. Eventually, she is made aware of the wounded man's true identity and devastated, unable to come to terms with the reality of what she has done, decides to go back to her Aunt's for a holiday with her wounded husband.

§ CHAPTER 1

Candor purchased an evening paper from the newsagent and tobacconist at the street corner. The week had passed quickly by but, having no plans for the next few months he had decided the payment for carrying out Jordan's job was too good to miss. Here was the chance to avenge himself and his wife on the Israelis and get paid to do it. No matter what the snags and difficulties might be, he was confident he could succeed.

He opened the paper to check his answer to Jordan had been printed in the personal column. He relaxed when he read the words 'To J, O.K. Will Do'.

So Jordan would have seen it too he knew. He folded the paper and deposited it in the first waste bin he saw, it had served its purpose and he had no further use for it. Only the advertisement was relevant, the rest was of no interest to him.

The following Monday evening at eight p.m. the weather cold and dank, Candor pressed the bell push on the club door. The eye appeared once more at the spy hole and then the door opened. The giant looked at him but said nothing, standing back to allow him access to the foyer, he was grateful he hadn't had to wait for long on the step. As he glanced across towards the office door,feeling some relief at the increase in temperature in the room, he felt a tap on his arm and looked around to see the attendant standing there with a sealed parcel. 'Hyam told me you'd be here; he gave me this for you'.

Candor took the parcel, surprised at its weight. It was tied up with string and this was fastened to the paper wrapping with adhesive tape at the knots. Not a fool proof method to prevent examination of the contents thought Candor. Although removal of the tape would damage the wrapper and show it had been tampered with, the whole thing could have been re-covered in the same manner and none the wiser.

'Still' he mused, 'I doubt if Hyam would chance the wrath of Jordan finding out he'd succumbed to temptation and opened it up'. He glanced at the attendant.

'This all there is?' he asked.

The man shrugged his shoulders. Candor turned and left the club, into the gloom of the poorly lit street and feeling the drop in temperature again, the parcel under his arm.

The club premises were strictly private, just tolerated by the law. The club boasted a carefully selected membership and admittance to non-members was restricted to those accompanied by card carriers. Located in a shabby back street of the country's second Capital, members and their guests arrived and departed at their own risk. Parking was restricted and Candor had been fortunate to find a space for the Jaguar for the second time. He waited on the top step outside the door for a short while, until his eyes became accustomed to the semi-darkness and keeping a careful watch for passers by. The November night was decidedly chilly and a faint dampness in the air made Candor shiver as he surveyed the street from his vantage point. Satisfied with what he saw, he descended the four steps to the pavement, keeping his eye on the man who was looking under the bonnet of a grey Granada parked a little way behind his own saloon.

He slid behind the wheel, keeping the man in view by the rear view mirror as he shut the door. The man slammed down the bonnet of the Granada and got in and Candor fancied he could then see two men sitting in the front seats. He knew he'd been followed away from the club on his last visit but had easily lost the tailing vehicle by his knowledge of the streets. His careful preparation and reconnoitre of the area before that last visit had paid off. This time however, he was interested in finding out who his pursuers were and their motives. He was unarmed. He rarely carried a weapon in the city unless he was on a specific job where a pistol was necessary. The risk of being apprehended by the police on some trivial driving offence, or other slight misdemeanour, might warrant a search of his person or the car, although a cursory examination would reveal nothing, but any ensuing investigations could be too dangerous for him and it was another reason why he seldom drank. He might need to drive at an inopportune moment, again risking police enquiry and an examination of his status. He had enough cover for routine questioning but could see no reason to jeopardise it by being caught armed or inebriated when it was unnecessary. He wondered if the two men in the Granada were armed. He smiled; he wasn't about to risk a confrontation with armed men. There were other ways of dealing with a situation and he knew most of them and in the past the knowledge had occasionally been invaluable.

One was the innocuous Volkswagon 'Beetle' parked about a mile away. Although Candor was a reasonably efficient mechanic, he only carried out emergency repairs to his vehicles such as wheel changing or pressure checking of the tyres. He believed in using the skills of experts whenever possible. The injection fuelled, turbo blown engine had not been fitted to the 'Beetle' by him, but by those experts. It had cost Candor a tidy sum, but it had served him well on more than one occasion.

He started the engine of the Jaguar, switched on the lights and pulled away from the kerb. After a few yards he saw, through the rear view mirror, the Granada follow suit. He smiled again, shaking his head slightly. If they only knew, he thought.

He took a left turn and then a right. Approaching a set of traffic lights at 'green', he judged the distance to them so that the lights changed to 'amber' while a few yards back from the white 'stop' line marked on the tarmac. He braked gently; then, as the red light glowed, he accelerated across the junction, narrowly missing a car from the left which was turning into the road he had just exited. The following car was trapped at the lights by the movement of the traffic and Candor took a left turn knowing his pursuers would see him do so.

The 'Beetle' was parked about thirty yards away on the left side of the street. He braked to a stop and hurriedly changed vehicles, accelerating rapidly away but taking care not to skid on the greasy road surface and turned right. Twenty yards down that street he did a three point turn and drove back, almost to the junction with the road in which he had left the Jaguar. He stopped the 'Beetle' in sight of the vacated saloon and switched off the engine and lights.

A few seconds later the Granada, tyres screaming, turned at speed into the road he was watching. There was a screech of brakes and the Granada's tyres left rubber on the road surface and the vehicle almost turned sideways across the road as the driver realised the parked Jaguar was the one they had been following. The driver realigned the car and pulled up in front of it and after a few seconds, seeing their quarry was no longer sat in it, the two men got out of their own and looked up and down the road, then had a quick look through the Jaguars windows, one of the men checking also that the doors were locked. This one, the passenger, gesticulated angrily at the other and then both got back into the Granada. A minute or so passed and Candor smiled as he could see the man in the passenger seat apparently remonstrating with the driver.

Eventually the Ford Granada made a turn in the road and left in the direction from which it had arrived. Candor started the 'Beetle' and followed. He soon spotted the car again and took station behind it at a discreet distance. He could see the shapes of the two men through the rear window of the Granada obviously still arguing. Candor smiled again.

The car took a different route from that which would have led back to the club and eventually stopped at a junction, where the passenger left the car and it then drove away.

Candor, who had stopped some fifty or so yards behind, watched the man turn into the side street. He vacated the 'Beetle, sprinted up to the junction and was just in time to see him walk up a short path to one of the row of semi-detached houses. In the dim glow of an adjacent street lamp the man fished in his pocket for his keys with which he opened the door. By his actions and the fact that there was no sign of lights from the premises, Candor assumed the house was empty of any other occupant, unless that occupant or occupants were early to bed.

There were no pedestrians to observe him as Candor approached the gate, slipped the catch and quickly walked up the path. As he did so, the glass in the front door was illuminated by the hall light so he moved round the side of the house to the back door and waited to see if the kitchen light would be switched on. That room's window remained in darkness so he carefully tried the door handle. The door was locked.

He hesitated for a moment then knocked on the door. There was no movement inside so he knocked again. He saw the kitchen light come on and heard the key turn in the lock. The door began to open. He kicked the door violently in and the man, who had been the passenger in the Granada, staggered back in surprise. Candor stepped in and with straight fingers hit the man just under the left collar bone, followed by a second straight fingered blow to the man's throat, before the man could cry out in his agony from the first blow.

The man collapsed like an empty sack, his left arm useless and full of pain, like fire from the damaged nerve, clutching his throat with his right hand. He writhed on the floor, choking and gasping, his face red and distorted and obviously in fear of his assailant, not having any previous knowledge how dangerous the man was. Hyam had not prepared him for this and in his fear cursing him for not making him aware.

Candor closed the door and quickly drew the curtains. He pulled the man's right hand away from his throat and turned him over on to his stomach as he reached for the towel on the rail by the door. He placed a foot in the small of the back of his victim while he expertly tore the towel into strips. With these he tied the man's arms and legs together and rolled him on to his side. There was even more fear as well as pain in the man's eyes as he lay there, knowing he and his partner had seriously under-estimated the man who was now expertly going through his pockets, checking for hidden weapons, of which there were none.

Candor dragged a chair up by the man's head and sat down, waiting for him to recover enough so that he could answer his questions. Eventually, the man lay quietly, moaning a little. Saliva mixed with blood ran from his mouth and a large bruise was gathering at his neck. A little harder, thought Candor and he would never have talked again.

He tapped the man's head with the toe of his shoe and the man winced, cringing, awaiting the expected blow.

'I'm going to ask you a few questions' said Candor, 'I don't want any rubbish answers or you'll regret it even more than you do at the moment. Understand me?'

The man was silent. Candor reached down and pressed on a nerve in the junction of the man's neck and collar bone. His body writhed and he gasped again, uttering rasping moans of pain.

'That was question number one' said Candor, releasing the pressure. 'I want answers. I haven't come here for the pleasure of your bloody company'.

'All right, all right', gasped the man in a husky, obviously painful voice, 'what do you want?' The words were spoken with difficulty.

'That's better' said his tormentor. 'Now we can get somewhere. First, who lives here with you?'

'Only the girl friend, but she's away for a bit'.

'Fine, fine. You expecting anyone else?'

'No'.

'What were you following me for?'

The man hesitated, but, as Candor reached down again, he thought better of it and was quick to reply. He wanted no more of Candor's persuasion methods.

'We was told to, me and Offton, the driver. We meant no 'arm' he offered.' We was on'y doin' wot we was told.'

Candor smiled. 'No harm received' he mocked. 'Who told you to follow me?' he demanded.

Again for a second, the man hesitated, reluctant to risk the acrimony of his employer, but unable to defend himself from further suffering at the hands of his inquisitor.

'Hyam. Hyam told us to find out where you was staying. I don't know why 'e wanted to know. I only do an occasional job fer 'im, guv, 'onest'.

Candor considered for a moment. 'As I expected' he thought, 'Hyam's not only careful, but wants to see if he can profit from the meeting I had with Jordan'.

'Where does Hyam live?' he asked.

'I don't know guv, 'onest, I only sees 'im when 'e sends fer me at the club'.

'No matter' thought Candor. 'What to do with the fellow though?'

As if reading his thoughts, the man on the floor gasped out, 'onest guv, yer know as much as me now. I won't split it was you wot done me. I ain't no threat ter you'. His eyes were wide and full of fear.

Candor had survived by taking extreme caution in every thing he did. Leaving witnesses to his activities was not his method. Without a word he got up and began looking in cupboards and drawers. Eventually he found what he was searching for, a roll of two inch wide, brown adhesive tape. He returned to the man on the floor and bound the tape quickly and effectively around the protesting, struggling man's head. He passed the tape under the man's chin and over the top of his head, preventing him from opening his mouth.

Then he wound it round and round the front and back of his head, completely covering the man's mouth, nose and eyes.

Candor left the man thrashing about on the bare, tiled floor trying to rid himself of his bonds. His head was twisting backwards and forwards, rubbing against the uncarpeted floor of the kitchen in a vain attempt to dislodge the adhesive tape.

Candor closed the kitchen door behind him and after wiping the handle; he had also wiped the kitchen chair before he left; walked around the side of the house; taking great care that no-one should see him leave. He shut the front gate behind him, knowing the man would be dead before he'd reached it. He walked quickly back to the 'Beetle' and had started the engine before he realised he hadn't even asked the man for his name. He shrugged; the man's name was of no importance. He had found out who wanted him followed and he was sure the man's death could not be traced to himself. What to do about Hyam was another matter. Perhaps he need do nothing and decided it would have to 'lie on the file' for the time being. He wanted to study the contents of the parcel. He switched on the headlights and dove away to the lock up garage where he put the 'Beetle' away until he required it again.

Walking from the garage to a phone booth, he called a minicab and took a ride to a public house near to where he'd parked the Jaguar. After the cab left, he walked to the car and examined it carefully with the aid of his small pocket torch before unlocking it and driving away. As he drove he reflected on the meeting

he'd had with Jordan only a few days before and the
subsequent events which had already resulted in the
death of the man who's house he had just left and about
which he had no regrets.

Those few days had passed quickly and as
he reflected on the way the meeting had gone he
remembered in his mind the manner in which he had
met Jordon and the man's obvious power over his
subordinates at the club. While ringing the doorbell
Candor had looked at the small round hole in the heavy
hardwood door. An eye had appeared there as the cover
on the inside of the door over the hole was moved
aside. After a couple of seconds or so, the cover had
been replaced and after another brief interval the door
had swung slowly open.

§ CHAPTER 2

A giant of a man, well over six feet tall, Candor surmised, with body to match, glared at him, barring his entry.

'Hyam in?' asked Candor.

'Who wants him?' retorted the giant.

'Candor. He's expecting me!'

The door slammed shut in his face and Candor took the opportunity to take a few deep lungs full of the air available outside the building before he was given entry. Another few minutes elapsed and as Candor was about to press the bell push again, the door re-opened.

The giant, making no comment, stood back giving just enough room for the visitor to enter.

Candor was glad he'd ventilated his lungs before entering the room. The atmosphere inside was thick with tobacco smoke and drink fumes. It was also evident that smoke other than the product of burnt tobacco was in the mixture. The dozen or so of the clientele who had donned evening dress for the occasion of their visit must have regretted their choice in the heat of that room. Candor had the impression the heat was turned up to ensure the continuous imbibing of the various drinks being distributed by the scantily clad waitresses. They, dressed in ultra short skirts, black net tights and high heeled shoes, might as well have been topless, Candor thought, for all the good the deep cleavage blouses did for their modesty. They were indeed, in great demand, supplying their various drinks, proving to him his belief about the efficacy of the heating arrangements.

The room hummed with conversation, the occasional shrill laugh from one of the long gowned females and the click of chips being stacked or drawn in by the rake of the croupiers. Dice rattled, as the bright eyed, sweating, but hopeful punters staked their bids on the right spots being uppermost when the dice eventually came to rest.

Cards were being dealt and bet upon at some tables; spinning roulette wheels determined solvency or bankruptcy at others as the nervous onlookers waited in anticipation for the benevolence, or otherwise, of the whimsical Lady Luck.

Candor stood for a moment surveying the scene with a slight look of distaste on his features, not being a gambler himself, searching for the person with whom he had an appointment. A door, with a mirror in the upper half, at the back of the room opened and a man appeared there, beckoning Candor across as he caught the visitor's eye. Candor descended the two steps into the well of the room and moved towards the door, ignoring the overtures of the waitresses whose hard eyes belied their seductive smiles. The man who had beckoned him stood aside, unspeaking and he entered the small room behind the mirrored door which closed behind him.

A large grey haired man sat at the desk and a smaller man, dressed in an expensive looking evening suit glanced at Candor from the comfort of a deep, leather upholstered arm chair. The man who had admitted Candor to the presence of the two men was waved away by the man at the desk and he left, quietly opening again the door to pass through and closing it behind him.

Candor did not fail to notice the book shelves behind the desk had vertical divisions about a door width apart. He surmised there was probably a bolt hole there, suggesting the large grey haired man was a careful individual who left as little as possible to chance, unlike the clientele in the larger room he had just left.

The large man spoke, surprisingly, in a high falsetto; Candor wondered if that had any significance, but decided the man's characteristics were not of any interest to himself.

'I'm Hyam' he said, 'Have you any identification?' the big man asked.

As Candor reached for his wallet, Hyam's hand went into an open drawer of the desk by his knee. Candor grimaced and hesitated for a second then undid the button of his jacket with his right hand, pulling it aside with his left. He reached slowly into the inside pocket and extracted his wallet. Hyam removed his hand from the drawer and held it out for the driving licence Candor proffered which he had removed from the wallet.

Hyam, not having taken his eyes off Candor since he entered the room, got to his feet and handed the document to the man in the leather armchair. He took it and obviously satisfied with a quick examination of it, nodded his head and gave it back to Hyam. The big man tapped it on the palm of his left hand a few times as though pondering on some idea he'd had, then with a shrug of his broad shoulders, tossed it back to Candor. The visitor replaced it in his wallet which he put back into the inside pocket of his jacket.

Hyam sat down again. He took a cigar box from a desk drawer and offered the opened box to Candor who declined the offer with a shake of his head.

Taking one himself, Hyam took off the band, snipped off the end and after passing it slowly under his nose, sniffing the aroma of the Havana tobacco, he placed the snipped end into a silver holder and gripped the mouthpiece in his teeth. He took up a monogrammed lighter, also of silver, from the desk top and carefully, sucking gently on the mouthpiece, lit the cigar. He puffed out clouds of the aromatic smoke.

Candor's nose wrinkled and he grimaced again. He was becoming impatient. He shifted his weight on his feet; the fact that there was no other seating accommodation annoyed him.

'How long does this charade last?' He asked, 'I came here on business at your request. This childish messing about doesn't impress me. If you've got a proposition, let's hear it, otherwise, I have better things to do with my time!

The man in the evening suit straightened himself in the armchair and said 'Yes, I think Mr. Candor should be informed what this is all about Hyam'.

The use of the title for his name and not for Hyam didn't escape Candor's notice. He looked at the speaker.

'You know my name' he said, 'I don't know yours. That places me at a disadvantage. I don't like that situation!'

'Never mind that' smiled the man in the armchair. 'I doubt it's your true name anyway, but, if you're not at ease about it, call me Jordan, most of my acquaintances do'.

'That will do for me', shrugged Candor, 'what's this all about then?'

'I've got a job for you, if you're interested' said Jordan.

'I wouldn't be here if I wasn't; who is it to be?' Candor asked.

'The name doesn't matter at the moment. In fact I should say; names don't matter. This is a big job and because of the importance there's a bonus, besides double the rate you usually ask for. A very large bonus; fifty thousand pounds!' He sat back in the chair, looking for signs of the impression the offer should have made on the man who stood before him.

Though intrigued, Candor's face remained unaltered. He did a swift, mental calculation. The figure arrived at in his head was a large sum, he had to admit. A hell of a large sum. There must be a catch.

'What's the snag?' he asked.

'This job isn't going to be easy' replied the man in the armchair, slightly disappointed at Candor's apparent lack of incredulity which he had expected. He continued; 'The people involved are very important, fully protected. Lots of security around and what's more, the job's got to be done on a certain date. That date is approximately five months from now. You may think that's a long way off, but you'll need that time to finish any other jobs you've got and to prepare for this one.'

'Where does it happen?' asked Candor.

'That's another reason for the large bonus' said Jordan. He looked at the gold wrist watch on his podgy arm and rose from the chair. He said 'the job's in Israel!'

He carefully straightened the black bow tie, the gold rings on his fingers glinting in the light from the room lamp. Candor noticed also the sparkle from the cuff links as the coat sleeves rode up above the white, silk shirt cuffs. The man was immaculately turned out, he admitted, but he, himself was unimpressed with shows of finery, especially in the male.

'I've got to go now. You've got one week to decide; to make up your mind about it. You put an ad. in the usual paper next Friday. If you accept, you'll get all the details on the Monday, after I've seen the ad. You stay here five minutes after I leave'.

Jordan turned, ignoring Hyam who had got up from his desk seat and left without a backward glance. Hyam sat down again.

'Take a pew', he said to Candor in his high falsetto and waved his arm at the armchair vacated by Jordan.

Candor glanced at him and without a word, sat down in the armchair. He looked at his watch. He waited the five minutes stipulated by Jordan and while he did so, speculated on what the job, as involved as it must prove to be, would entail. One hundred thousand pounds was a lot of money even in those inflated times, he mused. Who could be worth that sort of cash? And why in five months time? He mentally calculated what the date would be and decided the end of March or the beginning of April held no significance as far as he could see, but obviously had some meaning as far as Jordan was concerned. He decided his first priority was to consult a good calendar and see what important dates, during the period beginning in five months, would give him a clue to the job.

The location didn't worry him at all. He'd carried out dangerous assignments abroad before, both on British and foreign territory. He conceded Israel was a dangerous area, as he knew to his cost. The knowledge that a visit to that part of the world again was a probability, awakened old memories and feelings which he had, for some years, kept buried in his mind. The hate he had felt then and which had changed his life began to stir in him again. The mental pain, the grief and the loneliness he had endured then-and afterwards, welled up as he thought about Candy. He rose from the armchair, his face white and fierce as he forced the memories back, trying to concentrate on what Jordan's job would mean.

Hyam straightened in his chair behind the desk at Candor's movement, about to say something, but seeing the look on Candor's face, kept silent. He knew of the man's reputation well enough to be wary of upsetting him. He glanced at the watch on his wrist; the five minutes were past anyway, he decided and pressed the buzzer button on his desk.

The attendant who had beckoned the visitor from across the club's games room floor opened the door and came in. Hyam shook his head and the man stood back as Candor left, alert again, his mental control re-established.

He noticed that the door he had entered and left by, had a curtain covering the upper half on the inside. The curtain had moved slightly in the draught caused by the opening of the door. It was possible to see into the main room of the club through the top half of the door. The mirror was a one way window. It served to confirm Candor's suspicion that Hyam was a careful individual.

Observing his usual precautions, he'd left the club and seeing no-one behaving suspiciously, walked over to his car. The large Jaguar saloon parked at the kerb did not seem to have received any attention from would be assassins, as far as his examination of it had revealed. He always checked it thoroughly before getting in behind the steering wheel and feeling and looking under the dash board to see that no wires were added or disturbed and his few minutes of caution had paid off on several occasions.

As he'd settled himself in, checking the rear view mirrors for any sign of vehicular activity which could have meant the possibility of a 'tail' as he left, Candor had thought again about the job Jordan had underlined for him.

He knew there was a lot of security surrounding Israeli figureheads and the people generally, were fanatical in their support of them. He knew also of their hatred of external influences on their Nationality. When Jordan had mentioned the location his heart had quickened its beat, his long experience of remaining calm in a crisis had prevented his revealing to the two men there, his inner turmoil.

Then he had driven away to consider what would be the best for himself, but already convinced that he could carry out the task he had been asked to accept.

Thinking of its implications for himself now brought to him a feeling of pleasure. At last he would be able to avenge himself on those he believed were responsible for Candy's death and the misery her loss had caused him. The scene where she had lain in his arms dying, never left him and those he believed to be responsible, had to pay. The more he thought of it the more determined he became to carry out that revenge. He began to ache for the moment of retribution. Yes!

The job would serve Jordan's motives and give himself peace. He was anxious to right what he believed had been the injustice of the past.

'So, now it has begun' he mused, 'I wonder what's in the parcel'

He arrived at the rented garage close by the one occupied by the 'Beetle' and locked the Jaguar away, the incident resulting in the death of Hyam's hireling already banished from his mind.

§ CHAPTER 3

Commander Allfield was uneasy. He put down the small watering can by the side of the cupboard on which he kept the collection of house plants he had been watering. It was a ritual he carried out every day before beginning the day's work. He didn't trust his secretary to do the task. She either over-watered them or else forgot to carry out his detailed instructions at the regular time he had stipulated. His wife's Pomeranian dog lay on its temporary bed on the floor at the end of his desk and always seemed to keep an eye on the door, its head resting on its forepaws.

The Commander leaned over the desk and put down the 'talk' switch on his intercom.

'Yes sir?' his secretary asked.

'Get hold of Oakey. Tell him I want to see him as soon as he can manage it. Tell him it's important'.

'I think he's around now sir. I'll just go and see'.
She got out of her seat and wandered out of her office
to the veranda where below, standing on the next
landing, she spied the Chief Superintendent giving
some instructions to a junior officer. She waved to
him giving him a sign by holding her cupped hand to
her ear. He understood straight away that Commander
Allfield was wanting him and excused himself to the
officer with whom he had been talking and began to
climb the stairs to the Commander's office.

Commander Allfield just grunted when he heard the
secretary's reply and walked to the window, thinking.

A few minutes later there was a knock on the door.

'Come in' requested the Commander, turning to see
the door open and the tall, thin, balding man with the
insignia of a Chief Superintendent on his uniform and a
worried look on his features enter, keeping a wary eye
on the Pomeranian. He'd crossed swords with the animal
once and didn't want to repeat the experience, he still felt
the tingle of the scar on his ankle each time he saw it and
had been disappointed when the incident occurred that
his superior had only tutted at the animal in response to
its behaviour. Arthur Oakey had expected the animal to
have received some chastisement as a punishment.

'You wanted to see me sir?' asked the visitor. He
wore the uniform as litttle as he thought he could get
away with; he thought that to wear it all the time meant
that he couldn't always keep out of the sight of the
Commander; and his whisky.

'Yes Arthur, take a seat. Would you like a drink?'
The Commander opened the cupboard door and took

out a tray with glasses and a nearly full bottle of, which was unusual thought the Chief Superintendent, fine, malt, Scotch whisky on it, which he placed at the end of the cupboard top. Arthur Oakey knew that the Commander made use of any type of whisky. This must be a present he thought.

'No thank you sir' hopefully replied the Chief Superintendent. It was known throughout the building of the Commander's love of a dram or two at any time of the day, but the Chief Superintendent felt, that just after breakfast was really a little too early.

The Commander poured himself a generous measure and seated himself at his desk and took a sip of the amber liquid. He rolled it around his mouth with evident satisfaction before swallowing it. He put the glass down and said,

'You're sure you wouldn't like a drop?' The chief Superintendent waved both his hands in a negative gesture. 'All right then; now Arthur, I want to knock an idea about with you'.

'Sir?' queried Arthur Oakey.

'Yes, I have a bit of a problem. One of our people is keeping 'tabs' on a club owner named Hyam'.

Oakey nodded his head. 'Yes, this person is working at the club for me under cover' said the Commander 'You've knowledge of that gentleman eh?'

'Well he does have a reputation for having an interest in every dirty activity around sir' agreed Oakey.

'Yes. I've been having him watched for some time and now there seems to have been a development. Though to be honest, I'm not sure that Hyam is directly involved. Just an intermediary, I'd say. Anyway, our person was in a position to observe Hyam's club have two unusual visitors. Two men, one of whom she had never seen there before apparently; one who arrived about ten minutes before the other is known to us. He, along with others, is suspected of supplying weapons to various underground movements and not in this country; no! in France. Though a careful watch has been kept on this fellow and his accomplices, if that's the proper word, we've never been able to get him on a charge to get hold of his files and records. Were it possible to do that, we could probably substantiate our beliefs. Anyway, I'm working on that side of things as are the French too. 'By the way, this fellow was heard to be called 'Jordan' to this second visitor. Now that's odd you see because we know him as William Somers; that's definite. Be that as it may, our person was sure of his true identity. Definitely Somers she said. Ah', he gritted his teeth, 'how remiss of me. Now you know our person is female. No matter'.

Chief Superintendent Oakey could see the Commander was annoyed with himself for his slip, identifying the informer as 'she'. He liked to keep everybody ignorant of everyone elses activities, or at least, their identification. Even to reveal their gender was anathema to him. Probably due to his war training in Intelligence, Oakey thought; what one didn't know, one couldn't tell.

'What does matter' the Commander continued, 'is what he was doing there. He was taken into Hyam's office and when the second visitor arrived, as I said, about ten minutes afterwards, he was also taken in there. They had a 'pow-wow' for about a quarter of an hour and then Somers, or Jordan, as he was called at the club, left. He was followed about five minutes later by the second visitor; name unknown. He did give his name to the doorman on his arrival, but our person did not have any luck finding out what it was. Incidently we're trying to get a secret microphone hidden in that office so that we can tape any conversation between any people there, because of what goes on. We'll manage it eventually no doubt'.

He paused and took another sip from the glass.

'Would this second man be one of Somers accomplice's Sir, do you think?' Oakey asked, noting that the Commander had reverted to 'our person' instead of 'her'.

'Well, I'm not sure about that because we have a good idea who two of the other three are. That is, we think there are four of them working as a sort of 'Rogues Company'. One's name is Wessing and the third is Moorwood. Now it is possible the fourth man is this second visitor at Hyam's place, but we cannot be sure until we can check it out. It is believed he's really resident in France somewhere and what has brought him here we'd like to know. Unfortunately, though our person gave us a good description we have no-one in the records to fit it. That's something you can do for me Arthur. I'll get you the description and you can put a man on it. He may have more luck than we've had. Funny thing though' he went on 'our person knows that two men who do Hyam's errands for him were going to follow this second visitor. Apparently they made a hash of it and lost him and Hyam was not pleased. The other odd thing is, that he turned up again some days later and was handed a brown paper parcel.

'Now then, when he left, our person managed to get out of the club via the toilet and got round in time to see this fellow leave in his Jaguar. He was followed again by the same pair'.

'Do we know the Jaguar sir?' interrupted Oakey.

'We have the number but it proved to be false. As I was saying', he went on, looking a trifle piqued by the interruption, 'He was followed by the same pair; but, our person has since reported that one of those two men who were involved in that 'tail' was a man whom later, the local police found dead, in mysterious circumstances, in his home. He had been attacked and killed; his name was Ambrow'.

The Commander finished the whisky in the glass and got up from the desk. He rinsed the glass in the small sink he'd had installed, returned the glass to the tray and the tray back into the cupboard.

'That's the trouble I was talking about at the beginning. We don't know yet if this murder is connected with our second visitor or not. It may be he'd been a nuisance to someone else who he'd been following on Hyam's instructions-or whatever. There could be several reasons for his untimely demise. One thing we are sure about, it wasn't a casual killing, by a burglar, say. No,no! This man was killed by a professional; someone who knows 'martial arts' as they call them nowadays'.

Here his lip curled and he wandered off the theme for a second.

'In my day it was called unarmed combat'. He went once more to the cupboard, opened the door behind which stood the tray, bottle and glasses. But then, apparently, thought better of it and closed the door again. He sat down behind the desk.

'Anyway, that's beside the point. It was a cold blooded, merciless killing by someone who wanted him out of the way for some reason or, to make sure he didn't reveal the killer's identity. If it was the latter and that would be my guess, it seems a bit extreme to kill him just to prevent him revealing who you are to a man like Hyam. Unless and again this is my view, you wish to remain so covert in your activities you want no-one to know about you'.

He shook his head, his lips pursed.

'In other words, perhaps an agent for a foreign power, or and I hope to God I'm wrong, an agent for ourselves. Someone even I don't know about, belonging to the other lot; or again, which is more likely, a professional killer who kills for reward. The latter is, in my view the correct one'.

He looked away from the Superintendent towards the window.

'You know Arthur? I think I'm getting too old for this job. The villains we knew in our day; our young days that is; they were a different breed to this lot now. In some ways you had a kind of respect for them; perhaps not respect exactly, but maybe an understanding of their reasons. Their needs and motives for doing what they did. But this modern criminal, well, I don't know what to think of them. They're too callous by half, I'm still not sure that getting rid of the rope was a good thing in a lot of cases'.

He shivered and looked again at the Superintendent who, until then had said nothing, but was thinking the Commander was expressing his own personal view.

'Well Arthur. What do you think about it? I've told you all I know at the moment. I can't think of anything else relevant to the account'.

Chief Superintendent Arthur Oakey cleared his throat. 'I was thinking about what you said about your theory being that the murderer was an agent or professional killer. If he is, then he's made his first mistake in going to Hyam's club. We have his description. In other words, he's been brought to our notice. The only reserve I have there is that he might be cleverer than we think. He may have given a false description to-er our person, deliberately. In other words what our person saw was not the real him'.

'Yes, I think I see what you mean'.

The Commander pulled at his lower lip.

'In that case he is a professional. A false description, false number plates on his car. In other words we know absolutely nothing about him except that he visited the club twice and on the second visit took charge of a parcel. He was followed by two men after both visits; one of whom was murdered after the second visit; on the same night, incidentally, that this man left the club with the parcel.

'This leads me to believe that after he lost them he then followed their car and saw off this chap, found dead at his house. He, the murdered man, must have been dropped off by the other at his home, unless the one who dropped him off murdered him, which is a theory I don't and can't believe'.

'In that case sir, it's more than likely he changed cars isn't it?' suggested Oakey.

'Yes, I think you're right Arthur, he must have had two cars'.

The Commander made some notes on a pad.

'Yes, this fellow is very efficient; he seems to leave nothing to chance. My God, I'd love to know what was in that parcel'.

'I don't suppose there would be any point in bringing Hyam in?' asked Oakey.

'I doubt it. I did think of getting hold of the other man in the car that Hyam sent, but he probably knows less than us, but make your own mind up about that. Whichever way you look at it, we seem to be completely in the dark at the moment. No doubt Hyam has his suspicions about his hired man's death. He'll be very cagey now. Probably wondering what he's let himself in for, especially if, as I think, he was just the host in that meeting between Somers and our anonymous man. They were just using his club as a rendezvous point, it seems it's been done before'.

'Yes. It's a tough nut sir. We've little to go on', agreed Chief Superintendent Oakey.

'Well Arthur, I'm putting you in charge of this inquiry. No need for me to tell you to be discreet about what you let out to your men, keep a tight knit circle, I'll get our person in the club to keep in touch with you and pass on anything found out directly to you. Now, I've got to get on. I've a meeting with the Minister at eleven. But don't forget to keep me informed about what conclusions you come to from the knowledge you get'.

As the chief Superintendent was about to leave, the Commander said, 'Incidentally Arthur; if this fellow is who we assume he is, it's a pound to a penny he's not that fourth member of the organisation we were talking about. We've therefore still to find out who that gentleman is and where in France he keeps himself'.

'Yes sir, I'll bear that in mind', replied Oakey looking a little more worried than when he entered the Commander's office although he was pleased that the Pomeranian seemed to ignore his presence this time.

The Commander did not seem to have heard Oakey's reply. He was already shuffling papers on his desk. It was a dismissal.

Chief Superintendent Arthur Oakey turned and left. As he closed the door behind him he rubbed his chin and frowned. He had plenty to occupy his mind, but grateful he had not been coersed into drinking the Commander's whisky and had been ignored by the dog.

§ CHAPTER 4

Hyam paced up and down the office floor chewing on the cigar holder, blowing out clouds of smoke and muttering to himself in his high pitched voice. The man who had opened the door to Candor on his visits was standing quietly, wondering what would happen when Hyam eventually came to a decision. He had, on occasion, been the subject of Hyam's wrath and knew the man could be extremely cruel. Very few people had crossed him and got away without scars of one sort or another. Hyam was big, but seldom used his own muscle on his victims. He had plenty of subordinates only too willing to comply with his orders so that they could achieve favours of one sort or another. One of those men, Ambrow, trying to comply with one of Hyam's orders, was now dead and Hyam was convinced that Candor had been the instrument of the man's death, there could be no other explanation about who was responsible. He was also afraid. His attitude and his behaviour betrayed his fear. His thoughts about the man when he'd been in the club were now confirmed.

The man, Ambrow, was of no importance to Hyam, but the reasons for his death made him aware that the murderer killed without compunction. The death of the man was a warning to himself that any enquiry about the killer, in any form, would not be tolerated. Hyam had been warned off and didn't like it. At the same time he was very worried and at a loss to know what he could do about it without any danger to himself.

He was annoyed that the two hirelings had not been able to find Candor's base. Jordan knew how to contact Candor, but Hyam didn't want to just contact him. He wanted to keep him under observation for his own advantage. It had been his intention to use the meeting between Jordan and Candor to find out what Jordan was up to. It hadn't turned out that way. He had to be careful with Jordan too, who had a lot of powerful friends. Hyam knew that he, himself, was only tolerated whilst he was of some use to Jordan. If that usefulness disappeared, he knew he would have a hard time carrying on the activities he now did.

The club had been a handy meeting place for Jordan when his clients came to the city. Hyam had been compensated for the use of his club in many ways and he didn't want to alienate Jordan and lose the business contacts to whom Jordan had recommended Hyam. Besides it was not just the loss of business. Hyam knew that if he crossed Jordan, that gentleman would have no hesitation in putting him into permanent retirement. He decided it seemed as though he could do nothing about it, just play along and hope for something to turn up to his own advantage.

Whatever it was being planned by Jordan and he knew it was something big, it looked as though he, himself, was not going to make any capital out of it. The knowledge rankled and it ate at his ego which had taken a battering. Being warned off went against the grain. He had another worry. He wondered if Ambrow's death would have any repercussions on his relationship with Jordan should he hear about it and find out there was a connection between the murder and Jordan's business with Candor. A connection which could only mean Hyam's involvement, as the murdered man was acting under orders from Hyam when he died. It looked as though he would have to call 'pass' on it and he had better try to cover his tracks too. His frustration boiled and he vented his anger on the attendant by the door as he dumped the half smoked cigar in the cuspidor.

'Get out of here, damn you and send Rita in and be quick about it'.

The man went out without a word, glad of a respite from Hyam's ire. He felt sorry for Rita and had often wondered how the girl managed to tolerate the attentions of the club owner. One thing he was sure of, Hyam would have cooled down by the time he had to face him again.

CHAPTER 5

Candor looked speculatively at the object on the table. He considered that the whole affair could be an elaborate charade to get rid of him. A trap, set up by Jordan, perhaps as a favour for one of his cronies who had perhaps, in the past, been the object of Candor's attention.

On the other hand it might just be exactly what it was supposed to be, a parcel of plans and instructions. He had already taken some precautions. The thing contained no magnetic material, or conductive material; his attempts to pass an electric current through it from a safe distance had resulted in failure.

He had removed the outer wrapper, albeit carefully and not without a slight increase in his pulse rate His assumption that the brown paper covering would not be attached to a trigger device, because of the necessity for others beside himself to handle it, had proved correct.

On removing the wrapping, a cardboard shoe box, which had once contained a pair of size ten brogues, had been revealed. The lid was held down on the four sides by short lengths of adhesive scotch tape. He had earlier obtained an empty shoe box of similar dimensions and filled it with several sheets of writing paper. This he had weighed and compared that weight with the weight of the one he had been given. He was satisfied the slight difference in weight was acceptable.

The box didn't rattle when shook and he took up the roll of adhesive tape and a pair of scissors he'd found in the kitchen drawer of the man he had killed earlier that evening. He took them with the box out into the walled garden of the house he was renting.

Searching around with his torch, he found a piece of plywood board in the garage and taped the box securely to it, laying the box on its side. He placed this at the top of the garden and weighted the board down with odds and ends of stones, bricks and lumber from the untidy surroundings. He took down the clothes line from its posts and taped one end to the lid of the box, laying the thin cord backwards and forwards across it to get a good purchase on it. He removed the scotch tape from two of the sides holding down the lid and satisfied, laid out the cord along the garden path. He took refuge around the corner of the garage.

He had assumed that there was no danger at all from the box; if he had been more unsure about the thing he would have taken the whole arrangement to some more private spot in case there was an explosion needing explanation, but there was no sense in taking no precautions at all.

He pulled tentatively at the clothes line, taking up the slack. He took a deep breath and reached out from the garage wall, gripped firmly on the line and gave a sudden heave on it. The cord jerked loose. He waited a few seconds and then hauled it in until the torn lid of the box came into his hands.

He peered round the wall into the blackness at the top of the garden. He shone his torch to where the box lay on the plywood base. He saw something white in the beam of the light and throwing further caution aside, walked up the garden path. The box lay open revealing a pile of folded papers. To make doubly sure of its harmlessness he took the clothes prop and retreating as far as he could, considering the length of the prop, poked at it from an almost prone position on the garden path. He heard only the rustle of papers; nothing else. Satisfied, he got up and retrieved the box and the papers he had displaced, by his efforts to ensure his safety.

He tidied up, putting everything he had used back into its original place. Taking a last look round, he took the box and papers and the used strips of adhesive tape back into the house. He placed the papers on the table and burnt the box and tape in the kitchen grate. He didn't consider he'd wasted his time taking the precautions he had. By doing the same sort of thing on occasions before, he had survived several attempts to get rid of him.

It didn't take long for Candor to read through the papers after he'd got them back into the correct order.

The words were made up of letters cut from various newspapers glued onto backing paper. The instructions ended with two words. 'Destroy this'.

He read through them again, putting them into the box he had earlier used to compare the weight of the original package. This he took into the living room and placed on a card table beside an easy chair. He went back into the kitchen to make himself a sandwich and a cup of 'instant' de-caffeinated coffee, thinking about the instructions in the papers. Taking those back into the living room, he sat himself in the easy chair and chewed on the sandwich, occasionally taking a gulp of the hot dark liquid.

He meditated on the information he had been given and the instructions he was to carry out. He tried to imagine what the results would be if those instructions were carried out successfully; one thing he was sure of, the amount of money he was to receive didn't look quite so large considering what was involved and the expenses he would have to bear.

Jordan was not exaggerating when he said the job was not going to be easy. Candor, who had locked away in his mind a large part of his past found he had difficulty repairing and consolidating the barriers containing that part of his memory. Since Jordan had mentioned Israel, the two names being neighbouring countries had jarred, helping to widen the cracks in those barriers. He found it difficult to contain that which he wished to remain hidden away.

As he thought now about the job he had been set, the barriers began to crumble and Candy's face kept appearing before him. He could see the laughter in her eyes and sense her perfume in his nostrils. Then the picture would change, her beauty destroyed; only the blood and the pain was there; that and the sound of gunfire and shouting men. The weight of Candy in his arms as he held her close, knowing that she would never again look him in the eyes and tell him how much she loved him.

He suddenly got up from the chair and took the empty mug and plate into the kitchen where he washed them under the tap. But the vision would not leave him. He thought of the girl. His and Candy's girl and the song he and Candy sang together.

'Isn't she lovely, made from love'?

He groaned, let the mug slip and gripped the edge of the sink with both hands, head bowed, eyes tight shut. The picture would not go away. He went back into the living room and opened the door in the base of the sideboard. With wet hands he took out a bottle and a glass. He straightened up and poured out a large measure of the brandy and put the bottle down. He looked at the glass in his hand. The sweet aroma impinged on his nostrils and he closed his eyes, frowning as the ache from the past plagued him.

He opened his eyes again and regarded the measure of spirits. With an effort of will he turned, walked once more into the kitchen and slowly poured the contents of the glass into the sink, turning on the tap to wash the brandy away; the water gushed out, bouncing and splashing over the edge.

Candor reached out his hands under the deluge and threw water over his face. The harsh chill of the water made him shiver and he dried himself, rubbing the rough towel vigorously over his face and head.

He stood for a few minutes breathing hard at his exertions, regaining his composure, trying to forget, something he knew he could never do. He went back once more into the living room and took the papers from the box again, forcing himself to concentrate on the printed words there, pushing the memories back behind the wall in his mind.

As he read the papers again he knew that Jordan had little idea of the security which would have to be broken. His remarks didn't begin to describe the care taken by the police and the army to protect the Israeli leaders. Jordan's job would require a hell of a lot of thought and planning Candor decided. Even to get near those leaders was an extremely difficult task. But if you thought long enough and hard enough he knew that most things were possible if one gave enough attention to the difficulties.

Candor wondered if Jordan had any concept of what was involved, or any knowledge of the country's difficulties in maintaining its existence against the efforts of its neighbours to break through its borders. Only the determination of the Israelis to maintain their sovereignty had kept their enemies at bay. They had latterly repulsed all the physical and political attacks made upon it.

Candor knew of the role Britain had played in bringing about the State. In 1917, Arthur James Balfour once Prime Minister of Britain urged that Palestine should be shared by the Jews and Palestinians, but it didn't happen. When Britain had the mandate in 1922, they split the country into two parts. One part, consisting of three quarters of the land, to the Arabs on the East Bank of the River Jordan. The rest, on the West Bank to the Jews. This without reference to the League of Nations.

When the mandate ended in 1948 and the State of Israel was created by the United Nations, their Arab neighbours attacked them. The Jordanian army took a large part of Jewish territory on the West bank. This was known to Israel as Jordan and Samaria. At one point the Arabs almost reached the Mediterranean Sea, splitting the country in two. Intense advertising in Britain for men to join the Palestine Police to keep the peace then followed and many men responded.

In 1967, in the Six Days War, after being attacked by their neighbours the Israelis repossessed the area and against all disputes have held it ever since, only retaining that part they had originally possessed in 1948. The Israelis aver that a Palestinian State does exist, The Kingdom of Jordan where almost two thirds of the population are Palestinian Arabs.

Candor doubted if the man who called himself Jordan, knew of the true facts; probably only that the Palestinians wished to repossess that which they lost back to the Israelis in 1967. He considered why Jordan wanted Israelis leaders assassinated.

It was obvious there would be terrible repercussions at such an outrage. The P.L.O. would get the blame and the Israelis would reap awful vengeance on the Palestinian Arabs. Why would he want that to happen? What could he gain from such vengeance? The whole thing could again boil up into full scale war.

Candor began to realise what could be gained from such action. The demand would be for more and more weaponry. Probably Jordan was the person to supply that need.

Candor got to his feet and paced up and down, as the thoughts crowded into his head. That must be the answer, he decided; Jordan or whatever his proper name might be, was an arms dealer. Probably one of the illegal combines he knew existed and which was responsible for the slaughter of people in many parts of the globe. The riches he must have already made would not slake his appetite for more wealth and his, Candor's role which he was about to play, would increase that wealth for him and his confederates.

So, that was it. Stir up more trouble and the demand increased and men like Jordan and his gang grew fat on the proceeds. It was odd, he thought, that the fatter they got, the more their appetite for money became difficult to satiate. The misery, pain and death were of no significance to them; money and power were the only things of importance.

Candor sat down again, his countenance fierce. He also shrugged off the consequences of such action. Hadn't he known misery, pain and the death of his beloved Candy?

What was of importance he thought; was that here he had the opportunity to avenge himself on those he blamed for her death, the Israelis and his resultant agony and get paid for it. Candida, his lovely wife, had paid for her concern for his comfort with her life. He, a Captain in the Royal Marines, attached to the United Nations peace keeping force in Beirut had persuaded her to visit him for a short holiday.

They had met in Haifa and had spent a week of love and happiness there. They had made the decision to spend the following day touring Northern Israel. While returning towards the coast from Safed to Nahariya, about ten kilometres from the border with Lebanon, they had just begun to enter the town when it was attacked by terrorists.

In the confusion, as they tried to flee the area in their borrowed Land Rover, Candor and his wife mistakenly came under fire from a group of Israeli soldiers. The shot up vehicle burst into flames and Candor had great difficulty in extricating his wife before it exploded into an inferno.

Candida, badly burned and covered in his and her blood, died in his arms.

The tragedy turned Candor's mind and he was eventually sent to the Naval Hospital at Haslar. When he recovered sufficiently to face the world again he resigned his commission and went into exile in Scotland. Shunning for a while all human contact, he walked the river banks and camped on the mountain slopes, trying in the solitude he had made for himself, to rid his mind of the torment he suffered.

He abandoned his daughter to the care of her Aunt, feeling he was not fit company for anyone. She willingly accepted responsibility for the child, placating her own grief at the loss of her sister Candida by her love for her niece.

Candor's mental state was not improved by a further unfortunate occurrence. Making one of his necessary visits to a small town near the coast for provisions, he hoisted his now full pack onto his shoulders and set off along the cliff path, the ground to his left rising steeply to the summit.

About a mile or so from the town, he stopped and turned to look at the sea, the soft swell below the cliffs shimmering in the sunlight and the frothed edge where the sea met the rocks below. Suddenly he heard a stifled cry and the sounds of a struggle. Hurrying around one of the twists in the path he saw a man holding a partly clad woman to the ground. Most of her clothes were strewn about the grass and with his arm across her throat as she struggled, he was attempting to rape her.

Candor saw red. In an instant he had divested himself of his pack and like someone demented leapt at the man, dragging him to his feet. All his early combat training rushed to the surface and exploded into violence against the unfortunate would be rapist. Candor reduced the man to a moaning bloody wreck in seconds, venting all his hate and frustrations on him. In a blind rage he finally picked up the man and flung him over the cliff edge watching him fall to the rocks below. As suddenly as his rage had surfaced, so it disappeared; hearing a whimper, he turned and saw the woman, who, having recovered some of her clothing was standing there covering herself, one hand to her mouth, sobbing.

Candor stood for a moment looking at her as if not comprehending what had just occurred. Abruptly without a word, he turned, picked up the back pack and walked on past her, along the path.

Although he was not to know it, the incident was the final blow to his state of mind; he had changed. The man's death was the first by his hand, it was not to be the last; he was no longer the caring husband and father he had once been.

He had always called his wife 'Candy', now he would still be part of her by altering his name, using part of hers. He became Candor. Previously he had always cared about people who deserved care, but now that was in the past, he would care for no-one but his own.

Within a couple of days he was resident in a rundown street in a neglected area of one of Scotland's largest cities. His insinuation into the low life and their habitats accelerated his reputation for being a 'loner' and also a 'hard' man who would 'fix' anyone for a price. As his 'jobs' became riskier, his charges for those jobs became higher. Soon he had moved to Birmingham and then to London, sharing his time between each city.

His wealth accumulated and he started a trust fund for his daughter. She began to receive an allowance which increased with each of her birthdays and her Aunt a monthly sum for his daughter's keep. The money which his daughter received came to her anonymously and she never found out his whereabouts or his new identity, though of course she realized the money came from him, it could have come from no other.

CHAPTER 6

Chief Superintendent Arthur Oakey hurriedly gathered his papers together and stuffed them back into the folder. Only the timely reminder of the Commander's secretary Janet Brookfield, had prevented him from suffering the pique of his superior. He tapped on the door, still adrift by a couple of minutes, then obeyed the command from within and entered. The first thing he looked for was the Commander's Pomeranian dog, hoping it would not again attache itself with a growl to his trouser leg, but the beast was sat scowling in its basket by the Commander's foot.

'Sorry I'm a little late sir' he apologised, keeping a wary eye on the dog.

'Never mind that Arthur, what have you got for me? The Commander asked.

'Well, it doesn't seem a lot sir' replied the Chief Superintendent, noting that the cupboard door was shut and there were no glasses to hand.

'Still stymied eh?' His Superior grunted.

The chief Superintendent could sense disappointment in his tone, hoping that the little news he did have would temper the Commander's pique.

'Well' he put in, swiftly 'as a matter of fact I think we've solved the mystery of who Hyam's visitor was. The explanation is a bit long winded. Do you wish to hear it sir?'

'Might as well, I've nothing pressing at the moment Arthur' The Commander went to the cupboard and to the disappointment of the Chief Superintendent, took out the tray with the whisky and glasses. The pomaranian almost got to its feet to the hidden distress of the Chief Superintendent, but changed its mind to his relief as it settled down once more into its bed.

'Have one?' the Commander asked, pouring himself a large measure of the whisky.

'No thanks sir. Should I carry on?'

'Yes,yes, do'. The Commander carried the glass back to the desk, took a mouthful of the spirit, rolled it round his mouth and swallowed. His face showed a change from his earlier disappointment, to satisfaction. He leaned back in the large desk chair, his hands behind his head listening to the Chief Superintendent.

'Well sir, after chasing shadows for a bit I had Ofton brought in. You remember him sir? He was the driver of the vehicle who followed our unknown visitor; the mate of the man Ambrow, who was murdered'.

The Commander nodded after a slight pause to recall the name and the event.

'I gave him an uncomfortable few minutes; told him I was wondering if he'd had anything to do with his mate Ambrow's death. Ofton was easily scared and good fortune for us; he assumed we knew the identity of their quarry. He blurted out he'd only carried out Hyam's orders to follow this man Candor and lost him. He then dropped off his passenger and went home. I didn't let on we were pleased for his identifying him for us. Just gave him a hard time and let him go until we wanted him again'.

'Do we know this man—er Candor did you say his name was?'

'Yes sir. That is he let on the man's name was Candor, but no, we have had no knowledge of anyone by that name before. But, I had some checking done. That's when it got interesting. Over the past few years there have been several mysterious deaths, or serious injuries necessitating hospital treatment. Most of the mayhem was among the criminal fraternity. They don't talk much about their troubles to us as you know sir, not even from a hospital bed. Still, as I say, I have information from several districts around London, Birmingham and Glasgow and one or two other cities. The interesting factor as far as I am concerned, is that almost all the deaths I've mentioned which did occur, were as a result of injuries received in the same way Ambrow got his.'

'H'm, a professional killer then you think?'.

'Mm, yes sir. I then had enquiries made going back over the years, trying to establish a time when this type of murder began. It seemed to me that this man Candor, if indeed he was responsible for them, especially as no actual weapons were used, must have had his training by experts who use similar methods. Namely, one of the Country's armed Services'.

'Of course Arthur, yes! It's obvious I suppose when you think about it' The Commander took another mouthful of the whiskey, washing it around with his tongue, enjoying the feeling of warmth it gave as he swallowed the liquid.

'Yes sir', agreed the Chief Superintendent again, although it hadn't seemed obvious to him for quite a while, even though he had thought over the problem.

'Anyway', he went on. 'I plumped first for the S.A.S. but got nowhere. Then I thought of the Marines, the Commando force. I got in touch with the War Office and obtained a list of men who had left the Service for various reasons over the years. I narrowed the field down considerably, by finding out what happened to them after they left. Incidentally, I included all ranks, from humble 'boot necks' to Senior Officers. You never can tell'.

The Commander grunted again and looked at the glass on the desk, but then bent and stroked the dog's head instead and it licked his hand and wrist.

'It's amazing' said Oakey, 'how people can disappear so easily. I mean, these chaps, with a long service record, some of 'em, just simply get lost in Civvy Street and take a hell of a lot of finding. They go abroad, change their names; die. They get up to all sorts of tricks. In fact there are quite a few not accounted for, not yet anyway'

'Yes, yes get on with it Arthur', grumbled the Commander, picking up the glass and emptying the whisky down his throat and looking longingly again at the cupboard door.

'Sorry sir. Well there was one chap who particularly interested me. He was a Captain in the Marines attached to the United Nations Force in Beirut in the seventies. Miles Scholland his name was and, incidentally, he had been an 'unarmed combat' instructor in the Commando's'. He looked again at the dog.

'He was taking a spot of leave in Israel. His wife had gone over to be with him, to holiday together. There was a skirmish with some terrorists near the Lebanese border; Scholland was slightly wounded and unfortunately his wife died. The odd thing about it was that the Land Rover they were travelling in was shot up by the Israelis by mistake. That's irony if you like. Anyway Scholland resigned his Commission when he recovered from his wounds and disappeared. He'd got a girl—'.

Here Oakey shuffled his notes, then finding the errant piece of paper; 'yes here we are, her name was Patricia. Only a schoolchild then and she was being looked after by her Aunt. We had a talk with this woman. She's never seen Scholland since the Israeli incident, but apparently he went to Scotland; living rough, she said. The girl, just over twenty now of course and a student, gets an allowance which is believed to come from her Father though she's never seen him either since he disappeared. The money is paid into her bank account regularly, but they aren't forthcoming with any details yet. That's not important, except where her Father gets his money from. No doubt the Inland Revenue would be interested there too.

'As I said, Scholland apparently went to Scotland, so I did some back checking through the records of our Scottish friends. It took a few days but I had a bit of luck there too. I'd mentioned to Jim Dalgleish that I was looking for a certain specific type of injury in unsolved cases of death by violence. He came up with a few. The earliest, in 1974 by the way, was of a man whose death had been reported by a woman whom the man had been about to rape. 'It was a strange story, so I sent a man up there to check it out. He took with him some Service photographs of this Captain Scholland and the woman was interviewed. She repeated her story to my man. I have the interview on tape, by the way.

'When she was shown a bundle of photographs of different ex-Servicemen, she picked out Scholland straight away as her deliverer'.

'What do you mean about Scholland being her deliverer? How does he fit in?' asked the Commander, showing more interest.

'Well you see sir; the man had attacked this woman on a cliff path when she was walking her dog'. Here Arthur Oakey glanced across at the Pomeranian again, then carried on. 'He'd injured her quite badly and was on the point of raping her when Scholland appeared on the scene. According to her story, Scholland went berserk. He beat this fellow up quite badly and then slung him over the cliff on to the rocks below. Then he just picked up his gear and went off without a word. The woman spent an hour looking for her dog which had run off, before getting back to alert the police. She, of course, thinks Scholland is a hero, and who could blame her.

'Anyway, by the time the police got to the scene Scholland had disappeared. The man was dead of course, with the injuries, among others, which have become a pattern in these deaths, er—fractured larynx, ruptured spleen and liver and odd bruises on the body and a few broken bones and other injuries from the fall.

'These bruises apparently are usually on the pressure points on the surface of the body, which affect the nervous system. He knows his stuff, this fellow. Apparently, I'm told, one blow in the right place with the edge of the hand can completely disable a person. He's an extremely dangerous man.'

'H'm' grunted the Commander, 'that appears to tie in this man Scholland with a lot of unsolved crime then. I hope you've kept his identity to yourself Arthur. We don't want your Scottish friends around our necks trying to get him taken up there. Not till we've sorted things out this end. We want to find out what Somers, or Jordan, or whatever he calls himself, is trying to recruit Scholland for. I wish we knew what was in that parcel' he reiterated.

'We've kept quiet about Scholland sir. There's only you, me and Winfild, the Inspector I sent up there, knows about him. I'd given strict orders about keeping what he found out to himself. As far as the 'Jocks' know, his trip was a waste of time with no positive results. The woman knows we have a photo of him, but his name wasn't mentioned to her, or anyone else. Winfild didn't let on we knew who he was.

'There's another point here sir too. The physical characteristics from Scholland's Service records tally with what, er—our person, saw of the visitor at Hyam's club. Height the same, weight estimated similar and there was a scar on the man's temple which he could have got in that Israeli affair. His hair colouring was greyer and also he looked plumper around the jowls; perhaps cotton wool or something inside the mouth. He was darker too. Yes! I believe he had altered his appearance slightly when he visited Hyam's club. I showed Scholland's photographs to our person and she agreed with me that it was the same man, but that he'd partially disguised himself'.

'That sounds right to me Arthur'. The Commander got up and went to the whisky bottle again. His dog perked up a little at his movement then again re-settled itself in its basket bed.

'You must have a drink, lad. You've done well, getting on to him as quickly as you have'.

'Well sir, just a small one then', capitulated the Chief Superintendent, though a little put out at being called 'lad' by his superior.

'Good, good. Here!' The Commander passed a generously filled glass of the pale amber liquid to his subordinate.

'Your good health Arthur. Now—We've got to find out what it's all about, we don't know how much time we've got. There must be something serious in the wind for Somers, or Jordan or whatever he calls himself, to recruit a man like Scholland. You must make damn sure he doesn't get wise that we know anything. Not yet!

'When we do find out we'll fall on him like nobody's business. Right. You get on with it Arthur, you've got to find this fellow and keep tabs on him. We don't want to pull a 'boner' by letting him get away with something which will reflect badly on this department. Use your judgement about finding him; you know we have to keep our eyes on the budget, but use what men you think necessary, but for goodness' sake, try not to tread on anybody's toes, anybody that matters that is. I've enough problems without adding to them. All right? Oh and by the way use this man Winfild, he seems to have the right ideas'.

'Yes sir. Now we're sure who he is, it should make the task a bit easier'.

As Arthur Oakey opened the office door to leave, the Pomeranian left its basket with a growl, making a sally forth towards the Chief Superintendent who was quick to pass through and rapidly close the door behind him as he left the Commander's office. He wished he felt as confident as he'd tried to show to his superior. He did a swift mental calculation, but his pension seemed a long way off to him. He sighed and wandered past Janet, the Commander's secretary without hearing her ask. 'Everything all right Chief Superintendent?' She just made out his remark, 'that bloody pest'as he opened her door to leave.

His mind was also already grappling with the problem of how to find Candor, alias Scholland and the whisky wasn't helping at all. He had not yet discovered a way which would prevent the Commander from insisting he drink the whisky which always semed to be pushed upon him.

§ CHAPTER 7

The man standing at the edge of the pavement took another photograph of the Cathedral and after another searching look at the building put his camera away in its case. It had not been easy, there always appeared to be someone walking past and getting in the way. Anyway, seemingly satisfied, he walked to his car and turning for a last look, he opened the door and got in.

The Citroen bore French registration plates and Candor watched it drive away. He let out the clutch of the 'Beetle' and followed, he having no problem in keeping the Citroen in view as it meandered through the traffic.

The driver seemed to ignore other vehicles and kept looking first right and then left, bending his head so that he could see the tops of buildings and anything which took his fancy. Occasionally he would brake suddenly to the consternation of other drivers; then accelerate away until once again, he saw something else which interested him, at which the braking and accelerating routine would be repeated.

Eventually the Citroen pulled into the kerb at a small lay-by adjacent to a toilet block and the man alighted and entered the building.

Candor stopped the 'Beetle' and got out. He took a quick look round but the few pedestrians about seemed concerned with their own business as he followed the man into the toilet convenience via the 'GENTLEMEN' entrance. A man buttoning his fly, left, ignoring the notice about hygiene on the wall above the exit. Candor walked up to the Frenchman as he was about to turn on the tap at the wash basin and tapped him on the shoulder. The man turned, questioning the intrusion, but the words he was about to say were never spoken as Candor hit him in the throat.

As he collapsed, choking, Candor caught him under the armpits and dragged him, struggling, into one of the cubicles. All of which Candor had rapidly checked on entry as being vacant. The man with his legs kicking out against the wall, died as Candor, with his hand clamped firmly over the man's mouth and nose, leaned against and then locked the door.

Candor, seeing the blood on his hands from the man's mouth, rinsed them in the toilet flush bowl and wiped them dry on the toilet paper. He picked the man up from where he'd fallen between the toilet bowl and the wall while Candor had made his ablutions and sat him on the toilet seat. He rapidly emptied the man's pockets and placed everything he could find, including the man's wrist watch and a loose ring and car keys, into a Sainsbury's plastic carrier bag which he took from his jacket pocket.

He then took off his own jacket and hung it on the hook behind the cubicle door. He stripped the man of his clothes and shoes and put them into a second plastic carrier bag; all except the man's jacket and hat which he put on. Placing the bags on the floor by the now naked victim, he listened again for a moment and then hoisted himself up to look and make sure no-one else had entered the facility and glanced into the next cubicle. Satisfied, he transferred the bags and his own jacket into that vacant compartment.

He had a last look round at the dead man, wiped off all traces of his own finger prints from anything he could remember touching, with the dead man's handkerchief and climbed back over into the next cubicle leaving the dead man's cubicle locked.

He changed into the Frenchman's trousers, putting his own trousers and his jacket into one of the plastic carrier bags.

He then left, again first wiping his fingerprints off the door handle and that of the exit door. Carrying the bags and using the dead man's bunch of keys, on which he had identified the Citroen's ignition key, he got into the left hand drive car and drove off.

It had taken just eight minutes since he had entered the building. Twenty minutes later, having parked the Citroen in a quiet side street, he walked round the corner, back into the main road and hailed a taxi. He returned to about a hundred yards from where he had left the 'Beetle' telling the driver to stop there, got out and paid the fare and waited until the taxi was out of sight, before walking up to and getting into his own car and driving away after checking the comings and goings of people using the facility which housed the dead man.

It was evident that the dead man had not yet been found. There was no obvious change to the normality of the daily activity around the area of the toilet building, just various pedestrians minding their own business as they normally did, in the British fashion. He drove the 'Beetle' back to the lock up garage and returning to the main street, once again took a taxi ride back, near to where he had parked the Citroen. He drove that car to a quiet lay-by in the suburbs where he carried out a thorough examination of the vehicle. He scoured the interior of the car, its internal compartments and its boot. Everything he could find; maps, papers, cards and all the bric-a-brac that had accumulated, he put in yet another plastic carrier bag, for scrutiny later.

He drove the car back to another lock up garage he had rented that morning, fortunately in the same garage block as that in which the 'Beetle' was housed. Here he removed the rear seat squab to check there and ran his fingers between the front seat squabs and their backs to ensure he had missed nothing.

He checked the road licence against the number plates, satisfying himself the vehicle was 'road legal'. After a few minutes thought to convince himself he had missed nothing, he locked the car away and took his haul into his house for examination.

There he studied the photograph in the man's passport and decided he could not disguise himself enough to impersonate those features. He did not think that would be a problem and made a mental note to obtain a suitable photograph of himself for substitution.

The dead Frenchman's name was Andre Fonnis and Candor religiously read every line of print he had taken from the Citroen so that he could assume the man's identity.

He had been lucky also in that the man had only been in the country for a couple of days according to the date stamp in the passport and according to that same document, was on a month's vacation. No-one would be likely to be making enquiries about his absence from his home for quite a while.

Satisfied there was nothing of the Frenchman's possessions, found in the car, which could have any significance to anyone who saw them, Candor determined to replace them in the vehicle. After all, he decided, the more of the original owner's stuff lying in the car the easier he could carry out the impersonation, should he be challenged.

His next problem was to silence any query about the man not returning to his hotel. Candor had found in the man's wallet a receipt for a weeks stay at a small hotel near Peckham Rye Common. He picked up the phone and dialled the number given on the receipt. The uncultured accent of a young girl answered and Candor asked if there would be anyone on the desk that evening at nine p.m. who could book him in. He was not surprised at the girl's answer.

'Oo no sir, there'll be nobody 'ere arter five o'clock. If yer wants a room, yer'll arter ask for Mrs Stannedge an' if she's about she'll see ter yer. Otherwise I'm afraid it'd be better if yer come round at about say, 'alf arter nine in't mornin'!'

Candor asked if there would definitely be a room available then.

'Oo yessir. We've got several empty like; it's just there's nobody 'ere arter five o'clock in the evenin'. Yessir, you'd be best by comin' in't mornin'. All right sir?'

Candor said that that would be fine and rang off. That settled it; he would go and collect Andre Fonnis's belongings from the hotel later that same day and after five o'clock.

As Candor drove back over Westminster Bridge that night, he marvelled at the way in which he had so easily obtained the Frenchman's few possessions. He had seen no-one at the hotel and therefore no-one had seen him.

He had made himself to look as much like the late Monsieur Fonnis as possible and entered the vacant small foyer of the run down hotel. He had examined the half dozen or so keys hanging on numbered hooks behind the unattended desk at the side of that foyer. He'd easily found the one which matched the key on the ring taken from Fonnis, thus identifying the room and the floor. He went through the pigeon holes for any mail for the Frenchman but could find none. There were only two floors and he soon found the room rented by Fonnis. He had certainly been travelling light, thought Candor; except for a pair of shoes, a couple of changes of shirts and underwear he found nothing else of the Frenchman's. He assumed the traveller's alarm clock on the bedside table had belonged to the man so took it just in case his instinct was correct. He did find two pairs of shoes in a closet, but as they were of a smaller size than those Fonnis had been wearing, he assumed they must have been the property of a prior tenant. These he left in the closet.

He put the dead man's things, including the two plastic carrier bags he had brought with him and which were now unnecessary, in to a holdall he'd also found in a wardrobe, had a last look round and left, hanging the key with its twin on the appropriate hook behind the desk. He'd seen no-one and nobody therefore could challenge him. He was in and out in ten minutes. He had no doubt that the hotel staff responsible for taking in clients, when they reappeared the following morning, would see no significance in the Frenchman's departure with his luggage. Nor would they connect that occurrence with the phone call from a man enquiring about a room and then not arriving to secure it.

Candor put the Citroen away in the lock up, the luggage stowed in the boot. The first part of his job was over. He'd decided, regretfully to sell the Jaguar and afterwards travelled down from Birmingham in the 'Beetle', he'd obtained two rented garages and acquired the identity and transport of a foreigner, all in two days. He was not surprised that it had been so easy but knew also that the problems and difficulties would gradually increase as the time went on.

§ CHAPTER 8

Sergeant Peter Bracken, was in an excited state as he reported by phone to Inspector Seth Winfild.

'I think you might want to see this guv, it's what I believe we've been keeping our eyes open for'.

'Oh aye, I hope you're right Pete. If it'll get Arthur Oakey off my back it'll be more than welcome. What have you got then?'

'They've found a stiff in a toilet up Peckham way. Not the usual thing mind you, this guy's been snuffed in the way you told me to watch out for'.

'Isn't that Toadole's manor?' asked the Inspector, his interest increasing rapidly at Bracken's news.

'Aye guv, I asked 'Warty' if I could have a 'butchers' at the stiff and he was most obliging'.

'Where's your respect Pete, we don't want Toadole to get shirty. I'll get in touch and go and have a look myself. Where are they keeping it? Has it gone to the morgue yet?'

'Aye it has guv. Do you want me to come in?'

'No I'll meet you at the morgue in say, twenty minutes; don't let it run away. O.K.?

'Right guv. I'll try and keep the flies off my sandwich meanwhile'.

'Never mind the sandwich. See what you can find out while I'm getting there'.

Seth Winfild put the phone down. He pulled at his lower lip deep in thought. He searched among the papers on his desk and finding the folder he was looking for, he got up and took his jacket from the back of his chair. He went through the outer office and told the harassed looking woman police Sergeant there, he'd be gone for an hour or so and to hold the 'fort' until he got back.

She pursed her lips and sighed.

'Look' he said, 'I'm off to the morgue up Peckham. Keep it to yourself. Stall anybody who wants me and tell 'em whatever you like. O.k.? Anything but where I am and don't look so hard done by. If Oakey comes in, tell him I expect to have something for him when I get back. I'll bring you a nice fat cream cake when I do. Mind you, I'll want a smile or you won't get it!'

He laughed at her moue and went out. He didn't hear her say he knew what he could do with his cream cakes. She settled her ample frame in her chair and opened the drawer in the desk. She took out a strong mint and popped it into her mouth. 'Blow the calories', she muttered and dived once again into the pile of papers awaiting her attention.

The Inspector grimaced as he gazed at the form of the man on the slab.

'See guv', pointed out his Sergeant, 'same method again. Bruises and a busted larynx. Looks as though he drowned in his own blood. Messy, eh?'

'H'm' grunted Seth Winfild. 'It's the same M.O. all right. He was naked when they found him you say?'

'Aye guv. Apparently the cleaner was doing his rounds of the 'bogs' in his area and the cubicle this guy was in was locked when he got there and all the time he was slopping out the place. He had a crafty look under the door when nobody answered his knock. Saw this guy sitting there, or what he could see of him through the gap and being too old to go climbing up to have a 'butchers', called the 'plods'. He hadn't got a stitch of gear with him. No belongings at all. The guy who did it took the ruddy lot'.

'Did they dust the place for prints?'

'Yep. Not one guv. Wiped clean. The only thing left was this ring. He had worn another one and a watch, look'. He pointed out the lighter colouring of the skin on the third finger of the man's right hand and on the left wrist, where the ring and watch had shielded those areas from the sun and weather.

'This ring's too tight to get off. I suppose that's why he left it. Didn't want to hang about too long eh?'

'H'm', Winfild said again. 'Look Pete, I want this ring off so we can get a good look at it. You never know your luck'.

'I've tried guv. It won't come off, not without cutting it'.

'Get it cut off then Pete and when you get it off, let me have it. I'm going to have a word with our friend Toadole'.

He went out into the fresh air and breathed deeply, clearing his lungs of the air from the morgue. He made the short drive from the morgue to the building housing his colleague Inspector's office. A little later he was closeted with him, Inspector Lawrence Toadole.

'Now Larry, how's tricks? Still keeping the streets clean eh?'

Lawrence Toadole had a flat, almost expressionless mien. He always gave the impression of being thoroughly depressed, but his doleful look belied his intellect and Seth Winfild knew he was as sharp as a tack. He also knew he was no 'pushover' when being asked for favours.

'What can I do for you Seth? What's the interest this time? Why are you interested in a stiff on my patch? Haven't you got enough of your own?'

'Oh no! We don't get many interesting ones Larry; ours are always fully clothed, or at least from the waist up, that is, though we do also get the occasional ones with trousers on. Do you think this fella had pawned his?'

His banter cut no ice with Inspector Toadole and that Officer's suspicious nature remained unalloyed.

'H'm. Very funny I must say. I still can't see what you've got such an interest in this one for. First your man Bracken comes sniffing round; now you're here. What's going on? Is there anything I should know about?'

'Well to tell you the truth Larry' Winfild prevaricated, 'we've got a bit of interest in him. Pete Bracken heard his description, told me about him and I just wanted to check him out with someone we've been looking for. That's all, nothing of much interest to you I wouldn't think'. He held out both hands palms uppermost, in a gesture of innocence.

'H'm' muttered Toadole, unconvinced by Inspector Winfild's protestations, always wary of his colleague's machinations.

'Does he fit what you're looking for?' He asked after turning the minute, almost negligible, information given to him by Winfild over in his mind.

'Well, I'm still not sure Larry. He has got a ring on I'd like to take a look at. Er, I've told Pete to get it cut off for me'.

'Here, hang about. You ought to have asked me first. What good will his ring do you, anyway?' He sounded a little peeved.

'Now don't you fret Larry', soothed Winfild. We're not going to take it away with us. I just want to get a good look at it. Don't want to leave anything to chance in these matters you know. When a stiff is completely naked except for a ring, it just might give us a clue about his I.D. mightn't it?'.

Lawrence Toadole knew all right but still remained unconvinced that Seth Winfild was not holding something back that he should know about. Seth's placatory manner didn't soothe him at all.

'Well, see it doesn't disappear' he complained. 'Apart from the hair on his head and other places, it's the only thing he'd got left'.

'Yes, yes Larry. By the way, Pete tells me you didn't find any 'dabs'. Is that right?'

'Not one that didn't belong to that cleaner bloke. He who did it was a clever bugger. It's a bit of a devil if you can't go for a pee without your number being called. I don't suppose you do really know more than you're letting on, do you?' Toadole asked hopefully, knowing Winfild's methods.

'If I did know anything, you'd be the first I'd tell Larry, you can be sure of that', Winfild lied.

'Oh yes, I'm sure'. Toadole sounded a little sarcastic and a little disappointed. 'By the way, don't forget you already owe me one for that other job I helped you with. It's beginning to look like one way traffic'.

'Now, now Larry. I swear if I find anything, you can trust me to let you know. And I haven't forgotten I owe you one. We've got to co-operate you know, or the villains'll get an edge on us'.

His quasi-bantering tone changed. 'Now then Larry, here's Pete coming'.

Peter Bracken could be seen through the glass partition separating Larry Toadole's office from the main office complex. He approached and tapped on the door before entering. 'Here it is guv; I had to cut it to get it off, as we thought. That guy in the morgue was all for hacking off the poor sod's finger, but I told him I couldn't stand the sight of blood'. He grinned at his Inspector as he handed him the ring.

'Good man Pete. You haven't got a Sherlock's magnifying glass on you Larry, by any chance have you?' and he winked at Bracken.

Lawrence Toadole bit his lip, reached into his desk drawer and scuffling myriad items around, eventually found, among those items lying there, a small 'Gowllands' 10x magnification folding glass, which he handed to Winfild.

'Don't you people have anything?' he complained again.

Seth Winfild ignored the remark. He was already too engrossed examining the inside of the small, gold band.

'Take this down Pete' he said, 'ANDRE VOUS J'TAIME. FRANCINE'. He spelt the letters out one by one.

'Hang on, there's something else, but it's badly worn. Probably the date. No! I can't be sure. Larry, can we get a photo of this info here and of the 'stiff'?'

'You wouldn't like bed and breakfast as well would you? It's all want isn't it? And what do I get for all this eh? nothing' grumbled Inspector Toadole again.

'You get my undying gratitude Larry, you know that', said Winfild, grinning at his Sergeant.

'Go down to the lab. And tell them I said you could have it and the dead man photographed', surrendered Larry. 'And bring the damn ring back. Remember! Don't go sliding off with it'. Larry Toadole still sounded aggrieved.

'As if I would. And thanks Larry'.

Seth Winfild and Peter Bracken were already going through the door as Larry conceded the round.

When they were both clear of the office area, Inspector Winfild said, 'when we get to the lab. You go in and get me a photo of the inscription in the ring and see if you can wangle one of the stiff as well. I'll keep that old bugger Ogston gassing. You know what a stiff neck he is for chits and forms and rules and regs he'll want a complete dossier if we don't watch out'.

'Right on guv', agreed Bracken. 'No problem'.

The photographs were eventually obtained and the two C.I.D. men returned to their own department, Bracken to his desk and Inspector Winfild, feeling a little happier, to a meeting with his superior on the case, Chief Superintendent Arthur Oakey. He had a little success with their enquiry to report.

§ CHAPTER 9

'What have you got then Seth?' asked the Chief Superintendent, 'I hear you went to see Inspector Toadole about another killing?'

'Yes sir', answered Inspector Winfild, knowing that his Chief Super'. didn't miss much 'he was his usual cheerful self and he co-operated eagerly as you can guess'.

'So I can imagine' remarked Oakey, dryly, at Winfild's sarcasm.

'Well he did let us have a photo of the ring belonging to this dead man sir and we wangled a picture of the guy too. Here they are sir'.

He took the photographs from the folder under his arm and passed them to his boss.

'As you can see from the engraving inside, the ring is French, giving us the probable first names of the deceased and of the person who gave it to him. The date's there as well but indecipherable unfortunately'.

'Well that's interesting' said Arthur Oakey as he examined the photographs. 'What conclusions have you come to? If any'.

'Well sir, unless this guy obtained the ring from some other 'geezer', he must be French, or at least there's a good chance he was. If so, he was probably a tourist and Candor, assuming he killed him which I believe is likely, was after something he'd got that he could only get from a foreigner. His passport and other personal papers is my guess. Also it's a pound to a pinch of 'whatsit' this guy had a 'jam jar' as well. Now, Candor's got papers and a vehicle to match them. My next guess is, he's off somewhere abroad with a false identity on some job for Jordan, stroke Somers, sir'.

'H'm, I agree, that's what I'm thinking Seth' mused Oakey. 'Quoting Commander Allfield, if only we knew what was in that parcel he got from Hyam's club. Still, we haven't a clue about that, so, what are we going to do now we have these photos?'

'Well sir', suggested Winfild, 'there's a possibility that someone might recognise that engraving in the ring and the face of the dead man. If we 'have a go' at the 'Surete' about circulating them in the French press and if possible on television, there's just a chance that someone, possibly the woman Francine herself, may see them and get in touch with the French police. It's a chance don't you think? Though I think it would be a waste of time to circulate the info in this country. I mean, he must have been on his own or how else would Candor manage to separate them to be able to do what he did without the other person knowing. He wouldn't be 'sight seeing' on his own would he, if there was a partner or a friend?"

'I agree Seth. It's the only chance we've got. If he is-er, was French, there'd not be much use circulating the stuff over here'. D.C.S. Oakey shook his head, thinking.

'No, it would be a waste of time. Leave these with me and I'll see what I can do. The 'Surete' seems to be our best and only chance of making something out of it. They may also promulgate Scholland's picture for us if we can convince them he's going over there. I'm sure they'll be pleased to know they've probably got one of our most dangerous criminals wandering around on their territory' and he grimaced.

'I bet. Is that it then sir?' Winfild asked, moving towards the door.

'Aye Seth. Just keep your fingers crossed. We need a lucky break on this one and we haven't had one yet. Perhaps things will change eh?'

He laughed grimly as Seth Winfild left, but not with any amusement. He had little to report to the Commander and he knew that gentleman was impatient for results and could be very cutting when things didn't happen quickly enough for him and of course he'd have to watch out for that ruddy dog when he did report this fresh news. 'Why couldn't the Commander leave the blasted creature with his wife?' he asked himself.

Inspector Seth Winfild left him with his dark, but hopeful thoughts.

§ CHAPTER 10

Patricia Scholland sat quietly, though a little confused and flustered, mentally. She cast another quick glance from beneath her dark lashes at the young man at the counter. She became instantly more flustered. He was looking directly at her as he turned, with a tray containing a cup of tea and a couple of salad sandwiches and began to walk towards her table.

'Should she get up and leave?' the question in her mind plagued her. 'No, she couldn't leave', she dismissed the idea instantly. She looked down, picked up her empty cup, pretending to take a sip and unconsciously crossed her long tanned legs, as she did so she caught the under edge of the table with her knee, shaking it and its contents violently.

Her subconscious reaction, to stop the table and at the same time straighten her legs, caused her foot to bump against the opposite table leg, exacerbating the movement of the table.

Her confusion was complete, her cheeks crimson.

The young man stood before her, eyeing her quizzically and said. 'Excuse me, is this seat taken?'

Patricia swallowed hard. 'Er-no-er, no it isn't'.

'Do you mind if I sit here?' he asked politely.

'Er-no, not at all'.

Patricia wished she hadn't emptied her cup before seeing him enter the canteen.

'Thank you', he said, 'it seems rather full here this morning'.

Pat said nothing. She eyed him, then the queue at the counter, wondering if she had the nerve to go for a refill and return under the quiet, open gaze of the young man.

'Have you taken your 'finals' yet?' he asked.

'Er-no' she answered, cross with herself for being a bumbling fool. Then, with unaccustomed bravado, 'Have you? She asked.

She swallowed again. Why did this young man make her feel as she did? She felt the blush on her cheek spread down her neck as soon as she asked the question.

She thought she saw a smile in his eyes.

'Yes. More or less; last one next week and then to be thrown out into the cruel world to earn a crust'.

He laughed and took a sip of the hot weak tea.

'What are you taking? He asked.

'Social Studies' she managed to reply.

'I'm doing engineering' he said. Then, 'would you like me to get you another cup of tea or something?'

He had half risen to his feet.

'Er, thanks-thanks very much' she managed to gasp, 'another cup of tea would be nice please'.

He turned and went to the counter, soon returning with a fresh cup of the hot liquid. While he had left her alone, she had admired the way he walked. His assured, confident step and slight rolling gait made her heart rate quicken again.

She looked down at the table as he said, 'there you are. Nice and hot, though it's pretty weak stuff isn't it?'

She agreed with him and offered the cost of the tea to him and he declined. She put the coins away again into her purse and sat sipping the tea as he chatted on. She listened intently and occasionally answered a question as she gradually became more at ease with him.

She suddenly had a thought and glanced at her watch.

'Oh! Look at the time. I'm late for my next lecture. I'll have to go', she blurted out, reluctant, but required by necessity to leave.

'Look, I'll pick you up here when you're through for the afternoon. May I?' The request was more a statement of intent and she said,

'Oh, er-yes. Er, here at five if that's all right?'

'Fine, until five then. By the way, my names Hiram, Hiram Woolley'.

'Oh. My name's Pat. Patricia Scholland'.

Somehow she, with his help, managed to pick up all of her belongings, books and papers and her bag and left, looking back once, self consciously, to see him gazing after her. He waved and she returned the gesture with a slight, again self-conscious movement of her arm.

Her step was light, her head spinning and her heart beating fast as she quickly ran down the stairs and along the corridor to her next lecture room.

Hiram Woolley stayed at the table for another few minutes, thinking about the girl with whom he had been sitting. He'd been attracted by the girl's dark looks. Her coal black hair, eyes which matched her hair and dark complexion. She was pretty, very pretty he thought. He realised also, by her manner that she seemed as though she was attracted to him and was glad he had decided to approach her.

He left the canteen and went to the library of the college, to check up on a few more facts in preparation for his last examination of the 'finals', but had difficulty in giving the subject his full attention and concentration after what had happened earlier.

He was aware the girl had made a deep impression on him. He had first noticed her some weeks before but had not, for some reason which baffled him, dared to approach her until that day. The more he thought about her; now he'd had the courage to speak to her, the more he wished the afternoon would hasten on to their next meeting.

He also wondered what it would mean to him if he became involved with her. He couldn't put out of his mind the knowledge that he would soon be going home to where he had lived for most of his life, to Israel; back with his parents and to become involved in his father's engineering business.

He knew his Father had high hopes of him, but even though he was confident in obtaining his engineering degree; for himself there was little joy in it. That had been his Father's idea, so that he could follow on in the family firm.

Hiram's interest lay in an entirely different direction. His bent was travel and politics. He knew he would do some travelling for the firm, but not the kind of travel he envisaged. He was deeply, almost obsessively patriotic. When his parents had settled in Israel he had been brought up soaked in all the dogma, all the doctrine of the Jewish faith.

As he grew to adulthood his religious faith and belief were firmly established. His belief that the Jews were the chosen people and that Israel was the promised land of that people and their culture.

He felt he needed to visit other people in other lands to persuade them to accept the fact. Israel was for the Jewish people; their inalienable right to occupy it; their land inviolate.

The only way to achieve this he was sure, was through politics, but it seemed that first, he must accept his Father's wish and join the family concern.

He was young and almost brash in his conversation with others when his favourite subject was broached. Convinced that his faith, the only true faith, must, if not wholly accepted; was to be tolerated by all and his land, Israel, be accepted by all.

He asked himself, where the girl, Patricia Scholland, would fit in. 'Was there any room for her?'

He gave up trying to swot and left the library. He smiled as he told himself he was jumping fences that didn't exist. After all, he had only just met the girl. They were not even friends. But, somehow, he had the feeling they were to become somewhat more than just friends.

For her part, Patricia Scholland was intrigued by the young Jewish man. He excited her. She had secretly longed to meet him since she had first seen him, but had not had the courage to invite his attention. She had girl friends, but none really close, with whom she could make known her feelings about him.

Her Aunt's strict upbringing had made its mark on her. She knew of the manner of her Mother's death in a tragic accident during a terrorist raid on Jewish soil, where her parents were enjoying a holiday together.

Patricia blamed the Palestinian terrorists, not the Israelis for her Mother's death and the loss of her Father's company. He, who, in his misery had forsaken her, had completely departed from her life. She could not even recall what he looked like now; photographs which had included his likeness had disappeared from her Aunt's home as the years had passed on. For some reason, during those years, as she had grown older and more aware, her interest in things Jewish and the State of Israel had increased. She had visited the local libraries and obtained as many books as she could which referred to the Jewish culture, particularly it's people and their problems. She had a longing which she kept secret from her Aunt, to visit the place in northern Israel where her Mother had died. Any conversation by anybody about that country immediately took her interest and attention.

Perhaps her interest was the reason for her attraction to this boy with the Jewish looks, she thought.

Now, at last, the young man had approached her. He must definitely be interested in her she believed. Why else would she have caught him staring at her while she waited in the queue to be served in the canteen? Then, to her consternation and excited disbelief had made a direct approach to her table. There were other tables he had passed, with unoccupied seats, but he had chosen hers. He must be interested and to think, she was to speak with him again that very afternoon. It could not pass quick enough to the appointed time for her. She was ecstatic.

Thus they spent that evening and most of the following evenings, together. At first, ostensibly to help each other with their studies and then, they did indeed become more than friends. In less than a month they were lovers. Hiram Woolley did his utmost to proselytise her from her Gentile faith as they spent more and more time together, she a willing listener to all his tenet; all his descriptions of the people and country in which he held such firm beliefs about its future as he did.

Then one day he explained to her that the time had at last arrived when he had to return home to Israel. She was extremely upset and their last hours together were spent holding each other close, talking, making love, crying and then repeating such behaviour all over again and vowing undying love for ever to each other.

The following morning she saw him off from the airport, tears streaming down her face, disregarding the looks of other passengers or their friends who were also seeing off acquaintances and wondering what the future could hold for her and Hiram.

She determined that as soon as she had finished her degree course she would go to Israel to be with him. He wanted it to happen and now England had no ties for her. Her Aunt was amenable to anything she, herself wanted to do and would have no concrete objections, though no doubt she would be surprised. Even more so if she knew what they had been to each other, she and Hiram and most probably mortified at the possibility that her darling niece was to become Jewish. But yes! She decided she would leave as soon as she possibly could.

§ CHAPTER 11

Candor had made a fast non-stop journey south from the harbour at Le Havre and had almost reached Vierzon when he realised he needed petrol. At the road junction with Blois he spotted a run down looking garage and filling station.

He pulled in and parked the Citroen by the pump and waited for the attendant to appear. After a minute or so he became impatient and alighted from the vehicle to stretch his legs, absent mindedly looking for a lavatory for which he was beginning to feel the need.

A man, obviously the attendant appeared at the garage door wiping his hands on a dirty cloth, muttering at being disturbed. He perked up a little on hearing Candor's accent, when he asked for the tank to be filled and the oil and water to be checked.

Inquisitive by nature, the attendant began to ask questions about Candor's activities, his journey, destination, place of disembarkation and other questions Candor had no wish to supply answers to. He gave the man a lot of false information about his intentions, not caring whether he was believed or not.

Eventually, he cut the man short and asked for directions to the lavatory. The man waved airily in the direction of the garage, shrugging his shoulders at Candor's rudeness. Nevertheless, the barrage of questions continued as Candor walked over to the garage doors.

As he approached the entrance he heard the patter of feet. Looking round in the gloomy interior he saw a door swing shut in a small wooden walled area, obviously serving as an office. Ever watchful and suspicious, Candor, avoiding all the bric-a-brac lying around the floor, went over and knocked on the door. After a pause the door opened slowly, revealing an aged, lined faced woman who looked at him with sharp black eyes.

'Pardon Madame' said Candor, 'ou sont les toilettes? S'il vous plait', he asked.

The woman, whose eyes never left his face, reached her arm round the door and with a long, bent, arthritic finger, pointed in the direction of the back door of the building. Candor, his eyes becoming more accustomed to the murk, could see another door, behind some racks containing a variety of tyres and other automobile parts.

He strolled over and investigating behind the partly open door, could see a filthy toilet basin containing smelly discoloured water. He entered and partly closed the door again, behind him. He peered through the gap between the door edge and the frame and saw the bent backed woman emerge from the office and pad away on her bowed arthritic legs to the outside of the garage, obviously in as big a hurry as she could manage.

He could see both she and the attendant framed in the daylight by the open double doors of the garage entrance and she was gesticulating excitedly and waving her thin bony arms in the mechanics face, occasionally pointing towards the garage interior. Now and then she stamped a foot to emphasize a point. After a couple of minutes the pair returned to the office and went inside. Candor stepped quickly out from the lavatory and quietly negotiating the mess of junk and tins behind the racks, hurried over to the office door.

He could hear her urgent whispering and exclamations inside, but the rapid exchanges of French baffled him. It was obvious there was something seriously amiss; something which had clearly upset the woman.

The arrival of a foreign stranger looking for petrol should not have caused such concern in the old woman. The pair must surely see tourists, even in this sparsely populated area, Candor decided. He was determined to find out what could be irritating her. He could take no chances, it was not in his nature to do that.

He pushed open the door and stepped inside, pulling the door closed behind him. Like the rest of the building, the room was full of the bric-a-brac one would associate with an old fashioned garage business.

Heavily laden shelves containing well thumbed and oily, old car manuals vying for room among the half used tins of paint. Filter boxes, stacks of invoice files and other paraphernalia threatened by their weight to bring about a collapse of the whole conglomeration. Everywhere the piles of boxes and tins and everything covered with an encrustation of muck and dust. A gas ring, supporting a large, black, iron kettle stood on a wooden box. The red, almost perished, rubber gas feed pipe led from an old, large, bronze tap on the filthy brick wall. The room stank of old burnt oil and Candor was astonished at the lack of prudence in the use of an open flame for boiling water in the conditions which prevailed.

He also wondered at the relationship of the pair who stood there.

The man, holding a tattered newspaper, was pale and his eyes betrayed his fear as he looked first at Candor, then at the woman. Her black eyes stared at Candor. Her toothless mouth was tight shut and he could see a pulse in her thin neck as she, warily, watched him.

He reached out and took the newspaper from the man's unresisting hands. It had been opened at an inside page and he could see his picture staring out from underneath large black headlines. It was a print of an old photograph, taken during his time in the Marines. But, apart from his now greying hair, a good likeness that no-one could mistake and this woman certainly hadn't.

He inwardly cursed himself for his own arrogance, assuming a disguise would not be necessary during his journey across France. He was not well up enough in the language to read verbatim the accompanying article, but he could see enough to know that the police had solved his identity. He wondered vaguely how they had managed to do so and why this warning about him in the French Press. The theft of a French car in England was not unusual. Why had they assumed he was the thief and that he would travel abroad with the car? There must be an explanation for that but he couldn't think what that would be and didn't have the time right then to worry about it.

He had changed the number plates due to a last minute decision and he had papers to prove his ownership, sufficiently authentic to fool any but a thorough investigation. Now he had, by his own negligence fallen foul of the curiosity of this astute, crone. She had not missed the warning headline.

'Prenez Garde! Ce Homme est Dangereux'.

Her womanly curiosity had ensured she read the warning to be on the look out for the dangerous Englishman, driving a stolen French Citroen; and now, here she was, glaring at him and she had seen the Citroen he'd arrived in.

Her mouth dropped open a little as he laughed and said, 'Quelle Blague!'

She turned away from him for the first time since he had entered the room and looked at the man whose fear had partly eased at the joking dismissal of the article by the Englishman. She spoke in rapid French and the fear returned in the man's eyes; she was not to be put aside. She turned again to Candor and vituperation, in her rapid incomprehensible French assailed his ears. Candor could not but understand the words 'police' and 'Telephon'. He decided he had no alternative, despite the possibility that the woman had already summoned the police, but to ensure the silence of the two people there. He had no alternative if he was not to jeopardize his safety.

He shrugged and turned slightly as if to leave; then struck sideways at the man's throat. He felt the man's larynx collapse under the blow and he hit him again at the side of the neck as he fell holding his throat, blood pouring from his mouth.

The old woman's scream was cut short as a straight fingered blow to her midriff momentarily paralysed her. As she too fell, Candor administered a rabbit punch to her neck shattering the old brittle spline. She died immediately whilst the mechanic was thrashing about on the floor spitting blood and making choking sounds. Candor kicked him and this second blow to his neck broke it. The unfortunate man twitched, then lay still.

'What a bloody mess' cursed Candor aloud as he massaged the edge of his right hand which was numb from the blows he had delivered.

'Bloody Hell' he said again.

He went out to the front of the garage, looking for signs of passers by, but the road was deserted. He closed the large sliding door of the garage, got in the Citroen and drove it down the side of the building to where it was less conspicuous. He once again entered the garage looking for an empty can among the odds and ends lying about there.

He soon found one containing a little oil which he emptied on to the garage floor, went outside to the petrol pumps and filled the can with petrol. He returned to the office and placed the can without its cap, just outside the entrance to the room.

He lit the gas ring under the half filled kettle, with a match taken from a box on the small, rickety table, containing partly drunk mugs of tea. From a vantage point just outside the office door, he put the can just inside the door and pushed it across the littered floor with a long piece of oil soaked wood. The can eventually snagged against the fallen man's leg and overturned, spilling its contents onto the floor. Candor made a rapid exit and ran down to where he had parked the car, got in and drove swiftly away.

He hadn't travelled more than a hundred yards when he heard the explosion in the building behind him, as the petrol vapour ignited. A few yards later on he heard another explosion and by the time Candor had reached Vierzon he knew there would be little left of the garage or the two grisly occupants and he relaxed slightly. The oil soaked building, the old fashioned petrol tanks and the gas supply would have made sure of that, he knew.

He stopped in a lay-by a couple of kilometres from the town and applied a few simple, easily obtained cosmetic preparations, so that he could not so easily be associated with the photograph in the newspapers.

He decided he would have to change cars to lessen even further the possibility that he might be recognized as the wanted man by some other person, curious about his identity.

Again in his mind, he cursed Jordan for his instructions, taken from the parcel he had been given at Hyam's club, necessitating his driving through France. He had a meeting on the following day at a house just outside Thiers, about thirty five kilometres east of Clermont-Ferrand, that industrial city formed from two and the base of the Michelin Empire. He had no doubt that in Clermont-Ferrand, if not before, he would be able to change cars.

He had taken the precaution of bringing with him, hidden under the rear carpet of his present vehicle, another set of forged number plates. These would help to maintain his anonymity when he did obtain another vehicle.

He turned south from Nevers to Moulins and as he was driving alongside the River Allier, he realized there was a good possibility he could make a change there. He stopped the car on the grass verge and lifted the bonnet. He disconnected the low tension lead from the coil, cleaning the outside casing of that unit. Using a soft lead pencil he traced a path to 'earth' down the body from the low tension tag. He then replaced the lead and tried the engine on the starter to make sure the engine would not fire.

He got out again and leaned on the bonnet. He wasn't interested in the first couple of cars to pass and the third ignored his gesticulations to stop. The fourth and fifth carried more than one person and not wanting to complicate matters, he made no request for help from them.

Eventually a large Peugeot saloon appeared and the driver, an oldish small man heeding Candor's signals, stopped a couple of cars lengths up the road; got out and wandered back towards him.

Candor's expertise in unarmed combat once more stood him in good stead. As the 'good Samaritan' leaned over the bonnet to look at the sabotaged engine, operating the starter solenoid whilst chattering away, he succumbed to Candor's skill in serving out death with little fuss.

Watching to see he was not being observed, Candor hoisted him in his arms and took him to the driver's side of the Citroen. He sat him temporarily in the front seat of the car. He changed everything of his into the Peugeot and the dead man's belongings into the Citroen. He kept the man's wallet, money and papers. He removed the graphite from the body of the engine's coil, started the engine and turned the car so that it was facing at an angle towards the river bank, then switched off the engine again.

He moved the dead man into a driving position in the driver's seat with his foot depressing the throttle pedal, switched on the ignition and with the gear lever in top gear released the hand brake. He closed the door and at the back of the car rocked it backwards and forwards slightly, then with a heave, managed to get it in motion down the river bank.

The engine suddenly burst into life and the car accelerated downwards towards the water. Within a few minutes, the car with its dead occupant was submerged, stuck in the mud at the bottom of the slow flowing river.

Candor got in the Peugeot and drove away. He had seen no-one whilst he had made the change and eventually turned down a cart track off the main road and emerged a quarter of an hour later with the car carrying different number plates.

He had little difficulty in finding accommodation in Thiers, later that night and the three people he had that day killed, had been ejected from his mind and did not prevent him sleeping soundly, having carried out his usual exercise routine and instructed the concierge to wake him at seven o'clock the next morning.

§ CHAPTER 12

Chief Superintendent Arthur Oakey stood looking through the office window at the threatening dark clouds. He ran his hand over his head in contemplation. The line of balding seemed to advance each day he thought and he could actually feel the scalp under the sparce covering of hair. Not like in his youth, when his thick wavy hair had brought 'wolf whistles' from the girls on the square as he passed with his mates.

His spirits sank a little. The gloomy outlook from the window mirrored the state of his mind, there was going to be a downpour soon he decided and his mind turned again to his problem.

'This damn Candor business' he said aloud, wondering when they would get a lucky break in the investigation which would give them a clue as to what the man was after. They didn't seem to be able to get a line on the fellow at all. 'Like a Will o' the Wisp', he thought and the name 'Pimpernel' came into his mind. The French had tried to outsmart him to no avail according to the book. Now this other Will o' the Wisp was outsmarting everybody at the moment.

The buzzer on his intercom broke his train of thought. Irritated, he pressed the 'speak' button.

'Yes' he snapped.

'Inspector Winfild to see you sir', the receptionist, Janet informed him.

'Send him in', the Chief Superintendent said as he sat down.

There was a knock at the door and Inspector Winfild entered. 'Sorry to disturb you sir', he apologised. 'I thought you might like to hear the latest on Scholland,—er Candor, as he calls himself now'

'Yes Seth, let's have it then, I hope to God its good news for a change'.

'Well, I dunno whether it is or not really sir. Anyway, we've had word from the Surete about a couple of incidents which have occurred over there which, I think, confirms our suspicion that the man was making for France.

'The police have found a Citroen car, submerged in a river with a dead man in the driving seat'.

The Chief Superintendent sat bolt upright, his mouth slightly open.

'No! It wasn't our man sir, a local chap he was, but he hadn't drowned. Hardly! Killed just like Fonnis and the others we know about'.

Arthur Oakey slid further back into his chair, disappointment showing on his face. 'Good grief', he said.

'The point is sir, that the Citroen was traced to a man named Fonnis by the engine and chassis numbers. The plates were false. Having checked on the man Fonnis's whereabouts they discovered he was on holiday in England!'

'Some holiday the poor beggar had' said the Chief Superintendent; 'but why was this local man involved?'

'Well sir, a farmer type was doing a bit of hedging and ditching, whatever that is, in a field about half a mile away from this river. He noticed a Citroen pull up on the grass verge of the adjacent road and the driver got out and put the bonnet up. The farmer assumed that the car must have broken down and didn't take much notice for a while.

'Occasionally he had a look up from his work and after a short time there were two cars there. But! After another attention to his work he looked again and the Citroen had suddenly disappeared and the man, whom our friend, the farmer, was sure was the same man who had arrived in the Citroen, got in the other car and drove off. This farmer was a bit non-plussed about it all. He couldn't figure out where the Citroen had gone.

'Being by nature a guy with curiosity, he left his work and went to have a look. It took him about half an hour to get down to the roadway, then realized by the tyre tracks on the grass by the tarmac road, that the car must have been sent down the river bank into the water. He scrambled down and had a look round. He found he could see the vehicle down on the bottom, partly on its side and then, would you believe it? Went back to get on with his work. He forgot all about it, assuming, he eventually said, that the guy must have scrapped it.

'Fortunately, at breakfast the following day, he mentioned to his wife the peculiar goings on he'd seen. She gave him a fair quizzing and said he ought to have tried to get it out with the tractor as there might be parts on it worth salvaging.

'Any way it transpires that she happened to go to the local shops for supplies and spotted the article about the dangerous Englishman and the stolen car. She put two and two together and went round to the local police station, thinking there might be a reward if the car in the river was anything to do with the article in the newspaper.

'The police took a team round to where the farmer's wife said her husband had seen the incident and it wasn't long before they found the dead occupant. They retrieved him and the car.

'The man was recognized straight away. Everyone knows everybody else around those parts apparently. The car was traced as I've said sir and it was found that this new dead man owned a Peugeot; no doubt now being driven by Candor. They're trying to trace it by the number plates, but my guess is that Candor has some more, different plates on it. He's no fool; that we do know.

'Another thing sir. The French police have also come to the conclusion that our man Candor is responsible for some more mayhem and murder'.

'Oh God. What else has he been up to?' said Arthur Oakey, in his mind's eye seeing the next rung on the promotion ladder disappearing out of view.

'A garage owner and her son were found dead in their burnt out garage some one hundred and fifty kilometres, that's about ninety three miles sir, North West of where the Citroen was found, on the day the farmer saw the man change cars. They were already dead when the fire started. Forensic tests showed that although the bodies were almost completely burnt away, in both cases there was injury to the bones of the neck'.

'My God' said Arthur Oakey again, 'this man's a walking crime wave on his own. He must be damned determined to get where he's going. Nothing's going to stand in his way, it seems.

'That's five deaths which can, almost definitely, be tied in with him on this latest escapade'.

'Yes sir and we're not sure how many he'd done to death before this lot'.

'We've got to get him Seth, especially before the French do. If they get their hands on him we won't find out what this big job is he's concerned with. It's not just him; we want the others who are tied in with him. He's being used as their means of getting what they want'

'Look; you and your best man had better get ready to go over there. I'll get the Commander to square it with the French and as soon as he gives me the 'go ahead', I want you to go and find out what's happening. This could blow up in our faces if we don't see some results soon.

'Right Seth. I'll give you the word as soon as I can'.

'Yes sir. I'll take Sergeant Peter Bracken with me. He's keen to see some action'.

Inspector Seth Winfild opened the door as the Chief Superintendent picked up the telephone. He went out wondering what his wife would say about his proposed trip to France; she had made threats many times about his always being away from home. 'Still, orders are orders', he told himself. 'I wonder if she'll definitely press me for divorce this time. You never know what the day will bring when you turn out of the bed in the morning, it's a good job we've no children'. Oddly, he didn't seem too concerned with the threat of divorce by his wife anymore.

§ CHAPTER 13

As Hiram Woolley sipped the iced tea his mind was far away. He was mainly concerned with the passage of an aircraft over the Mediterranean Sea and which was rapidly approaching the Ben Gurion Airport in whose terminal building restaurant he sat. Also he wondered what Patricia Scholland would have to say about his decision to give up his job in his father's business, that which he had himself built from nothing and in which now his son seemed to have no interest.

Hiram had not been too successful and his father had been disappointed with his progress, often wondering if Hiram's degree in engineering had been worth the bother of studying for—and that disappointment didn't seem to bother Hiram. The son's lack of interest had not been born easily by the parent and on several occasions heated exchanges had taken place between them, Hiram's mother finding it difficult to keep the peace between them without compromising herself with her husband.

Hiram's after work activities had been at the bottom of their arguments; his associates had been denigrated by his father who considered them to be hot heads, rabble rousers and worse. Hiram defended them as patriots, eager to advertise their belief in the legality of the recovery and retention of lands once taken from them, the true inhabitants, by hostile neighbours.

The son's heated and impassioned arguments, his public haranguing and his obvious fervent patriotism brought him to the attention of the Mossad. He was watched and noted; his behaviour monitored and eventually he was approached and to his delight, recruited by them.

He was now in a dilemma. What to disclose of his secret activities to his beloved Patricia? She had finished her studies and having obtained her degree, they had decided she should join him in Israel. He was both excited and apprehensive. His family, while not totally opposed to their marital union, were not entirely convinced of its wisdom. Even though Patricia's agreement to conversion to the Jewish faith made her more acceptable as a family member, rather than would have obtained had she refused the abrogation of her Gentile status.

Hiram unconsciously shook his head as he mentally wrestled with the problem of what to reveal and what not to reveal. He asked himself, 'Why is life so full of problems? Even when it could be simple and straightforward something always happens to damn well complicate matters'. His features registered his concerns about his parents doubts about his behaviour and what restrictions they may try to impose on him.

His reverie was interrupted by the airport loudspeaker system announcing the imminent arrival of the flight from England. He rose from his seat at the table and wandered into the reception area, joining the throng of others awaiting the arrival of passengers from the flight.

When she appeared, he greeted Patricia with a passionate embrace and she responded eagerly, happy at last to be with him again. They gathered her luggage onto a trolley and eventually, after entry formalities were completed, piled her belongings into his car and drove away. Soon they would be alone together in the flat he had rented; their temporary home. There they would stay, in love and happiness until, together, they could choose their permanent marital home.

After the initial excitement of their meeting Patricia thought he seemed a little withdrawn, apprehensive even. She, a little worried, turned and watched him as he drove, taking his left hand from the steering wheel and holding it in both hers.

'How far is it to Tel Aviv Hiram?' She asked gently.

'Oh, sorry; I was miles away' he said, after she posed the question again. 'It's about twenty kilometres; say twelve miles or so'.

'Is everything all right Hiram, you haven't any misgivings have you?' she queried, a little disconcerted at his quiet behaviour. 'What about your parents, have you been able to bring them round to your way of thinking?'

He turned quickly to reassure her.

'No misgivings my love. None. It's just something which I think you ought to know about and it has nothing really to do with my parents, although when I tell them they're not going to like it much, I was somewhat in a quandary, wondering how I could tell you'.

'Tell me? You must tell me everything Hiram. I want to know everything about you. Everything that happens to you, or concerns you, happens to and concerns me too. I couldn't bear it if you kept things secret from me. I want to be part of everything with you, you know that'.

'Yes, my darling. I know. I feel the same way as you. There will be no secrets from you; it's just that what has happened means a great deal to me and needs to be told in such a way that you understand what it means—and to us both.

'I don't want to say any more until we get home. There we can sit and talk and I'll tell you everything'.

He squeezed her hand and she responded.

'All right Hiram. Until we get home. Our new home together'.

She stretched over and kissed him on the cheek. He turned again and smiled at her.

'We'll soon be there darling; our new home—yes, but it's only temporary until after we're married. But at least we'll be together'.

She snuggled down on to his shoulder. Happiness suffused her being. She and Hiram were once more together and now, no one could separate them again.

Later that evening Hiram related how he had been approached by an agent of the Mossad, the Israeli Intelligence Service. After a great deal of thought he had agreed to become involved with them.

Patricia knew nothing of the activities of the organisation and accepted the situation; if that was what Hiram wanted to do and what he thought best for himself, she could not disagree. Hiram did not deliberately gloss over the implications of membership, nor the covert methods used by the Mossad to obtain information.

On the other hand, neither did he press the points he had raised; sufficient that she knew and could accept and keep secret the knowledge. She would begin to understand what it would mean as time went on, but he didn't want to raise any doubt in her mind about its importance, or its possible difficulties yet.

All she knew at that time was that she felt that the country needed an ever watchful system to maintain its independence and its sovereignty. She was thus proud that her husband to be was already part of that system.

She would support and assist him in any way she could. She was now happy and content and felt there was nothing which could come between them and their contentment.

§CHAPTER 14

Aaron Plaistot eased his bulk into the driving seat of the little Citroen. The steering wheel brushed against his paunch even with the seat in its very rear position and he eased the saloon out of the line of parked cars, squinting as he did so, through almost closed eyes against the curl of tobacco smoke from the ever present cigarette between his lips.

He kept the big Peugeot in view though several vehicles behind it and the smoke from the cigarette, partially obscured his vision. He was an expert at surveillance, gleaned over years of similar work and following the Peugeot was no problem to him. He was confident the driver of the other car would not realise he was the object of Plaistot's attention. Simplicity and casual, natural behaviour was his watchword.

Aaron wound down the window, discarded the cigarette stub through it and closed it again. He skilfully extracted another cigarette from the packet on the seat beside him and lit it with the vehicle's cigar lighter, steering as he did so, with one hand lightly gripping the top of the wheel, always keeping his eyes on the vehicle in which he was interested.

His quarry turned into a side street and Aaron eased the Citroen into the kerb a short distance before the turn off. He alighted and surprisingly agile for his size sprinted up to the junction. He could see that the Peugeot was parked a hundred metres or so up the street and the driver was just leaving the vehicle. Aaron walked casually across the opening, looking out right and left in case traffic might be wanting to turn into the street, nonchalantly removing the cigarette from his lips to flick the ash away.

He took no apparent interest of the Peugeot or its driver and cast a glance at his watch as he reached the other side of the road. To a casual observer he was just another person quietly going about his business.

Candor ever watchful, saw the big man cross the end of the road as he locked the door of the Peugeot; he then turned and walked back to the corner of the main road. There were few people about and he looked along the pavement in the direction which the big man had taken. He saw the big man throw away his cigarette and light another, stopping as he did so, to cup the flame of the match in his hands to protect it from the light breeze. He seemed to be unconscious of Candor's presence and interest.

Candor saw him discard the burnt match after examining the lighted end of the cigarette and he then turned and entered a door. The sign above the entrance advertised the business as being a cafe and Candor decided to investigate a little further. He strode up to and entered the premises. The big man was sorting out a handful of coins to pay for the cup of coffee and the pastry he had just ordered. He turned and casually looked at Candor as he entered and then picked up the food and drink and sat down at a corner table. He took a tattered newspaper from his pocket and put the cigarette, still smouldering, in the ash tray; picked up the cup of coffee and sipped at the hot liquid. He seemed to Candor to be soon engrossed in the reading matter.

Candor ordered coffee as he looked around. There was only one other male occupant, also sat reading and Candor took his coffee and sat down near the door, a position which allowed a complete unobstructed view of the interior. The big man occasionally uttered a suppressed laugh at the comic strip he was reading but Candor was not entirely convinced by his apparently innocent behaviour; that he was as guileless as he appeared.

After a few minutes another man, tall, slim and dark, entered. He looked tired and a trifle unkempt. He gave a seemingly uninterested glance at the other three male customers and approached the counter where he purchased a cup of coffee and with it a croissant and sat himself at one of the vacant tables. His countenance was glum and wearied and he attacked the coffee and croissant with little enthusiasm; gazing down at the floor beyond his table with sorrow in his eyes. He was apparently completely oblivious to the cafe or its occupants.

Candor watched him for a minute or two and then turned his attention back to the large man who, still chuckling, was putting the paper away in his pocket.

Aaron brushed the crumbs on the table with one hand into the palm of the other and emptied them on to the vacant plate. He put the cup and saucer on top and picked it up and returned the crockery to the counter. He paid the charge and left, bidding the cafe owner 'Bon Nuit'.

The night was approaching fast and black clouds made the evening seem darker as a sprinkle of rain encouraged Aaron to turn up the collar of his jacket. He walked hurriedly to his car trying to dodge any large drops especially from those from an obviously cracked roof guttering, to try and escape the threatening weather. The water was alreasy beginning to pool in some places at the edge of the road gutter. He took a large handkerchief from his jacket pocket as he climbed into the driving seat, with which, when he had settled himself he wiped the spots of water from the lenses of his spectacles. He started the engine and drove away past the cafe front; out of the corner of his eye he saw Candor standing inside the door obviously having watched Aaron's departure.

Aaron smiled to himself. He had seen the innocent small Renault saloon parked by the pavement edge, adjacent to the side street. Hassan Mradmoor had chosen the right spot to follow Candor, whichever way he should choose to take the big Peugeot. The tall miserable looking individual had played his part well, he thought. He was sure Candor had not suspected Hassan of any involvement with himself. He smiled again, also sure by the man's actions that he was indeed Candor, the one who's movements he was to observe.

Hassan's demeanour had served him well in many situations; to look at him one would not suspect his sharp, shrewd brain. Many a villain had lived to regret his under-estimation of Hassan's grasp of a situation and his resolve; his unflinching dedication to the job in hand and its conclusion. His skills and ability were well known and appreciated by the Mossad. He was ostensibly a member of the French police force, but was in fact, a double agent. All information he thought might be pertinent to the Mossad was reported by him to them.

An Algerian by birth, he had been brought as a boy, to France by his parents. Subsequently he had joined the police and eventually met and married a Jewish Frenchwoman, he having little or no interest in any religion. However, as her beliefs gradually exerted their influence on him he decided to embrace the Jewish faith.

He was just what the Mossad were looking for. It was another opportunity to recruit someone who could give them valuable information about the French police and their activities. So it was that Hassan became a willing double agent. The Mossad's interest in anything to do with terrorism resulted in their being made aware of the English assassin; the man Candor, reported by the British police as having, murdered a

French National on holiday in England and suspected by the French police of further mayhem and murder on his way south in their country.

Aaron Plaistot had been dispatched to France from Israel to contact Hassan Mradmoor and having been briefed by him, Aaron had been informed of the probability of the identity of the assassin's contact to be an ex patriot Englishman, Adam Buckland, living just outside Thiers, a French town near Clermont—Farand although rating only sporadic interest from the French police and their C.I.D., the Surete, Buckland's activities were watched with interest by the Mossad who knew of his ability to supply explosives and small weapons which he obtained from criminal acquaintances. The Mossad's agents kept tight surveillance on him but did nothing to hinder his transactions although it was believed he had a considerable quantity of the goods. He was responsible for leading them, albeit unwittingly, to several of Israel's enemies.

If he had been put out of business it would only have meant that another supplier would begin operations somewhere else. They were content to watch and take steps further down the line to eliminate any danger to their country or countrymen. Buckland's carefully built up business had been allowed to continue.

Aaron and Hassan had studied, carefully, the reported route taken by the man Candor and assumed he was heading for Thiers and Bucklands abode. Thus it was that Aaron and Hassan had spotted the big Peugeot, driven by the man they believed to be Candor. Their pre-arranged and often used method of keeping contact with a quarry had met with success. Aaron was now sure of the identity of the driver of the Peugeot and knew that Hassan would do his best to maintain contact with the man. Aaron decided to make for the house of the criminal, Adam Buckland and left the town in the drizzle.

It was getting quite dark when Aaron arrived at his destination and was glad he had brought with him a hat and a raincoat. The drizzle had worsened and he knew he had to leave the vehicle out of sight and keep watch on foot. He therefore drove off the road, negotiating between the trees into their shelter in the thicket just along from the gates of Buckland's building and having donned his wet weather wear, left the vehicle to cross the road and looked for some means of getting a view of the premises over the high wall. Unfortunately there was no broken down tree stump or anything else of use so walked along to see through the gaps in the ironwork of the gates.

Buckland had done well for himself, Aaron thought. His house was a large, detached, cut stone building with a private drive and a gated stone wall. The latter was a good two and a half metres high, perhaps topped with broken glass he wondered and a substantial hedge again about two and a half metres high on the house side of the wall gave even more cover. The gate, a strong wrought iron affair, gave access to the seemingly red chippings drive which twisted through a second hedge, forbidding any sight of the premises beyond. At least Aaron believed the chippings to be red as they reflected the light from the security lights. The only part Aaron could see from the road was the roof and chimneys which reflected those ground security pole lights.

Aaron thought it would have been interesting to see the meeting between Buckland and Candor, but knew it was not essential. Candor, if he was indeed to see Buckland, was obviously after either weapons or explosives, or both; sufficient that the meeting, if taking place, was known and reported to Aaron's higher authority. Aaron, a staunch Israeli and confirmed member of the Mossad had only instructions to keep watch on Buckland and now the man Candor also. He had never been a member of that branch of the Mossad, the kidon,or their helpers the Sayanim who were licensed to sought out villains, perhaps for execution or extradition from countries where they had been given succour and protection. His own particular hero,Isser Harel, the then head of the Mossad, had been instrumental with seven others, in kidnapping the Nazi Adolf Heikman in Argentina were he had resided since the Second World War having escaped to there at that war's end. He had been kidnapped and brought to Israel in Nineteen Sixty where he was tried for, among other things, war crimes and found guilty and executed. The first and only execution carried out in Israel. David Ben Gurion had at that time been the Premier of Israel. Isser Harel resigned in Nineteen Sixty Three and Aaron often thought of him during his own, often tiresome surveillances.

Aaron having parked his Citroen hidden some way further along the road, decided to go and sit in it out of the rain until any car's headlights coming along the road would indicate to him he may have to make a foray into that rain which by this time was quite heavy. The carriageway was deserted and the only house, that of Buckland, was about a couple of kilometres beyond the last house in the road leading out of town.

Aaron eventually got out again, side stepped the puddles beginning to form and hearing in the noise of the downpour the almost musical tinkle of the rain running down between the bars of the road drains. After about a half hour and leaning against the bole of a tree, cursing to himself as the rain steadily became worse,he longed for a cigarette but daren't smoke in case Candor should arrive, get out of his car at the gate and smell the tang of the cigarette smoke. Besides, he knew it would be impossible to keep a cigarette dry. His normally even temper gradually deteriorated; he wondered whether Hassan had managed to keep track of Candor should he not follow their hunch about his visiting Buckland.

Perhaps Hassan's cover had been blown and Candor had gone to ground, or again, maybe he wasn't Candor at all but just some nervous individual trying to maintain his privacy. Then of course, there was the possibility that Candor, if indeed it was he, had seen through his own and Hassan's charade and waited for the Algerian and—but that didn't bare thinking about.

Aaron unconsciously reached for a cigarette, extracted it from the packet and lit it. He had taken a couple of lungsful of smoke before he realized what he was doing. Only as the cigarette broke up in his wet fingers as he put it to his lips again did he remember why he dare not smoke. He stamped the offending soggy mess into the rain soaked ground, remonstrating with himself for his lack of discipline and cursing under his breath for the conditions which were prevalent as the water dripped on him from the greenery of the branches of the tree under which he stood.

He tried to think positively and his self doubts eased as he remembered Hassan's reputation and skill. The craft the man had learned as a boy in his native Algeria. He smiled to himself as he recalled Hassan's ability to extricate a man's wallet. He would accidentally stumble against him, apologize profusely, castigating himself for his inept clumsiness, to the victim. Accepting that person's forgiveness he would then make off with the man's belongings. His victim, feeling a better person for accepting Hassan's craven apologies with good grace would happily go on his way, to regret the loss of his property later.

Feeling better, Aaron leaned back against the tree again, turned up tighter his coat collar and resigned himself to his vigil.

§ CHAPTER 15

Candor stepped back inside the cafe, thinking. For some reason he felt uneasy; the big man had driven past apparently without a glance, but Candor did not feel very reassured. He sat down again and attended to his coffee.

The tall miserable looking individual was gazing sadly into his coffee cup as though wishing it would refill itself, saving him the effort of going once again to the counter.

Candor felt that something was wrong somewhere. The man's behaviour seemed to him to be too studied, almost an act. A warning bell sounded in Candor's subconscious and his eyes narrowed.

That was it, he thought. This man was a partner of the big man who had just left; they were a two-some and had just carried out a switch in observation. He wondered if perhaps, they were part of a three-some, if there was a third man, or woman somewhere nearby, to take over again. He decided to find out. He paid for the coffee and left.

The only addition to the few parked vehicles near the cafe was a scruffy Renault, almost leaning against the kerb on its sagging springs. Candor walked quickly past it in the drizzle and dived into a shop doorway. The shop boasted a sun blind, still extended and side curtains at each end of the frontage. Although it was now drizzling quite sharply Candor could see the cafe door through the gap between the side curtains and the wall. He had time to compose himself there before the dark, miserable man appeared at the cafe entrance. He looked quickly up and down and seeing no one, hurried to the side street where he carefully investigated the position of Candor's stolen Peugeot.

Candor's face became grim as the man sprinted to the Renault, opened the door and got in.

Candor left his hiding place and quickly moved towards the Renault, reaching the driver's door as the engine burst into life. He opened the door saying 'Pardon Monsieur'. Hassan, surprised, turned towards Candor, his mouth dropping open in surprise. A few seconds later Candor was engaging the car's gears and driving them both out of the town.

The tall dark Algerian was collapsed choking against the passenger door to where Candor had heaved him, his breathing laboured. His eyes were streaming and blood flecked the spittle which dribbled from his open mouth.

When the car had left the last house behind, Candor stopped it and turned to the stricken man who was beginning to recover slightly. The rain hissed down and beat on the car roof. It was quite dark by then and Candor switched on the courtesy light; he turned to the man who was regarding him with eyes full of pain. He searched the man's pockets and was not surprised when two of the items he turned out were a police identity card, together with a badge. There was also a small automatic pistol, about point .22 calibre he surmised. There was little else of interest except the man's driving licence and insurance documents. As an afterthought he hitched up the man's trouser bottoms and there in a small holster was another pistol similar to the other and a small stiletto.

'So, quite an arsenal eh?' he said.

The man just looked at him saying nothing, giving no indication whether or not he understood Candor's English.

On the key ring attached to the ignition key, Candor identified the key which opened the glove compartment; inside which he found some cartridges which obviously fitted the two weapons and little else of interest.

Candor thought for a moment; he wondered where the big man had gone and what he, himself, was going to do with his passenger. These two then were from the police and he wondered if any others knew of his presence in Thiers. The obvious thing to do, therefore, assuming they did, was to contact Buckland immediately, get the stuff from him and disappear. It was apparent there was no means of communication with police headquarters, or anywhere else in the Renault and he wondered if the big man had the means in his car to contact his superiors and perhaps was at that moment doing just that.

He looked again at the man in the passenger seat who, though still in great discomfort, was taking more interest in Candor.

'Parlezvous Anglais?' Candor asked.

At first the man made no indication whether he did or not. Swallowing with difficulty he just looked at Candor, the pain showing in his dark eyes.

'Where's your chum, the fat man?' Candor asked, this time in English.

Mradmoor made a gesture with his hands, palms uppermost and shrugged his shoulders. A croak came from his lips.

'So you do understand English' stated Candor. 'Are you trying to say you don't know the fat man?'

Mradmoor shook his head and said with great difficulty, 'I know of him'.

He swallowed again, painfully.

'Don't try to fool me 'said Candor; 'it's obvious the two of you were working together. I've been in the game too long not to spot your play-acting'.

His voice was scornful. The man shrugged again and Candor continued, 'I am interested to know where the fat man has gone. However, I don't care to hang around here waiting for your friends to come along, so we'll go for a little ride'.

He took off the man's tie, meeting with no resistance to his roughness; Mradmoor meekly accepting the tying of his hands together in front of him. Candor felt the man was no danger to himself, he was still obviously distressed from the blow to his throat, but as an afterthought he took off the man's waist belt and with it tied the bound hands of the Algerian, now bent forwards, to his legs. He then switched off the courtesy light and drove off.

Eventually, about a kilometre along the road, his searching eyes spotted a lane with a closed gate. He stopped the car and taking the ignition keys with him, got out to have a look round. The gate was easily unhooked and he got back into the Renault and drove the car some way along the muddy lane and then off into a clump of trees. He stopped and turned to his passenger.

'I doubt we'll be disturbed here' he said.

'Now then! this fat man, he is your associate, or assistant, or whatever you like to call him, isn't he? He also looked Jewish to me'.

He saw a change in the man's eyes as he spoke. He untied the waist belt so that the Algerian could sit more upright.

'So, he is Jewish eh?'

The question betrayed a certain contempt, Mradmoor thought. He decided the only thing he could do to gain time was to co-operate with his captor.

'Yes, he is Jewish. So what of that? And yes he is my assistant. As a matter of fact, I too am Jewish. I am proud to be accepted as a Jew'.

He spoke slowly and with difficulty, the painful articulation of the words caused his eyes to fill with tears he could not restrain. As he spoke he saw his tormentor's face harden from mocking contempt to something more sinister.

'So that's it is it? the two of you working together and both Jews'. Candor spat the words out.

'I didn't know the French were such Jew lovers as to take them into their police force; and you, you're not French anyway. You look like an Algerian to me. Now that's something; an Algerian Jew'.

Candor laughed, a grim sound of derision.

'I would never have believed it'.

Mradmoor looked at him warily, wondering how far he could go before the man who held him captive became his executioner.

'What have you got against Jews?' he asked. 'They only wish to be left in peace. They do not want to interfere with anyone else. They are non-aggressive. They just wish to be left alone, others are the aggressors'. His throat burned with the effort of speaking and his pronunciation was an indication of his pain. His admittance to being a Jew and his words about them was the worst thing he could have said to Candor who was enraged at his utterance.

'Left alone! left alone!' he almost shouted, his face white with anger; 'why, you Jewish bastard. So they weren't aggressive when they killed my wife? A curse on you all'.

He hit the Algerian under the rib cage with another straight fingered blow and Hassan doubled up again in agony. His body felt on fire and he retched through his protesting throat. He felt the nausea shrouding his brain, whilst realizing that he had hit Candor's nerve on a raw spot due to his own ignorance of the man's reasons for his hate. Above his own torment he heard his captor curse him again.

'We'll put paid to your bloody Jewish regime. You'll all suffer; first those bastards in the Knesset, then the rest of you will follow the same fate'.

Candor wrenched open the door and went round to the passenger side. He shackled the weakened mans hands once again to his legs by his belt and dragged him by the scruff of his neck to the boot of the car, into which he dumped him with little ceremony. He struck him another blow to the back of his neck as he forced him in. The Algerian, lying in the foetal position, jerked once, then relaxed into unconsciousness.

Still in a highly aggressive state, Candor got in the driving seat, started the engine and roared back down the lane to the main road, By the time he had opened the gate and got back in the car his rage had subsided. He wiped the rain from his face and hair with his handkerchief and sat for a minute thinking. More certain now of the necessity of haste in his visit to see Buckland.

He realized he had been foolish to allow his anger to overcome his circumspection. His lapse in advising his prisoner of his intentions regarding the Jews, had signified that persons' demise; but he told himself, he had meant to kill the Algerian anyway. He could not have been spared to tell his story to his superiors. He also chastised himself for not finding out more about the 'big man', the Algerian's accomplice. In venting his spleen on the tall miserable looking individual, he had lost the advantage. The fellow would never talk now, he decided.

He was about to drive back up the lane to the copse again, when an idea struck him. He smiled to himself.

'Yes' he thought, 'they don't know I have the miserable bastard's Renault. I'll go and check on the Peugeot. If there's no one about I'll leave them a gift. By the time they find him I'll be well away'.

Candor could not resist the idea of cocking a snook at the French police yet again; even the danger of the situation could not deter him. He knew there was a possibility that the 'big man' had already reported his presence in the area but he laughed at the risk. He drove back into the town in the pouring rain, his wet trousers clinging to his thighs as he peered into the gloom, through the mist condensed on the windscreen. The wipers, flicking the water away had difficulty maintaining an area on the glass through which to see a passage through the downpour. The raindrops glistened and reflected the light from the headlamps, like falling tinsel.

The Englishman returned to where he had parked the big Peugeot, stopping a hundred metres or so away and sitting in the Renault with the lights extinguished. He searched the area with keen eyes for any suspicious activity, remaining in the car for a good ten minutes. The street seemed deserted.

Eventually, taking the chance that the Peugeot was not under observation in the filthy weather, drove the

Renault up to it. He got out and with a thorough last look around, opened the driver's door of the other vehicle. He quickly collected everything of his and transferred them to the Renault. He was about to get in the smaller car when, on second thought, he went to the rear of the Peugeot and opened the boot. He removed the number plates which had originally been fitted to it and with a roll of insulating tape from his own belongings took them also in to the Renault.

It did not take him long to bind the mouth and ears of the man in the boot of the Renault with the tape. He got in the driver's seat and did a three point turn in the street and reversed the Renault back up to the rear of the Peugeot, leaving a short gap between the two cars.

He got out and opened the boots of both cars after another intensive perusal of the street. He began to bundle the Algerian across the gap from one car boot to the other and in the rain, almost dropped him between the two vehicles. He heard a door slam somewhere down the street and looked up. In the darkness he could just make out a female figure approaching, holding a large umbrella in front of her and leaning against the driving rain.

Candor grabbed the man's body and with a desperate heave hauled him up and into the Peugeot's boot and slammed down the lid. He pretended to look for something in the Renault's boot as the woman passed. She did not even give him a glance; nevertheless, he felt it had been a close call and was glad of the darkness and the rain. Another scan of the area revealed nothing; he once again opened the Peugeot's boot. Taking the tape he wrapped it round and round the struggling man's head, finishing the job he had started; he, weakened by Candor's blows and restrained by his bonds, had no chance to prevent the Englishman from completing his task.

By the time Candor had closed the boot again and got back in the Renault, Hassan Mradmoor had suffocated. For once the Algerian had made the mistake of underrating the skill and the ruthlessness of the subject of his surveillance, paying the ultimate penalty for his mistake.

Candor drove off in the Renault to his liaison with Buckland, the body in the boot of the Peugeot, another marker on his journey to the destination ordained by Jordan.

§ CHAPTER 16

Inspector Seth Winfild could not help but feel a little frustrated. He and Sergeant Peter Bracken had been in France for two days trying to find out from the French police what they knew about Candor. They had just left the Poste de Police in Clermond-Farand and Seth aired his displeasure with a little vehemence.

'Do you think the buggers' know more than they're letting on Pete? We've been here two days and learned nothing, we might as well have stayed at home'.

'It seems that way guv' agreed Bracken, 'we're no wiser than when we left London. My guts haven't got over that crossing yet either'.

'Never mind your insides Pete, there's a cafe over there. Let's drown your guts, as you call 'em in coffee, while we take stock. You've brought the map I hope'.

'Aye guv, we don't want to get lost do we?'and he grinned.

They entered the cafe and Winfild ordered coffee. His school French easily translated by the waitress into understandable sense. Her experience with English tourists, who believed everyone should be able to understand English, once again proved effective, she had shown no surprise at their lack of the basics required; she'd had plenty of experience.

The two C.I.D. men sat at a table in the corner and in the manner of police officers, unconsciously scanned the tables and other customers. They examined the surroundings and their eyes took in all the details of the interior. The waitress brought their coffee and they thanked her then, sipped it slowly, neither saying anything for a minute or two. Bracken was the first to break the silence between them.

'The Super'll be wanting another report any time' he offered. 'What're we going to tell 'im?'

'God knows' Winfild blasphemed, unlike his usual ebullient self. 'The trouble is, that here you can't understand what they're 'gabbling' about. Them that can speak our lingo don't tell you anything you don't already know, it's like trying to draw water out of stone'.

'Too right guv' sympathized Bracken, 'er—you did let on to the Super you don't know much French?'

'All right, all right, Pete. Less of the 'mickey' taking. Get that pocket map out and let's have a 'butchers'. Maybe we can 'suss' out where the bugger's heading for. I heard one of these Surete fella's mention something about a place called 'teeay'—or something like it.

130

They were definitely on about explosives. Their word for it's nearly the same as ours and he also said 'armes portatives'. Small arms, I reckon. Another thing; they mentioned a guy called 'Monsieur Bucklan'. That's Buckland more than likely but the name doesn't ring any bells with me, so I'll request information about a Buckland from London. They might be able to throw some light on it. I've a feeling that if I asked the 'plods' over here they wouldn't be forthcoming; so, we'll try and find out for ourselves first'.

Bracken had taken the map from his pocket and spread it over the table, pushing the coffee cups to one side. They pondered over it for a while and then Winfild called the waitress over. She thought they were wanting something to eat perhaps, but was surprised when he asked her if she could point out 'Teeay' and with a somewhat suspicious look at them both, wondering if they were 'ribbing' her, she pointed out Thiers on the map. 'That is the town you want monsieur'.

Winfild thanked her, then, as she moved away, turned to Bracken.

'It's their bloody accent you know and nothing's spelt out the way they say it. Mind you, when you think of places in England like—er, Worcester and Gloucester, Slough and Brough, we can't complain I suppose.

'Anyway, now we know where it is, I'll get in touch with London about a Buckland and get them to pass it on to us in this place Thiers; that is, if they've got a police station there'.

'Right guv' said Bracken. 'It don't look as though we're goin' to learn anythin' 'ere, so we might as well push off, eh? D'yer think we might get a few sandwiches before we go, just in case we can't get 'em later?'

It was more a statement than a question and Winfild grunted his agreement.

'Aye, we might get hungry and it doesn't look like they're going to tell us anything more than we know already. We might be able to get a line on this Buckland bloke in this other place. That's if I did hear his name right'.

They finished their coffee and Bracken went to the counter, returning with a supply of sandwiches, Seth Winfild also got up and thanked the waitress again and they left to go back to the police station. There, to make their report by phone to London and to request information about a suspected arms and explosives dealer named Buckland.

After their business at the police station had been concluded they returned to their 'digs' and packed their bags having been informed that there was indeed a police station in Thiers also.

'How far is this place guv, do you think?' asked Bracken, munching on one of the egg sandwiches.

'About thirty eight kilometres, that's say twenty four miles or so, according to that big wall map they've got at the station. I checked up while I was there; we should be able to get lodgings there I reckon, there's usually someone who will put visitors up. We may as well move there as stay here; it's a lot smaller place and easier to find your way about and pick up information I should think. Pass me a sandwich and then we'll go'.

Winfild was correct in his assumption that Thiers was much smaller than Clermont-Farand, but the streets above the fast flowing river Durolle surprised them by their steepness. They discovered some beautiful 15th Century timbered houses and a couple of interesting churches, but Bracken was more interested in their finding some sort of accommodation. Only by a visit to the police station they had been told about and an explanation of their presence there, were they eventually recommended to a Madame Charpentier, by a phone call. She said to send them round whenever they had finished their business at the station.

Following the police directions they arrived on her doorstep and knocked on the door. There was a rattle of bolts and the door opened a fraction, restrained by a large chain.

A small, bald, bespectacled man; his thin, pinched face, the lower half almost hidden by a huge, black and grey moustache, peered over the spectacles with narrowed eyes through the gap. He reminded Winfild of a character he'd seen in silent films but couldn't remember the name. He smiled at the fellow and explained as best he could how he had been advised by the local constabulary that Madame Charpentier had accepted them as temporary house guests.

The man just blinked at Winfild and said nothing; he made no movement to open the door further either. Seth Winfild looked at his Sergeant and shrugged his shoulders.

'Ask him if he speaks out 'lingo' guv' suggested Peter Bracken.

The little man looked at Bracken as the Sergeant spoke and then back again at Winfild.

Suddenly his face registered surprise, disappeared from the door edge and the door slammed shut. There was a rattle of chain and then the door was flung wide open.

A huge, red faced woman, with dyed black hair, bosom heaving, waved them in. Her breathing was quick, noisy and shallow, almost asthmatic. The two visitors squeezed past her, dropping their bags on the hall floor. She bolted the door behind them, saying, with some pauses for breath.

'He don't speak English, 'e's my 'ubby, met 'im in the war an' 'e couldn't be bothered to learn English. Yer wouldn't think 'as 'ow 'e were good lookin' then would yer?' and she laughed, which called for more heavy gasps of air.

Her accent was a mixture of several English Counties with a harsh French intonation for good measure. Winfild smiled. Monsieur Charpentier stood with an expression of guilt, on the worn carpet, further down the hall; his shirt, collar missing and open at the neck had shed a couple of buttons, revealing a bony white chest. The large red braces supported over-length trousers whose liberal waist size suggested they had been designed for a more rotund individual, either that, thought the Inspector, or Monsieur Charpentier had been seriously ill; an illness that an occasional wheesey cough from the man gave witness. Each of his large felt slippers sported, at the instep, a knitted rabbit's head, complete with button eyes. He stood stiff, slightly bent and still, holding his hands clasped together in front of his thin stomach, head down, peering over his thick-lensed spectacles at them. A yellow canary,fluttering from perch to swing and back again, in a golden coloured cage twittered its song near his shoulder on the bookcase there.

'Mind you, 'e's not a bad old so and so' the woman continued; 'e'll do any thin' for me, but I canna say as 'ow 'e takes to strangers much. Still, things as they are these days, yer canna blame 'im can yer? Call 'im Bert. It's Bertrand really, but I allus calls 'im Bert. My name's Mabel. The 'bobbies' said yer'd be wantin' somewhere fer a day or two an' bein' English bobbies yersel' I said it'd be a' right. Will yer be wantin' supper?' She took a few quick gasps of breath now and again during this declaration.

She stood looking at them both; her torrent of words had hardly been restricted by her shortness of breath and the sudden interjection of a question took them by surprise.

'Er—no thanks', answered Winfild at last, 'we have eaten and we just need a room'.

'That's a' right then, wot about breakfast? English style I suppose? Mind you, yer canna beat a good breakfast inside of yer, I allus say. Makes a proper start fer the day. This way then, I'll show yer where yer room is. Yer don't mind both bein' in't same bedroom eh? Mind yer it's only room I've got empty anyway, but there's two beds, both singles'.

They picked up their bags and she led the way slowly, ponderously up the thick, worn carpeted stairs, pausing now and then for a breath or two as she continuously rambled on about this and that and nothing in particular. By the time they reached the room earmarked for them, which she opened with a key from a large ring full of keys taken from her apron pocket, they had heard most of her personal history; about her family, her meeting with Bert while serving in the A.T.S. at the end of the Second World War. Also her courtship, marriage, move to France and her life there; most of Bert's short-comings and blessings, the town, the local people, the tourists and a hundred other subjects.

Seth and Pete followed on behind, marvelling at Mabel's ability to keep up a continual chatter whilst obviously in some, not inconsiderable physical discomfort.

Eventually their hostess left them on their own, having pointed out the usual plumbing and toilet appurtenances. Both the English C.I.D. men breathed a sigh of relief as the bedroom door closed behind her and dropped their bags on each of the two beds.

'No wonder the poor bugger says nowt' said Peter Bracken, 'e never get's the chance. I dare bet 'e's forgotten how to talk, English or no English'.

Seth Winfild laughed as he opened his travelling bag.

'You may be right Pete. Have you wondered how the poor sod managed to pop the question? I bet she couldn't speak French either then. He doesn't know any English and couldn't have got a word in edgeways if he did. That's a mystery I bet will never be solved. 'Anyway, it looks a comfortable stable; I wonder how many other lodgers she's got? And can I have another sandwich? I didn't want to prolong the attention of our host by accepting her offer of food'.

'There's no telling how many lodgers she's got guv. They perhaps keep out of her way. Can't stand the ear bashing I'd say' and he passed the packet of food to Seth.

'Thanks. He picked a sandwich out of the packet and handed it back. Right then Pete. I'll toss this double headed penny to see who goes down for breakfast in the morning. There's no point in us both getting clobbered. Loser has to bring the other's up here'.

'Thanks a lot guv. I guess it's my ear'ole that's for it then'.

He jumped on the bed allotted to him and bounced up and down a few times. There was a twanging and grating of springs.

'Anyway' Bracken continued 'it won't matter if you snore, these springs'll keep me awake anyway. Listen to 'em'.

Seth Winfild threw a pillow at him, picked up his toilet gear and made off to the bathroom, swallowing the last bite of the sandwich. A joke and a laugh were a necessity sometimes, he thought, if only to prevent them going 'bananas' on a job like the one they had. His face became more serious as he began his ablutions and his thoughts turned once again to the man Candor.

How were they going to stop him? He always seemed to be that one jump ahead of everyone else while they only seemed to follow a trail of dead bodies. He looked at himself in the mirror as he asked himself the questions; what would tomorrow bring? Where was the assassin? The result of his wondering and worrying about the case only seemed to etch the lines deeper in his face. He rubbed his hand over his jaw.

'Curse the sod' he said to the reflection in the mirror. He finished up and went back to the bedroom, Bracken taking his turn in the bathroom. He lay on top of the bedclothes with his hands behind his head, going over in his mind again all they knew about the killer they were following. He supposed it was even possible the man might very well be in the same town as themselves, that very minute. He turned to the door as Peter Bracken returned from his ablutions.

'Say Pete; have you thought about the possibility that this guy we're after could be here in Thiers with us?'

The Sergeant thought for a moment.

'Aye guv you could be right', then—'what if the bugger's staying here in this house? He must be getting his head down somewhere mustn't he ?'

'I think that's carrying hope and coincidence too far Pete' Seth laughed, 'still you're right about him having to get his head down somewhere—but where? I wonder if he sleeps in his car? He must have quite a pong on if he's not using proper facilities; people will be giving him a wide berth; Eh! That's perhaps the way to spot him, people giving him the cold shoulder' and he laughed.

'Aye and I wonder' said Bracken, 'supposing Buckland is the man whom he's going to meet, if in fact he's been to see him yet? Snag is, we won't know about Buckland until we hear from London tomorrow. There again guv. We don't know if there really is a guy named Buckland; where he lives, nor even if Candor's really going, or been to see him anyway. We might be all wrong and Candor miles away'.

'You're a wet blanket Pete', reproached Seth Winfild. 'We've got to try these things haven't we? O.K. we may eliminate Buckland, or a supposed Buckland from our enquiries tomorrow. But, at least, if that's what happens, we'll know if Candor is making for somewhere else. Also we know the French police will be keeping a sharp lookout for this guy; they're pretty well fired up about him. They want him almost as much as we do.

'That's another thing. I want to beat them to it if I can. Same as Oakey says, we've got to get him first. So, tomorrow we've got to get cracking. Keep our eyes open and our ears pinned back. We don't want to miss the slightest bit of information'.

'Right guv! I'm with you all the way' agreed the Sergeant as he unfolded his pyjamas from his bag.

'O.K. Pete get your head down. See you bright and early in the morning and don't forget about breakfast. I don't think I could face the charming Madame Mabel Charpentier first thing'.

'Thanks a lot guv. Good night. I bet I dream about tomorrow's confrontation with the lady, will it be a nightmare d'yer think?' and he switched off the light from the bare bulb hanging from the ceiling.

⁑ CHAPTER 17

Hiram Woolley slammed the door behind him. He went straight from his father's office to his own and picked up his hat and coat and left the building. The quarrel he had just had with his father simmered in his mind. He had told his father some weeks before that he was determined to give up his role in the business, to follow a different path in his life. The ensuing scene then had been as unpleasant as the one in which he had just taken part.

On that first occasion his declaration of his intentions had been met with accusations of betrayal, followed by pleadings to reconsider, a lecture by the father on duty and charges of irresponsibility; refutation and recriminations by Hiram about parental responsibility. Eventually, in the end, Hiram had agreed to stay on for a while longer and think about what to do.

Now his father appeared to have forgotten Hiram's initial notice of his belief that his future lay away from the family business. His intentions seemed to have been shrugged aside; no importance had been given by the father to his son's decision. It seemed to Hiram that his parent believed it to have been a mere, temporary aberration, a slight deviation from the smooth path of obedience to his father's wishes. Why couldn't they get it into their heads that he was no longer interested in pursuing the reponsibilities of engineering management? That his whole interest was outside his father's interests and he had tried his best to instigate that into his father's mind.

Since his marriage to Patricia Scholland, Hiram had imagined that the relationship with his parents would have improved, especially as Pat had embraced the Jewish faith.

'If only they could understand my feelings about our Country and its enemies' Hiram thought. 'They can't seem to accept that we're here, only on sufferance. We only have to become complacent and the whole lot of them will be at our throats again'.

His father had again remonstrated with him for spending too much time away from the job. He could not see that Hiram should have any interests that were foreign to the business.

'The business first and last' he had said. 'What's going to happen to the business if you neglect it! I am getting old now and soon you will have to take it on your shoulders. If you don't put more time in now, how are you going to cope in the future when I am not here?

What will happen to the business then? The business is your inheritance. You should cherish it; help it to grow. You must put more time in it Hiram'.

No! He had ignored and given no importance to Hiram's earlier declaration that he wished to make his own way. The lecture had been the same as always. Hiram's argument that the business would not be his to have if their enemies kicked them out of Israel made no impression on his father.

'There are others whose responsibility it is to keep the boundaries safe Hiram. The military have their job, you have yours and yours is the business. You have served your time in the I.D.F. (Israel Defence Forces). Let others serve their time and you concentrate on your correct occupation—the business'.

It was always the same ending. Hiram could not persuade his father that responsibility for the business could be delegated to more able men who would look after it and work for it; because so to do would be to their advantage as well as the family's. It always ended up in accusations and recriminations and so it had again. Was there ever going to be an end to it?

Hiram drove fast through the light traffic out of the town and pulled up off the road. The sun's rays through the windscreen were hot and he divested himself of his hat and coat. He took off his tie and rolled it up neatly, putting it in one of the coat pockets.

To ease his frustration he reached for the car phone he'd had installed and reported in to the area headquarters of the Mossad. He received a message that they had been trying to get hold of him as he was to meet his immediate superior at their usual rendezvous that evening. Something important had come up and he was first to prepare for a journey which might take several days and to pack ready, clothing and toiletry sufficient for such a journey. His contact refused to say more over the phone line and now, excited, he returned to the town and his home, the quarrel with his father thrust aside.

Hiram greeted his wife with an unusually long embrace; he was both excited and apprehensive. She sensed immediately that something was afoot and it seemed her heart missed a beat.

'What is it Hiram? What has happened?' she asked, pushing him away so that she could see his face and perhaps get a glimpse of what was exciting him.

'I—I have to go away for a few days. It's a job for the organisation. I was told today'.

'Oh my God!' She exclaimed, 'why you Hiram? Couldn't they send someone else? You are new to all this. You've no experience with what they're up to'.

She was white and distressed. She slumped down on a chair, feeling suddenly weak in her legs. Her obvious distress alarmed him for a moment.

'Calm yourself Pat'. Hiram knelt beside her taking one of her hands in his. 'Don't take it so hard. It's nothing exceptional for a fresh face to be sent on a mission. Besides, it's to meet another man and liaise with him. It will only be observation; I'll not be on my own,—no arms, fireworks or anything like that, none of that sort of trouble'.

He got up, not letting go of her hand. He pulled her to her feet and led her to the sofa. They sat down together and he put his right arm around her, kissing her on the cheek, taking her hand in his left hand.

'Look' he said, 'everyone has to start somewhere in any job. But this is not a dangerous escapade we're talking about here. Although there can be danger in certain circumstances—it can't be all talk and no action all the time—this is not one of those occasions; but, we have to show that we can help. Not just by talking about it, but also by actually getting up and doing something.

'This is my chance to get involved in the physical side of the job. If that's the right term, to actually be seen to be doing something useful'.

'But Hiram' she interrupted, 'it might be dangerous. You might get hurt—might get—. Oh Hiram I'm afraid. I wish you'd never got me to agree with you about you joining the Mossad in the first place'.

'Now don't Pat. Don't put more into it than there is. I know I'm not explaining it very well. Look, we know that here we live with danger all the time, in a way. There's no saying when some fanatic band or perhaps just one individual, will commit suicide just to take another few of our people—our children even, with them. No matter where we are, where we go; as Jews we are in constant danger, have been for years and years and not just under the Nazi regime. You know that yourself without me having to tell you and there's no knowing when that condition will change; probably never in our lifetime and as a consequence we have to be wary all the time, as I explained to you months ago. You seemed to understand then.

'I told you all this before we were married. I didn't want you to marry in ignorance of the situation here and I thought you understood, you seemed to then'.

'Oh Hiram, it did seem all right then. I love you so much; I don't want to see you hurt, or worse. I'm frightened for you; what will I do if anything happens to you?'

'But I tell you. Nothing is going to happen to me. That is—there will be no more danger where I'm going than there is here, than there is anywhere in Israel. Our enemies are all around us, possibly with the exception of Egypt now. They have honoured their agreement with us since Sadat came here. We are a strong nation now and we have to remain so. This sort of job I have to do is typical of the way we maintain our strength; by vigilance and the gathering of intelligence. The use of that intelligence is the best way to make sure none can assail us again. We have to get it right, we have to know everything that goes on. We all know what happened to millions of our people by the Nazis and some others in that Thirties and Forties war, we must never let something like that ever happen again. I think that some of our country's present neighbours would have liked to do what the Nazis tried—tried to exterminate us that is, it would have been to their advantage'.

As he spoke his eyes were bright; his fists clenched and unclenched with emotion. He stood and looked down at her.

'Every Jew, man or woman, in Israel must work to preserve and maintain our position; to show that we can keep our strength. That we can become self sufficient and prosper without either help or interference. Israel is our land. We shall never again be driven out, by anyone, never, even if we have to give many of our lives to prevent it'.

At first Patricia said nothing else. She could see that further argument was useless. Her eyes though, betrayed her concern and tears trickled down her cheeks.

'Well then' she managed to say at last, 'if that is how it is to be, then I shall join the Mossad too. I can learn. I can be of use to them'.

Hiram looked down at her and smiled, a little more relaxed at her remark. 'Well, it's nice to see your spirit my love, but I don't think it is necessary to do that. Just support me and understand that we must prepare to be parted now and again'.

He reached down and lifted her to her feet, kissed her and wiped the tears from her face.

'There. Go and freshen up; we'll have a meal together; then I must go'.

He released her and she dutifully went away to do as he bid. She entered the bathroom and looked in the mirror at her reddened eyes and smudged mascara. She washed and repaired her make-up, then sat quietly for a minute or two. Her thoughts were about what Hiram had said, about strength and unity and everyone working together to maintain that strength.

'So' she thought 'it's not necessary for me to do anything eh? Well, I'm not going to sit here just waiting and worrying. Other Jewish women are in the Services aren't they? Right, they must have something I can do too'.

She got up and went into the kitchen to prepare a meal for the two of them. She said nothing about her resolve to Hiram, not even when they sat together after the meal was eaten. She had checked his packing for the trip and made sure he had enough for the needs he'd said he would perhaps have.

They talked about other matters. She mentioned nothing about her decision and he nothing more about the job in hand. Eventually it became time for him to leave and she kissed him ardently then wished him 'good luck' and watched as his car left the drive. She waved him 'goodbye', turned and went back into the house, her determination to do something herself having become certain in her mind.

That evening Hiram sat drinking coffee in a cafe in a quiet quarter of the town, early for his appointment. His superior arrived punctually and brought his coffee to Hiram's table. He explained that Hiram was to proceed immediately to Ashdod on the coast; there he was to go to a certain 'mis'ada' to meet an intelligence courier, Vernon Pegton. He had just returned from France where he had been in contact with one of the two agents on surveillance duty there. One of those, a man named Hassan Mradmoor, a double agent who was really a policeman, but worked for the Mossad, had disappeared and it was believed he had been murdered. The suspect was believed by the other agent, Aaron Plaistot, to be on his way to Israel and he was obviously up to no good, it was believed he'd killed several people on his journey south through France and he had to be identified.

Hiram was to go to France to assist Aaron Plaistot in his surveillance and give any other aid required by that agent. Hiram's superior handed him an envelope.

'It contains an air ticket to Marseilles and sufficient funds to cover any other expenses or journeys you may have to make Hiram' he said and asked him if he was sure he had his passport. Hiram answered in the affirmative, thinking it an odd question, but supposed the superior probably thought Hiram was very inexperienced and wanted to make sure there was no possibility of a mistake jeopardizing the issue.

'It is well Hiram' he said. 'Good luck to you, but I tell you, you must be very careful. The suspect, whose name we now know is Candor, is extremely dangerous. Don't forget he is responsible for the deaths of several people; no one stands when he passes. They all fall before him, but only because they are not prepared for any eventuality. We have good intelligence to rely on and the determination to prevent the enemy from succeeding. Many would like to see us fall and they have tried; yes they have tried. But, if we are again vigilant and have the determination to make sure our actions succeed, we will prevail. They will never succeed in bringing about that fall. God speed and protect you Hiram. Farewell'.

He stood up and took Hiram's hands and clasped them between his. He turned and left.

§ CHAPTER 18

Aaron Plaistot, idly and unconsciously rotated the glass backwards and forwards by the stem between finger and thumb. What was left of the liqueur swilled up and down the sides of the bowl; almost to the brim, each time the motion was reversed. Aaron, sitting in the Auberge, wasn't seeing the glass or its contents. His mind saw only the Renault arriving in the rain at the gates of Buckland's house.

Aaron's heart quickened its beat a little as the headlights of the vehicle he'd seen coming, turned in towards the gate and revealed its identity. It was the battered old Renault of his friend and accomplice

Hassan Mradmoor. He relaxed and turned away from the tree behind which he had been concealing himself from the lights of the car and stepped out towards the road. He had to ask Hassan what he was doing there and what had happened to Candor. The man might turn up at any moment and he was about to shout and ask him where he'd been.

Almost immediately he realized his mistake, just as he was on the point of shouting Hassan's name. He dodged quickly behind the bole of another tree. The water dripped from the brim of his hat and he wiped the droplets from his glasses. His heart sank a little as he could see that the driver who had just emerged from the car and was pressing the bell push on the wall in the arch of the gateway, was the man he believed to be Candor himself. He could even hear the man's voice as he said something into the security microphone above the bell push.

The gates swung open and the Renault passed through, the gates closing again as the car went up the driveway.

Having concluded his business with Buckland and somewhat annoyed by the man's attitude and he himself in his usual high state of nervous tension, Candor was about ready to leave when he took umbrage with the man's remarks and having earlier not been impressed with his arrogance, what little patience he had ended and he lost control of his feelings as he had many times in the past. He turned on Buckland and threatened him if he did not keep his remarks to himself. Buckland just laughed and told him to watch his manners or his colleagues in London would teach him some. Candor again lost control completely and attacked Buckland without any further warning. Buckland was taken completely by surprise as Candor hit him in the throat and then grabbed him by the neck, covering his nose and mouth with his other hand.

Madame Pentriche had heard raised voices from where she was sitting in the library and went to see what the commotion was about. As she turned into the hall she saw the visitor with Buckland in his grip and panicked as Candor turned his head towards her. She ran back into the library and through a door into an adjacent annexe, locking it and ramming home the two bolts there. The door was steel framed as was the room's window and the door itself was steel; a security against any onslaught, be it human, animal or fire. The window glass was bullet proof. Buckland had, years before Candor's visit, taken no chances though in this instance he had under-estimated Candor's reputation, not being so knowledgeable about it as some others did. Buckland's neck had been broken and Candor soon gave up the attempt to get at the woman, she was of no consequence, he decided and anyway he had lost his ire; he had what he had come there for and he wanted to waste no more time. He put the large, heavy suitcase by the side of the other one already there, in the boot of the Renault and left.

Eventually after about an hour the swarthy, black eyed, extremely attractive, dark haired Madame

Pentriche, who was in her late thirties and had felt some affection towards Adam Buckland though she believed he seemed to act almost as a misogynist, risked opening the annexe door and hearing no sounds also opened the library door into the hall. She peered round the door and could see Buckland lying there. The front door was open and she carefully looked out and saw that the Renault was gone. She ran back to the prone figure whose glazed eyes were partly open and tried to find a pulse, but it was obvious that her employer was dead. After a little thought she decided she must phone the Police to inform them of the murder of Adam Buckland, but first she decided she must first phone a number in London to report what had happened, to Buckland's partners there; she had to cover her own safety before any other consideration.

Aaron was not only puzzled but fearful. 'What could have happened to Hassan? Why was Candor driving Hassan's car? Where was the fellow in whom he had placed so much trust?' The questions ran through his mind in rapid succession.

Obviously something awful had happened. The Algerian was usually so skilful in his work. 'What mistake had he made then, to betray to the Englishman his interest in him and which had allowed the assassin to gain an advantage over him?'

Aaron suddenly realized he was thinking of Hassan in the past tense. 'My God' he thought, 'is that the case? Is Hassan dead?' While he pondered on the puzzle he saw the flash of headlights through the hedge in the house grounds and then heard the sound of a car engine. The gates swung open again and the car arrived at the exit, probably thought Aaron, the lights of the car had triggered the sensor which supplied the power to open the gates, or an electronic beam had been broken by the car's motion, doing the same job, or maybe they had been opened from the house; whatever had been the cause, the gates had opened.

Hassan's car accelerated through the gateway and spraying a fountain of water from its tyres roared off up the road away from Thiers.

Aaron stepped forward and looked after the fast disappearing rear lights, then hastened to his own car, his rain soaked clothing forgotten in his concern for the missing Algerian. His feet sloshing through the water gurgling down the gutter and into the dripping trees of the copse, Aaron flung open the car door, squeezed his frame inside and operated the starter, blessing his luck as the engine roared into life. He drove away after the speeding Renault, with one finger trying to wipe the water from his spectacle lenses, he wanted to keep it in sight, but not get too close behind it that Candor might see he was being followed.

Some of the liqueur in the glass splashed over the rim as Aaron unconsciously accelerated the twirling motion. Startled, he jumped in his seat, looked guiltily around and took out his handkerchief to mop up the small pool of liqueur on the table. He needn't have shown any anxiety, no one was paying any attention to him. The few customers in the Auberge were each too concerned with their own business.

He sighed. Hassan his colleague, friend and assistant was dead he was sure and the man responsible for his death was upstairs above him in that Inn. He knew that because he had seen him drive into the adjacent car park in the Renault which belonged to Hassan. He had watched through the window, concealed as he was in the darkness and the rain and had seen Candor sign the counter ledger and pass on upstairs.

He even knew which room he was in. He had stood back and seen the light come on in the first floor window. He had watched and waited, still in the rain, listening again to the water running down the gutters and gurgling into the drains. Mercifully it was beginning to abate and he had decided to wait until the light had been extinguished. He had waited a further half hour after that and seen nothing of the man, so taking the chance of being seen by the assassin, he had entered the Inn himself.

Taking his bag from the car, he had obtained a room for the night where he'd stripped himself of his wet clothing and donned the change of clothes he always carried in his bag. He had washed and shaved; his wet apparel littered the radiators in the room and the bathroom and he had gone downstairs for a snack and a drink, taking great care that the man he was following was not in evidence, knowing that he, Candor, must be aware of his relationship with Hassan.

He finished the rest of the liqueur and left the bar room, returning to his room and lay on the bed, restless, trying to decide what his next move should be. His original instructions from his superiors in no way meant that he could approach Candor, not even with back up if he had any at hand. No! His job was to monitor the man's movements and report to those superiors when he had the opportunity. He wrestled with the problem of what to do next and one thing he was sure of; it was gross stupidity to stay in the same Auberge as the probable murderer of his friend. It was odds on that he would at some stage be seen by him. Candor was not likely to have forgotten his time in the cafe in Thiers. Besides he wanted the man to believe he was safe from observation.

Candor had obviously tumbled to what Hassan had been up to and no doubt tied Aaron in with him, so it was imperative that Candor should not know that Aaron was still at his heels. Making up his mind he gathered up the still damp clothing and the rest of his belongings. Taking great care once more that he was not taken unawares by the man Candor as he left his room, he went down to the reception counter.

He told the concierge he had decided to continue his journey North to Dijon now that the rain had ceased, as he was anxious to arrive there as soon as possible. He paid his bill, tipping the man generously in the hope he would forget his curiosity, unspoken but apparent, about Aaron leaving his car somewhere, instead of parking in the area provided by the Auberge; then walking in the rain instead of driving to the hotel. As Aaron left, he trusted the concierge had seen stranger behaviour from guests which would put his own in the shade,-not worth the recounting to anyone else. Then he found himself wondering if he had tipped him too much, perhaps thus drawing attention to his odd conduct. He shrugged, giving up the attempt to draw any psychological conclusion to what the man might or might not do. He had other worries to ponder.

The night was then almost clear, the rain having ceased and the clouds thinned considerably. It was nevertheless quite dark and because of the loss of cloud cover, turning cold. Aaron, though now dry, shivered and hurried to where he had parked the car. He got in and deciding that Candor was fixed up for the night, drove the car a little further down the side street to a more secure position. He slid the driving seat back slightly on its rails and operated the tipping lever, canting the back of the seat to a more comfortable angle. He settled himself, hoping he would not fall into a deep sleep, but if he did, that he would not overlay on the morrow.

He woke with a start, trying to make sense of where he was. It was pitch black and he was cold and stiff. One leg had gone nerveless and he moved it gently, gritting his teeth against the 'pins and needles' of the returning blood supply. He fancied he heard a noise and froze, straining to hear, but nothing stirred to disturb the stillness.

He got out after glancing around through all the windows, which for his large frame was a not too easy an action; exercising his arms and legs vigorously for a minute or two, he tried his best to get warm. He looked at his watch, which showed half past three o'clock. He suddenly had an idea.

He collected the small torch which he carried in the glove compartment and from the car boot, underneath the damp clothes he had dumped there, a short stiff wire. He locked the car doors and went off to the car park of the Auberge, keeping a sharp look out for unwelcome observers.

He soon identified the battered Renault which had belonged to Hassan and tried the doors. They were locked, but a couple of minutes careful work with the piece of wire on the passenger side window soon unlocked it. He listened again for a while but heard and saw nothing, so entered the car and searched it thoroughly. There was nothing of interest in it anywhere. Only bits of rubbish, empty packets and plastic cups and soiled sandwich coverings in the main.

He carefully wiped every solid object he had touched with his handkerchief and got out. He tried the boot lid; that was also locked. With some difficulty he managed to get in the rear seat of the car and by removing the back rest retaining pins, he leaned the 'rest' forwards gaining access to the boot catch. Straining his muscles and swearing at his bulk which was jamming him in the confined space, he could just reach in far enough to release the catch, grunting at his exertions which were beginning to steam up the windows. From what he could see in the boot from his position inside the car, he didn't have much hope of finding anything there. He replaced the rear seat back rest, wiped off any prints from the solid objects he had again handled and went around to the rear of the car. He jumped as a nervous reaction to the sudden bark of a fox away over the hedge at the extremity of the park, shuddered and had another look round.

After opening the boot, in the torch light he fancied there were traces of blood on the false bottom and not being sure, he wiped them over with the handkerchief for examination later. He lifted the false bottom of the boot and searched there but beside the spare wheel could find nothing of interest. He replaced the panel and after a last look round in the torch light reached up to close the lid. He took a sharp breath.

There in the grime on the underside of the lid, outlined by the torch beam, was clumsily scrawled 'C'est le Knesset'. He read the words over and over again. So, he decided, Hassan must have been stuffed in there like a parcel, but his confinement hadn't prevented his leaving a clue to Candor's intentions.

'But why hadn't Candor himself seen the message?' he wondered. Then he knew. 'Of course' he thought 'the rain; and he probably unloaded Hassan in the dark without the benefit of a torch. It must definitely have been Hassan who was responsible for the message, poor sod. I wonder how he died'

He looked again at the handkerchief in the torchlight, 'it must be blood' he decided, shaking his head. 'Poor sod' he said again.

He searched the boot for a piece of rag and finding none he took the rubber mat from the floor of the passenger side of the car and obliterated the scrawled message. He replaced everything as he had found it, as far as he could remember and relocked the doors and the boot lid. He returned to his own vehicle, had a last look around seeing no-one and got in. He looked at his watch and decided he had time for a good nap. As he settled himself down once more he realized he must report Hassan's message and probable death.

He knew the monthly courier had left for Marseilles only the day before with Aaron's last report to his own contact in Lyons. He would have to make contact again, it was impossible to maintain surveillance on Candor by himself now Hassan was gone. He resolved to phone for help the first thing in the morning in the hope that his contact would be able to get in touch with the courier before that individual left for Israel.

He woke again with a start, chilled through and desperate to relieve his bodily functions by finding a lavatory, hopefully not too far away. He cursed the cold early morning light. His eyes were sore and he looked at his watch and stretched as best he could in the confined space. He reckoned he'd had only about three hours sleep in total all night and he felt jaded, his mouth dry as dust and he passed his tongue around it, trying to stimulate the saliva glands.

'Too many damned cigarettes' he said aloud whilst hunting in his jacket pockets for the packet. He inadvertently pulled out the soiled handkerchief in his search and remembered Hassan. He examined the square of cloth in the morning light.

'Bloody Hell' he said. There were definite bloodstains there, mixed with the grime from the boot of Hassan's car, dried in the material. He turned it gently over and over again in his hands.

'The bastard' he exclaimed; then, 'Poor Hassan'.

He got out of the car, lit a cigarette whilst still examining the handkerchief. He folded it carefully, almost reverently and put it away in an inside jacket pocket.

He took deep lungsful of the cigarette smoke, recharging his system with nicotine as he flung his arms about and stamped his feet to increase the circulation of warming blood. He cast around for a telephone kiosk as it was getting lighter by the minute and the necessity to make a visit to a toilet area was getting more urgent. The chill in the air was gradually easing and there was evidence of a fine day forthcoming.

He decided that, toilet or not, he'd better have a quick look to make sure Candor hadn't left. Hands in his pockets, shoulders hunched and smoke drifting behind him from the cigarette drooping from his lips as he walked quickly on avoiding most of the rain puddles, he reached the top of the street.

The battered Renault was still there and looking around, he spotted a Cafe in the opposite direction to the Auberge and its car park. Signs of life in the village were now apparent and there were two men walking towards him as he went to the cafe. They acknowledged his 'Bon jour' but, it seemed to him, not without a hint of suspicion. Someone they had not seen before and therefore did not know and wondered what he was doing there so early in the morning.

Soon, having used the cafe toilet and breakfasted on croissant, jam and coffee and purchasing a packet of sandwiches for later, therefore his feeling for the need for sustenance being satisfied, he went to make his report. He had obtained trom the proprietor the location of the nearest public telephone box and decided to walk there after a further check on the Renault's position, it had not been moved. He felt he needed the exercise, but every step which took him away from the Auberge increased his concern that the murderer might leave during his absence. He increased his pace as he realized the cafe owner's estimate of the distance to the phone kiosk was in error. Eventually however, he spotted the 'TELEPHON' sign with relief and he searched in his pockets for the coins to make the call as he approached the box.

He told to his contact his suspicion that Hassan Mradmoor was certainly dead and the necessity for another assistant. He informed his contact of the message on the inside of the boot lid of the Renault which Hassan had managed somehow to scrawl there and his belief that Candor was already in possession of explosives as he had seen Candor drive Hassan's Renault through Buckland's house gates and then some little time later, leave. Receiving orders to maintain surveillance and knowing his report would be transmitted to those who needed to know it, he returned to the Citroen and sat thinking while warming up the engine.

Eventually he drove up to the main road and turned away from the Auberge until he found a spot where it was possible to turn the vehicle around, then headed back towards the hotel and parked at the road side between two other vehicles, thus pointing in the correct direction he assumed his quarry would leave, should Candor appear. Yet, far enough away so that, should Candor look about for anything suspicious, he would not be able to be seen, parked there.

He took another cigarette from the packet and lit it with the cigar lighter from the dashboard, switched off the engine and settled down once again to wait, blowing smoke hrough the partly open window.

❦ CHAPTER 19

The two British policemen's arrival at the Police Station in Thiers the following morning occasioned little interest to those on duty there. The few officers whose local headquarters it was and whose attendance at that time was required, were too involved in other matters to be curious about Seth Winfild and Peter Bracken's visit, giving them only a cursory glance and then carrying on with their hurried movements carrying out their own business.

'What do you think's caused all this ruddy 'hoo-ha' Pete?' Seth quietly questioned his assistant of the apparent haste of movement and busyness of what staff there was.

'Beats me guv! Something's livened them up though; where's that one who speaks our 'lingo'? I can't see him about anywhere' was Bracken's reply. He had been searching the faces of the French officers in his endeavours to find the one he knew would be able to help them.

'He's probably cuddled up to his missus now after his night shift, if he's got any sense. I don't expect they're daft enough to work all hours of the day and night to make a few bob like us. But, I suppose one of 'em must speak English' Seth said. He held out his arm to a hurrying, passing policeman, partially blocking the way through the door by the vacant reception counter.

'Excuse me chum, do you, er, I mean parlezvous Anglais?'

The man looked at him. 'Non! une moment sil vous plais'.

He called a name through the hatch above the counter and eventually a young officer came through the door to them. An exchange of rapid French followed and the new arrival said, 'Pardon; I can speak with you and would like to try out my little English. What is it I can do for you?'

'Well' said Seth Winfild, 'we came here yesterday evening and on the recommendation of one of your officers, we spent a night at a Madame Charpentier's house. It was quite late when we arrived you understand and we had no pre-arranged lodging waiting for us. We'd like now some further assistance please'.

He showed his identity card and explained they were expecting a call from England to this station. He also asked what all the commotion was about and was told to his surprise, that a police officer had been found dead in the boot of a stolen car.

'Where did this happen?' asked Winfild, all attentive now.

'Here in Thiers' was the reply.

'Good grief!' said Winfild. 'By the way; was this car a stolen Peugeot?' he asked.

'Why, yes it was. How did you know about that?' the officer was instantly suspicious.

'Well; I'd better tell you what we're doing here and perhaps you'll tell us what you know about this business' Winfild bargained.

'Very well! I think the Inspecteur had better hear what you have to say about this. Pardon me a moment'.

He left them and Seth turned to his sergeant.

'There you are Pete. We've made a good move coming here. Right on the bloody spot eh?' He rubbed his hands together showing his pleasure, believing he knew who was responsible.

'Not 'alf guv. Candor can't be very far in front of us if this has just happened. This dead man must have been found since we left Clermont-Farand, or they'd have been as jumpy as this lot are now'.

'Yeah! We've got to make the most of this Pete. We'll try and find out everything they know, if you think of anything that I don't ask them, feel free to ask them yourself. Hold it! The young geezer's coming back'.

The young officer asked them to accompany him and escorted them through all the lively commotion of officers hastening in several directions, squeezing past other officers down a narrow corridor to a small room, probably, thought Winfild, where they interviewed the local criminal fraternity.

The Inspecteur was middle aged and although obviously angry and upset about the murder of a brother officer, was very patient and friendly towards the two British C.I.D. men. He spoke excellent English and they spent a half hour talking about the case, though they were frequently interrupted by officers on station business.

'I am sorry for all these people coming in and out', he apologized, 'but the work has to go on. I think you know as much about this sad affair now as we know and I believe you are expecting a communication from your headquarters in London?'

Seth nodded and the Inspecteur pressed a buzzer on the desk.

'Well then. I'll leave you with Officer Bonnet who will help you'.

He rose and shook hands with them. The door opened and the young policeman they'd been speaking with previously appeared and the Inspecteur went away to carry on with his duties.

They had a few words with the helpful young man and he asked; 'Would you like une cup of cafe while I go to the radio room?'

They accepted his offer and he took them to the almost deserted police canteen where he fetched them their drinks before leaving them to find out about their message from London.

The man soon returned with the message they had been waiting for.

'Here you are. It arrived just a few minutes ago'.

Seth Winfild thanked him, read the paper then handed it to Peter Bracken. 'There you are,' he said, 'this 'info' ties in with what the Inspector said. This guy Buckland must be the one Candor's making for. By the way, it was a good guess eh? The name, I mean. Just shows you, it pays to keep your lug'oles open, you never know what you might find out' and he smiled at Bracken.

'Yes guv I must admit it. It was pretty fair that. Mind you, I bet Buckland's place is crawling with Gendarmes now eh? They're bound to go and see if Candor's been there aren't they?'

'You're right Pete. We'd better get over there ourselves. It's not far out of town according to the Inspector and we might just be able to see something and find out a bit more there. Better than getting corns on our backsides here don't you think?'

They got up and having found the exit again, went to the car. Seth had the key in the door lock when a shout alerted their attention. Seth looked up and the officer they had been talking to in the canteen waved them back in. The two C.I.D. men looked questioningly at each other and Seth shrugged his shoulders.

'Now what's up?' he muttered.

They turned and went over to Officer Bonnet and followed him back to the Inspector's office. The young policeman knocked lightly on the door and opened it for them.

'Ah good', said the Inspecteur, indicating to them to be seated.

'I thought perhaps that you may have already left. I have just received word that Monsieur Buckland is dead, apparently his housekeeper phoned in to us to say that Buckland had been attacked and that she thought he was dead. She herself had escaped the assailant by locking herself in an adjacent room to the library where the assailant couldn't get at her. She waited for some time then had a look round, found Buckland's body and phoned us'.

He examined their faces to see how the news affected them but could only see questioning surprise there as they looked at each other with eyebrows raised.

'Crikey' said Bracken, then. 'Er sorry guv, but he's been at it again then?'

'It appears that is so' said the Inspecteur. 'I suppose you mean of course, that Monsieur Candor is the, er, how do you say it, the culprit?'

Seth Winfild nodded in agreement.

'Yes it must be him. It would be too much of a coincidence for it to have been someone else I suppose?'

He sat back for a minute, thinking.

'How did he die?' he asked, after a few seconds thought.

Well', said the Inspecteur, 'as I mentioned in our earlier conversation, we became in possession of the search warrant I had requested and I sent out four men to carry out the search. The gate at Monsieur Buckland's residence is operated by remote control from the house whenever entrance is requested by a visitor. There is a switch operated microphone in a panel in the wall by the gate and also a camera to check on the identity of anyone requesting admittance. My officer's were ignored and they decided to force the gates open. It locks electronically and it took quite a time to gain an entrance. As there was no answer to their knock on the house door either, which was also locked, they had to force an entry there too.' He hesitated a moment.' You see Madame Pentriche was afraid to operate the gate or open the door and was hiding again in the library annexe until my men announced themselves.

'Of course when they did get in, it did not take them long to discover the body there'.

Seth looked at Peter Bracken.

'The body was definitely that of Buckland?'he asked

'Yes. That was Adam Buckland; his housekeeper was very upset and badly frightened'.

Here the Inspecteur raised his eyebrows and shrugged his shoulders.

'Buckland was not an old man by any standards and quite rich, but he was a bachelor. Madame Pentriche was a widow, her husband died of a heart attack some years ago, it was a surprise to all who knew him because he was quite young and it is rumoured that Madame Pentriche and Buckland were not just master and servant. But that is only rumour by the way, you understand how these rumours can get about in such circumstances, it is—was their affair if affair there was and I doubt its truth because others we know who have met Buckland say he was a misogynist and anyway, as I say, it does not concern us. Whatever those circumstances were which did prevail, it was their business and no-one elses, it was to do with their own private lives'. He hesitated again, he seemed sad.

'Well Inspector, how did he die?' Seth repeated his original question.

The Inspector recovered himself.

'He was partly strangled and had a broken neck. He did have other injuries, but this fiend killed him with his bare hands as he did our officer'. The Inspecteur held out his own hands and looked down at them.

'He is a monster, this Englishman. He spares no one. He leaves a trail of death everywhere he goes'.

The officer sat back and shuffled papers on his desk, his face bitter.

'I have a written report here. It was taken down by one of my men over the telephone from another officer at Buckland's house. He says they have searched the house and cellar thoroughly and have found nothing which would indicate Buckland having been in possession of arms or explosives or anything else illegal.

'Sniffer dogs, I think you call them, were used but my men couldn't say for sure they were positive there were no traces, though the dogs did sometimes seem more interested than others. However, nothing was found. It is the old story. We have kept an eye on this man for a long time, when I could afford the manpower that is.

'We have raided his house at odd times when there has been a whisper of something, on suspicion of him being in possession but have never found anything. He even had the nerve to complain to our Mayor that he was being harassed and for a while we had to be very careful in our investigation into the man's activities.

'Now it has come home to him with a vengeance and he has paid the ultimate price for those activities. In the past we have occasionally been lucky, our surveillance resulting in the apprehension of some criminal in possession of arms or worse. That is why we have tolerated Buckland's presence here. But we could never tie him in personally. No one would implicate him in their being supplied with arms or anything else. But now it is finished for him.

'What we do not know is whether this man Candor is now in possession of arms or not. We suspect that he is of course, we expect that was the reason for his visit to Buckland, was it not? but why he should murder Buckland and frighten his housekeeper is a mystery. He must have had a reason I suppose; he is a very dangerous man indeed. We have interviewed Madame Pentriche but she says she knows not that the assassin went away with explosives and she was too frightened to be positive anyway about anything. I suppose she didn't necessarily have knowledge of whether he did or not; if he did, where in the house had they been kept? That is a mystery'.

'I agree there' said Winfild. He could see and understand how upset the Inspector was. He had lost an officer and now another person on his patch and literally hadn't a clue where the killer was or where he was going next.

'By the way' Winfild asked, 'have you found out where the car of that officer of yours is yet?'

'No. We are keeping a look out for it as you can imagine. But it is such a big job to check so many. There are hundreds of such vehicles around in this area and now, of course, the murderer has probably left the district. He could be many miles away'.

'I see' said Seth Winfild, 'I don't suppose you've come to any conclusions about why your officer was murdered? I mean, was he specially detailed to hunt for Candor?'

He thought the office looked a little embarrassed by his questions and was instantly alert.

'He was on the case I suppose?' he asked.

'Well', the Inspecteur hesitated. 'All our officers of course, were watching for the man Candor, should he enter the district. By that, I mean everyone was on the lookout for a Peugeot strange to the area. You see, in a town like Thiers, there are always the regular users of one kind of car; many of them are known to us. We were just keeping an eye open in case there was a suspicious driver of a Peugeot, one unknown to us. We had the bulletin from Clermont-Farand about the stolen one and of course we weren't just looking for one with a certain number plate. We were sure, more or less, that the number plates would have been changed'.

Seth wondered why he had side stepped the question about the murdered officer but didn't pursue the matter any further.

'Would it be all right if we went and had a look at Buckland's house?' he asked hopefully.

'Er-yes! However I don't suppose you will learn anything there. Incidentally, I hope of course that you will reciprocate in the matter of evidence or any clues you might glean from your enquiries. After all, you know everything now that we know and we would expect the same courtesy'.

'Of course, of course', Seth vowed his intention, then, 'will there be any problem from your men? About getting into Buckland's house, I mean'.

'I will give you a note which will give you free access to the property with the consent of the housekeeper there of course and you must treat her with respect and sympathy, you understand?'

The Inspecteur took up his pen and a sheet of paper and wrote that the two English officers were to be allowed to enter the premises of the late Buckland with the consent of the Housekeeper, Madame Pentriche and armed with the pass, the two C.I.D. men left.

When they got out to their car Peter Bracken spoke. 'I think he was a bit cagey about their bloke who got 'is, guv'. He offered.

'Yeah; too bloody right Pete. I wonder why? The crafty old fox was hiding something all right. Then he wants us to cough about anything we might find out. Well, he might be lucky!' he concluded; but then, not forgetting about all the information they had been made aware of he continued, 'I suppose he was pretty straight with us on the whole really though and deserves some of our consideration.

'Let's get over to Buckland's place and have a 'butchers' anyway. You never know, we might just happen on to something. We might also find one of their blokes there who speaks English. He might tell us some more'.

He laughed as he let in the clutch and drove away and Peter Bracken grinned at his superior's comment.

CHAPTER 20

The tapping grew louder.

'Go away, dammit' Aaron said, but the tapping continued; not a persistent drumming, but a sharp intermittent rattle.

'I'm not going to let you in, you might as well go—' Aaron's voice tailed off and declined into a mumble.

The tapping increased in volume.

Aaron slowly regained consciousness, slightly opening his eyes. He began to move his head to see where the noise was coming from and winced at the pain in his neck. The sharp twinge made him hunch his shoulders and brought him almost to full consciousness.

He turned his trunk to enable him to look out of the window; vigorously massaging away the discomfort in his neck, trying to collect his wits and yawning widely.

A bluetit was pecking at some hidden insect under the roof guttering above the car door. He could just make out its shape through the misted door glass. The sudden realization of his whereabouts cut short his yawn.

He looked at the clock on the dashboard.

'Bloody Hell!' he exclaimed, suddenly wide awake. He jumped forward, his left hand still holding his neck and wiped the mist of condensation from the screen with his right hand and also frightening away the bluetit. He peered anxiously up the road towards the car park of the Auberge.

The Renault was still in the same position as it was when he had settled down in the Citroen. He looked at the dashboard clock again and then put his own wristwatch to his ear as it agreed with the time displayed by the former; it was still ticking.

'Bloody Hell' he said again.

The two timepieces informed him he had been asleep for an hour and a half. Only the discomfort of his position and the tapping of the bird which had interrupted his dream, had eventually wakened him.

He rubbed his eyes, massaged his neck once more and wiped away more of the condensation from the windows. He glanced around. He wondered if the Renault had been driven away by Candor and returned while he had been asleep, but then dismissed the idea. The Renault was obviously in exactly the same position it had been in when he visited it and he couldn't understand why it hadn't been moved, it didn't make any sense to him.

He sat thinking for a minute then decided he couldn't stay there much longer without something more to eat and drink and he preferred a meal to the packet of sandwiches he had purchased earlier. Also another visit to the lavatory would again be welcome. He would have to take the chance of Candor moving without his knowledge; he assured himself of the logic of his argument by believing that if Candor did decide to leave it might be hours before he again got the opportunity to partake of sustenance, apart from the sandwiches. He lit another cigarette, realizing the packet was almost empty and he had forgotten to restock on his last visit to the Cafe. That convinced him. He vacated the vehicle and went to the Cafe, glad of the chance to get some more exercise.

At the Cafe he visited the toilet again, where he managed to swill water over his face at the small wash basin there. As he dried himself with the warm air from the swivel outlet of the air drier, he rubbed his hand contemplatively over his chin, regarding his reflection in the mirror, wishing he'd brought his shaving kit with him. Then decided he wouldn't have been able to afford the time for a shave in any case. He left the toilet and went once more into the body of the cafe.

He sat again by the window of the Cafe and ate his fill of eggs, bacon, sausage and beans; also consuming two large mugs of coffee. Armed with two tins of soft drinks, a further wrapped packet of sandwiches from the glass display cabinet on the counter and a replenished supply of cigarettes, he went back to the car. His enjoyment of the meal had been somewhat tempered by his concern that Candor might have left whilst he was absent from his vantage point in the Citroen. His return allayed his fear that it had been a mistake to leave to take advantage of the Cafe's amenities, the Renault was still parked there in the same spot in the car park of the Auberge, obviously having never moved at all during his absence. He got in his car and lit another cigarette, meditatively picking his teeth with the split end of a matchstick as he again settled down to wait for developments, watching all sights of movement of people moving around, all the time wondering why there was no sign of the man he was waiting to see. Where the hell was he and what was he waiting for? Surely he was taking a big chance that the police might be making searches for that type of vehicle and its driver. Again he knew it didn't make any sense, a man like he knew Candor to be wouldn't have behaved in this way or was there some other, perhaps more sinister reason for such behaviour, if so how could he find out what it was?

After a further hour of restless observation and with somewhat nervous tension, he got out and walked up and down for a while, bringing life back into stiff muscles, fretting at the lack of activity and unsure whether or not to move his car, because the vehicles which had been in front and behind his car when he had parked there had now left. Indecisive, he walked away looking for a newsagent, thinking that if he should see Candor he would be able to dart behind one of the trees planted near the edge of the pavement in their small square of earth and hope not to be seen himself.

After a walk of about half a kilometre and at every step wondering if it would be better to abandon his quest, he found what he was looking for. With some relief and anxious to be back at the Citroen he hurried off with the newspaper rolled up in his hand. The Renault had still not moved. He swore, got in the car and opened up the paper. With a start he saw the article reporting the death of the local police officer. The account confirmed his suspicion about Mradmoor's fate and his ire was rekindled. There was however, no indication that the officer's car was being searched for. He cursed Candor and his own inability to do anything about avenging his associate's death.

His own allegiance was to the Mossad. Unlike Mradmoor, he was not an officer of the French Police. They knew nothing of him at that time and he wished to keep it so. Mradmoor's dual roll as Police Officer and Mossad agent had been of great assistance to him, both in past liaisons and the Candor affair. They had been firm friends for a long time and he felt sadness at not being able to repay his debt to the Algerian, but with the restrictions placed upon him there was nothing he could do about it.

His superiors in the Mossad wanted the assassin alive, if indeed he meant harm to Israel and Aaron Plaistot's job was that of supervisor and reporter of Candor's movements; nothing else. He must not prejudice that task by possibly losing contact with the man, or risk losing his own life by accosting him. The latter action did not appeal to him anyway, knowing of the man's reputation, but he cursed him once more just to allow himself to cool down a little.

But reading about Mradmoor's death, though the officer had not been named, Aaron was sure he was the man reported dead in the article in the newspaper; it not only inflamed his anger, but also increased his frustration. He decided he must do something besides sitting in the Citroen watching the Renault. He looked at his watch for the hundredth time and resolved to wait one more half hour only, then he would reconnoitre the Auberge and try and find out what Candor was waiting for.

The half hour seemed an age to Aaron and after frequent references to his watch he sighed with relief when, at last, the interval he had decided upon had expired. He got out and locked the Citroen and walked gingerly up to the car park. He could see that the Renault hadn't been moved at all and as casually as he could he surveyed the Auberge's surroundings.

Carefully he had a tentative look into the reception area from the side window. Seeing no one he slipped inside and moved across to the dining area and examined the interior from the doorway. There was a couple sat at one of the tables but no sign of Candor.

He heard a step behind him and his heart rate increased; he turned, seeing with relief the concierge walking to his position behind the desk.

Giving up any attempt at further caution, Aaron went across to him. The man greeted him with a 'Bon jour Monsieur' and Aaron noted the faint sign of identification of him in the man's manner.

'I was here last night, after the rain' Aaron said.

'Ah yes, I remember!'

'I changed my mind again' laughed Aaron, keeping a wary eye on the stairway to the upper floors. 'I was going to carry on to Dijon but I had a puncture and my spare tyre was under inflated'.

He shrugged his shoulders. 'I gave up. I spent a bad night in the car waiting for someone to take a message to a garage for me. Still these things happen, do they not?'

He laughed again but he was also puzzled. His eyes had scanned the key rack and noticed there were two keys on the hook for the room he knew Candor had rented, whereas occupied rooms' hooks usually only boasted the spare. The other obviously being in the possession of the guest whose room it was, whether he was in it or not.

Was Candor out then? If so, where had he gone and when and in what car?

'It is fate which has brought me back here no doubt', he continued, but could see that the concierge had little interest in his explanations.

With a bored expression the man asked if he required a room again or a meal. No doubt he was immune to the vagaries of the multifarious clientele he came into contact with, thought Aaron. His long association with guests having inured him to their little foibles and dulled any empathy he might have with their troubles. Aaron however, though feeling some sympathy with the fellow also had his own problems.

'Er-no', he said, 'not a room or meal. But you could help me'.

He took out his wallet and extracted a crumpled fifty franks note. He rubbed it between finger and thumb, his hand resting lightly on the counter. The concierge seemed a little more attentive, but not too impressed as he cast a glance around and back to the proffered note.

'I observed a gentleman come in here yesterday evening' Aaron began. 'He, like me, had been caught in the deluge'.

He described Candor's physical characteristics. 'I saw him go to his room, but have not seen him leave yet. I wondered perhaps if he had left while I was away, perhaps in the night?'

The concierge looked at Aaron then at the bank note.

'I'm afraid Monsieur, it is against the rules of the hotel to give information about clientele' he said.

Aaron extracted another note of equal denomination to the first and carefully, in a studied theatrical manner, smoothed out the two notes together, one on top of the other. He turned them over and again held them loosely between finger and thumb as before.

'You see' he went on, 'it is a matter of friendship. I will be frank with you. This man is the husband of a friend of my wife. She is worried about him and prevailed upon me to keep an eye on him so that he might not get into any trouble. He is ill you see, not physically you understand, but he sometimes does things out of character, he has been under a psychiatrist on occasion. She trusted me to look out for him without his knowing, otherwise I would go and knock on his door and talk with him. As I am on vacation and have nothing of any urgency better to do, I agreed to follow him when he left home and let his wife know his whereabouts and what he was doing. It seemed last night that he was on his way back home; also to Dijon. So, I decided to go on before him, until my bad luck with the car, that is. Then, having to come back here to the garage I thought I might as well check whether or not he was still here'.

The concierge did not give any indication whether he believed Aaron's story, or for that matter whether he disbelieved it. It sounded a bit thin to Aaron himself, but he knew also that the concierge was playing for another increase in the proffered remuneration for his information. He was obviously wondering if Aaron was willing to pay more for what little he, himself, knew.

Believing that Aaron might retract his offer if he got tired of the concierge's presumed reluctance to respond to the proffered bribe, he capitulated. He reached out and took a grip on the two bank notes. Aaron though did not immediately release them.

'Well' he asked.

'The gentleman in question left at about eight o'clock this morning' the concierge said.

Aaron was dumbfounded.

'But his car is still in the car park' he protested.

'I don't know about that Monsieur' he said, frowning and hunching his shoulders, but not letting go of the two notes.

'Nevertheless, a man arrived and asked for me to inform-er-your friend that he was here. The two men left. I, myself, with my own eyes, saw them get into a pick-up truck and drive away'.

'Do you know who this man is?' Aaron asked.

The man looked at the two bank notes and gave a little tug at them.

'Perhaps' he said.

Aaron released his grip and the two notes disappeared into the concierge's hip pocket.

'He is a local man. He works for the airfield at Valeille. It is about six kilometres South East of Feurs. That is all I can tell you'.

'Just one more question' insisted Aaron. 'Is this an international airport?'

'It is not Aerospaciale. That is all I know'.

The concierge dismissed him with a wave of his hand and walked away towards the dining room.

'Damn and blast' said Aaron aloud and the couple, still sitting at their table stopped talking and looked at him. He turned and went out into the car park. He cursed again. 'That's what comes of having no colleague' he comforted himself.

Deciding not to use the telephone in the Auberge, he hurried away to where he'd made the call to his contact that morning. He reported his latest information and received orders to go to the airfield and find out what he could. His contact assumed that this latest manoeuvre of Candor meant that he was probably heading for Marseilles and he gave Aaron some new instructions.

Aaron Plaistot was to verify this destination, if possible and if it was so, he was to go there himself. It had been arranged for another agent from Israel to meet him there and he was given an address near the Aerospaciale Airport where this other agent would be. If, on the other hand, he found out that Candor's destination was different, he was to report in immediately. Further arrangements would then be made regarding his meeting with his new assistant.

Aaron returned to his car feeling that once again Candor had slipped the net. It was apparent from the newspaper article he had read earlier that the police were not even as wise as himself about Candor's whereabouts. At least he knew that the man had gone to an airfield and its identity. Cheered a little by the thought, he lit another cigarette and drank some of the contents of one of the cans. He belched loudly. He'd just had another thought. Suppose the police had men at all the small airfields, he wondered.

Then he dismissed the idea, thinking it would take a small army to cover all the airfields. No! It was possible however, that they would have men at the International airfields. Still, he himself was of no interest to them and they might not know what Candor looked like now. He did; he knew that Candor had changed his features; just enough to nullify the newspaper photograph. Now the police,wherever they were would have difficulty recognising him. He finished the contents of the can, belched again, complaining to himself that the contents of the can he'd just emptied always made him belch, started the engine and drove away leaving the Auberge and Boen behind him.

When he arrived at the airfield at Valeille he asked similar questions of the receptionist there as he had at the Auberge. She was more loquacious than the concierge had been and freer with her information. Yes! The man answering Aaron's description of him had left that morning on a flight to la Malouesse, a small airfield about seven or eight kilometres South of Aix-en-Provence. Yes, there was a flight leaving for la Malouesse at seven o'clock that night, so Aaron booked a flight on it. He went back to the Citroen and ate the sandwiches and drank the other tin's contents. He took a few articles of clothing and his raincoat, still damp and locking up the car he put its keys about two or three centimetres up the exhaust pipe making sure no-one saw him do it. He went off to the departure lounge, mixing with the few other travellers there.

He phoned his contact once more and informed him of his destination and the whereabouts of his car and its keys, then sat to wait for his flight and began glancing at the magazine he'd purchased from the news stand. He felt slightly miserable; it was a long time to hang about waiting, knowing that Candor could have left the other airfield before he got there. But, didn't think there was much he could do about it; he lit another cigarette, blowing out smoke and shrugging his shoulders in resignation.

CHAPTER 21

As the small four seat aircraft banked and turned into wind for the descent to the little airfield at la Malouesse, Candor looked more intently through the window. He sat next to the pilot and there were no other passengers; the flight had been arranged as a private booking by the man Adam Buckland before his demise. Indeed Candor had been by the telephone when Buckland made the call.

It wasn't the first time Buckland had arranged a private flight. He was adjudged a valued customer by the tiny airfield's management who took pains to satisfy his requests for transport to various airfields around France. They, of course, knowing nothing of his business and criminal dealings would not have entertained his custom if they had, but it was not part of their procedure to check their clients veracity or integrity with the police before accepting the proposed business.

'When the bill for this flight falls on Buckland's mat' thought Candor, 'they'll probably have some explaining to do. That's if the police find it before the termites eat it'.

He smiled to himself, unaware that even at that moment the police were studying Buckland's books, records and bank statements, having obtained them from various sources by order of the Court.

As the aircraft bumped on to the runway, puffs of smoke spurted from the rubber of the wheels' tyres as the friction of contact with the concrete accelerated those wheels into rapid rotation. The plane sped along the runway veering slightly from side to side and the pilot adjusted the rudder trim with his feet on the pedals to counteract the yaw at each variation of direction. He braked, slightly at first, then with increasing pressure as the machine lost momentum.

The plane was taxied to the 'visiting aircraft' park where, on coming to rest, the wheels were chocked by a ground attendant. The pilot 'cut' the engine and Candor got out. He didn't fail to notice the look of surprise on the pilot's face at the weight of Candor's luggage, as he handed the two imitation leather cases, which were not a definite pair he could see, down to him.

Candor, standing on the concrete, accepted them from the pilot, turned and without a word walked away.

'Funny beggar' the pilot commented, 'hardly a bloody word from him all the way here'. Then promptly forgot about his passenger in the business of reporting to the control and requesting the refuelling of the plane for the return journey whilst he carried out the 'between flight' inspection.

Candor went into the tiny restaurant and ate a light meal while cogitating on the journey he had made so far. He felt no remorse for the deaths he had caused. He felt them to be necessary to ensure his own safety and the success of his task. All, that is, except Buckland and his attempt to silence the man's housekeeper. He now felt that had been an error. No doubt he would have to explain his action to his employers on his return. The explanation would have to be sound; he knew Jordan would have no qualms about putting out a contract on his life once the job he was to do for them was concluded and not just for them; for himself, for his own reasons.

Buckland had been an objectionable fool he thought; for a man in his position he had asked too many searching questions. To someone as touchy as Candor about his security, that was his mistake. Buckland's condescending arrogance had roused Candor's ire and the man hadn't known when to accept that Candor was just there to collect what had been paid for and that was all he needed to know. The man had paid the penalty for not realizing the danger signs his interference and arrogance would cause and his being unaware of Candor's reputation. The attempt to silence the man's housekeeper had not been successful, but that had not mattered to Candor.

He had the explosive and when his contact showed up he would be on his way again and he believed, unhindered.

He had purchased a newspaper from the vendor at the counter in the reception area and he soon found the article about the murdered French Algerian policeman. He read it with some difficulty but it roused in him a feeling of disdain. From what he could gather from the story it gave the impression the police had no clue who had carried out the killing, or why, or where to look for the person responsible for the murder.

Candor felt that was a blind to lure him into a false sense of security.

'Let them look anyway' he thought, 'I'll not be here to find in a short while'.

Candor's feeling that Buckland's death had been a mistake was an understatement. Buckland was the unknown fourth member of the criminal syndicate comprising himself, William Somers alias Jordan, Wessing and Moorwood, the three latter being known to and watched by, the British Special Branch and their residences were all known to them, they being not far from each other and all in the London area.

Buckland had not so far been connected with the other three in the minds the Special Branch but enquiries by the French Police were to acquaint them with the connection. Not however before the anger of Jordan had been aroused by the phone call he had received from Buckland's housekeeper, Madame Pentriche informing him of Buckland's death. He now knew that Candor was responsible and was already plotting revenge on him as soon as he had completed the task set for him, as that individual sat waiting for his contact to arrive. A contact again organized by Buckland.

He was sat, as instructed by Buckland, at the first table by the door. Buckland, prior to his murder, having sorted out the whole of Candor's journey in an orderly manner, before the man had arrived in France.

Never a very patient man Candor fretted at the delay. The longer he stayed in France the more dangerous it became; especially in a small airport like the one he was at. He would have felt better at the large airport at Marseille-Provence where he could have hidden among the multitudinous milling travellers there. He had the impression, that in the small confines of the restaurant in which he had been instructed to wait, he was much more obvious a target for suspicion of his business. On the other hand, he knew there were likely to be more stringent checks on traveller's persons and luggage at the larger National Airports.

He was just about to succumb to his fears and move outside, when a man, himself with a furtive air, approached the table. He hovered about for a few seconds then, 'A very pleasant day for a long journey Monsieur', he offered.

Candor was instantly attentive; with some relief he responded. 'If the journey is in good company' was his reply. At that the man sat himself down.

'Ah yes!' He seemed ill at ease. 'I am sorry but I have for you new instructions. There has been a delay. You are to leave here and return at seven o'clock this evening. You are to sit at this table again and your guide will meet you here with the same greeting, except that the word 'day' will be changed to 'evening' to identify you'.

Candor, surprized at the information that he had to hang about further and always on a short fuse, could feel his anger rising. He was to be subjected to further danger by being kept waiting about there in la Malouesse. The man could see the change in Candor's attitude and quickly spoke an explanation.

'It is no use blaming anyone Monsieur. The aircraft which was to take you from here has developed a small problem; that is all. You can be assured you will be met at seven o'clock this evening. I would suggest that you leave your luggage here and hire a car for the rest of the day. It can be arranged at the reception desk'.

He rose and said quietly. 'Goodbye Monsieur, have a good flight'. He turned and left.

Candor was furious but, as the man had said, it was no use blaming anyone, aircraft sometimes did have problems and there was no way that other arrangements for another plane could be made. He would do as the man had suggested except he would take his luggage with him, there was no way he could leave the suitcases in the custody of someone else.

⚜ CHAPTER 22

Hiram sat and wondered where the man he had to meet had got to. He had arrived at the Aerospaciale at Marseille-Provence nearly an hour before. It hadn't taken him long to pass through the Airport Customs and Immigration controls and once outside the Airport grounds, he had easily found the small Cafe where he was supposed to make the acquaintance of Aaron Plaistot.

He felt conspicuous after drinking his second cup of coffee; sitting and reading again the magazine he had bought at the Airport and now his cup was empty again. Dare he ask for a third cup? Or should he get up and leave, to come back later?

While he was making up his mind what he should do, he heard the ringing of a telephone in a small annexe adjacent to the counter. Almost immediately the call was answered. Then the woman serving there came to his table.

'Could I have a word with you please Monsieur?' she asked in a low voice.

'Certainly Madame' answered Hiram, puzzled, wondering if he was going to be asked to either buy something else or leave.

'You are Hiram Woolley?' she enquired

'Yes Madame' he said, wondering how she knew his name.

'Can we have a little talk in private? Then follow me'. She almost whispered the question at his confirmation of his name and her face now had a conspiratorial look. She turned and walked away, back through the flap gate in the counter, into a back room, holding the door open for Hiram to pass through. Hiram, following on behind and carrying his duffel bag, slightly bewildered at the sudden change in events, was grabbed by the arm and quickly drawn in by the woman. She partly closed the door behind him leaving a gap large enough for her to keep an eye on the few customers left in the Cafe dining area.

'May I see your passport Monsieur?' she asked and Hiram, again wondering how she had known his name, handed the document to her.

She studied it for a moment and apparently satisfied, handed it back to him.

'I am sorry, I have little time to explain. You are to leave immediately. My husband will take you by car to a small airfield at la Malouesse. I have just heard from him on the telephone and he will be here at any moment.

'Your contact was to meet you here but it is feared the man you are to watch for has already arrived at la Malouesse. My husband will explain everything to you during the drive to get you there.'

Even as she spoke the back door of the room opened and a dark complexioned man with a two day growth of stubble on his chin beckoned him.

Baffled, wondering; a host of questions in his mind, Hiram followed the man outside to the rear of the building. There he was led hurriedly, through an alleyway to a side road.

The man opened the door of a taxi parked there and waved Hiram into the back seat. He obeyed and the man got in the driving seat and immediately drove off.

He spoke for the first time.

'My friend Aaron Plaistot has been unable to get here yet and the man Candor is believed to be at la Malouesse already. You are to find him and observe his movements. You have his description and photograph I believe?'

Hiram answered in the affirmative and the driver continued.

'Good. You must understand that you are on no account to approach him. It is not an easy surveillance. The man, I must warn you, is very suspicious and extremely dangerous.

'Try and find out where he is going without him knowing and report to this number'.

He handed his passenger a piece of paper over his shoulder.

'When my friend Aaron Plaistot arrives at la Malouesse from Valeille you will obey all his instructions. Do you understand?' The man spoke with authority and Hiram answered with a question.

'How will I know him?'

'Don't worry about that. He will know you. But anyway, you can't mistake him. He is built like an ox and will have a cigarette in his mouth. He always has a cigarette in his mouth'.

The man laughed and Hiram asked another question.

'How did you know who I was, or the woman at the Cafe know, I mean? Did you say you were her husband?'

'Yes, she is my wife. You must accept that we are all but small cogs in a very large wheel, my young friend. Do not worry your head about these things. Just do as you are told. You have friends you do not know about, friends who know you though.

'You doubtless, are convinced that you are alone here, but for Aaron and me. That is not so, there are many of us but we each have our duty, our own role to play and not interfere with others. Yours is to watch and report the movements of the man Candor. That is all. On no account, as I said before, are you to try and get in a tangle with him. Believe me it is folly to do otherwise. Don't even give him the least suspicion that you are interested in him'.

'Yes, all right' Hiram answered. Though surprised at the turn of events, he was also relieved and reassured at last, knowing he was not in it by himself.

The taxi eventually arrived at the visitor's entrance of the small airfield in well under an hour, the roads not being too busy and Hiram got out with his duffel bag. He thanked the swarthy man and was about to walk away when the man whispered.

'What about paying the fare my young friend?'

He had a twinkle in his eye and the cigarette dangling from his lips trembled up and down as his shoulders shook with silent mirth.

Surprised, Hiram took out a bank note from his wallet and passed it to him. The man took it, then with it screwed up in his hand he handed it back.

'There is your change Monsieur' he said aloud; then in another whisper, 'We have to keep up appearances, do we not? Good hunting'.

His shoulders shook again and a length of cigarette ash dropped down the front of his open necked shirt. Then he was gone.

Hiram looked after the disappearing taxicab wondering what other surprises he was going to have. He shouldered the small duffel bag and turned and went into the foyer of the reception hall.

He looked at the arrival board while trying to make sense of what he was supposed to do; he felt out of his depth and tried to imagine what the fellow Aaron Plaistot would do if it was he who stood there. It seemed that circumstances were passing a little too quick for himself; he didn't now feel he had the time to adapt and take stock of events so that he could adjust to them. Things were beginning to feel different from what he had expected, he had never thought it would be like this, despite the taxi driver's assurances that he was not on his own.

He had believed he would be met, introduced to and then set off together with the agent Plaistot. He, Plaistot, the man of experience would have taken charge and accepted the responsibility of any surveillance they had to make, explaining everything to him, Hiram and completely putting him in the picture.

Instead here he was, thrust into the thick of it and unsure what to do about it. His experience of small airfields and their procedure was almost none existent. It was strange and foreign to him; there seemed to be no sense of urgency anywhere. None of the frantic hustle and bustle of a large airport such as the one he had so recently left. No people rushing hither and thither, faces excited or perhaps anxious. Here there were few people about and all was calm and quiet; just the opposite of what he had expected to find. In some ways it was an anticlimax.

On impulse he walked over to the reception desk to ask if they were expecting a flight from Valeille, the Airfield the taxi driver had mentioned, when he noticed the entrance to the small restaurant. So, instead of approaching the young lady with his question, he decided to go in for a coffee while he thought out his next move and probably from where he would be able to identify his contact. Smoothing out the banknote which the taxi driver had screwed up he approached the counter.

He took his cup and a packet of sandwiches he had purchased over to a seat by the window and settled himself down. While spooning the sugar into his coffee he looked around the small dining room at the few people there. The place was almost deserted. He was about to tear open the plastic cover of his sandwich pack when a man walked into the room with two, obviously heavy suitcases.

Hiram's heart missed a beat. He was the man whose photograph he carried in an envelope in his inside jacket pocket. The man wanted by the British and French police; the man under surveillance by his own organization the Mossad, the Israeli secret service; the man with a string of deaths to his name.

There was no doubt about it; it was Candor all right, though it appeared he had tried to make himself look somewhat different to the photograph Hiram had and Hiram tried not to look at him, that he was showing no interest.

But what he could see, was that the visitor's features looked plumper, his hair was greyer and receding. He looked to be somewhat different in skin tone; but the eyes were the same. He had been told to examine the eyes and those eyes he had seen scan the tables when the fellow entered could belong to no-one but Candor.

Hiram managed to force himself to look away as the assassin surveyed the room. He concentrated all his effort on removing the plastic cover from his sandwiches, feeling as he did so that he stood out from the others there. That Candor was bound to know he was an enemy. He felt as conspicuous as if he stood alone in the middle of the floor with a placard on his chest carrying a notice to that effect. He tried as casually as possible to un-wrap the sandwiches and suddenly his racing pulse quieted and slowed, the drumming in his ears subsided and he felt an air of bravado overcome him.

He got up from his chair and walked across to the next table and took from it an un-wrapped packet of tomato sauce. He almost giggled to himself as he returned to his seat and slowly, deliberately, tore off the corner and squeezed the contents on to his opened sandwiches.

He took a bite and looked up, chewing slowly.

Candor had taken a seat at a table by the door. His suitcases stood upright on the floor beside him.

He seemed to Hiram to be staring directly at him and his show of ennui evaporated. He became tense again, the bread and meat suddenly tasted like sawdust as his mouth dried up and the drumming of his pulse became again, louder in his ears.

He shifted his gaze, forcing himself to look with apparent boredom around the room; he knew he was afraid. The man's reputation, the recalled words of the taxicab driver about caution and the closeness of the man himself, brought home to him the realization of the danger of his situation should Candor become aware of his interest in him. He took a mouthful of coffee to assist him to finish the sandwich and was glad when he managed to force down the last bite. He wrapped up the remainder of the packet in the plastic though his hands were a little shaky and undid the string of the duffel bag, placing the packet carefully inside.

He risked another glance around the room as two of the people there got up noisily from their table and left. He saw that Candor was watching the couple as they passed him and he relaxed slightly and turned to the window looking out onto the visiting aircraft park. He determined to quell the uneasiness he felt,trying to reduce his pulse rate and then he heard the sound of a planes' engines. It was now quite dark and the noise grew louder as a taxying, twin engine aircraft appeared into the post-lamp lit area of the hard standing adjacent to the building he was in.

It came to a halt a few metres away from where he sat and the engine noise ceased, the propellers stopped and a ground crew man unhurriedly wandered over to it and placed yellow chocks to the main wheels.

There was another, smaller plane parked between Hiram's window and the newly arrived aircraft, but he could see enough of it to identify it as an old Dakota D.C.3. The type which had remained in use as a workhorse since before Hiram was born. He had become a little calmer, being interested in the older type of aircraft and knew something of the history of that particular aeroplane and knew that many had been built and especially the role they had played in the Second World War.

A refuelling bowser had drawn up beside it and in the poor illumination of the post lamps Hiram could see someone talking to the tanker's driver, looking up into the cab as another man was refuelling the aircraft.

As the person moved towards the building Hiram realized it was a woman. She carried no luggage and it appeared to him, she must be the one who had taxied in the aircraft. He could see no-one else out there; just the woman and the ground crewman and the man delivering the fuel into the aircraft's tanks. She moved out of his line of sight as she walked around the angle of the building, but a few moments later, to his surprise, she entered the restaurant and went to the counter.

She said something to the woman serving there and they both laughed, then she, the pilot, came away from the counter carrying a cup and saucer. Without any hesitation and much to Hiram's perplexity and disbelief she went straight to Candor's table ignoring several unoccupied tables further in and sat down opposite him. She was tall, fair and moved with confidence and grace. She wore a white bandana restraining her hair and a white blouse, while matching jacket and slacks set off her figure. Her shoes were sensible flat heeled footwear, light and comfortable looking.

Hiram thought at first that she must be aquainted with the man he was sure was Candor; had he made a mistake about the man's identity? but could see by the surprise on Candor's face that he had no foreknowledge of her, but when she spoke to him, his face changed. A look of relief Hiram wondered? As the woman spoke to the assassin he wished he could hear their conversation. She was speaking earnestly to him and Candor now seemed more relaxed than he was before she entered the restaurant.

Hiram, frustrated, looked again at the plane which had just arrived, obviously taxied in by the woman who was now seated and holding Candor's complete attention. On impulse he got up, picked up the duffel bag and walked past the pair, through the reception lounge and out of the exit.

He circled round the building and back to the aircraft park. The bowser driver's assistant was just replacing the hoses on the vehicle and Hiram waited until the man got in the cab beside the driver and the tanker had been driven away. He looked around for the ground crewman but he was not in evidence, so taking his chance, as no-one else seemed to be about, Hiram moved up to the fuselage door. He looked first towards the restaurant but realized that as Candor and the woman's table was on the opposite side of the room to where he himself had sat that they would not be able to see him.

Also, as the area was poorly lit he decided to investigate the interior of the aircraft if the door was unlocked. He tried the door handle which he could just reach, standing on a wooden block, put there by one of the ground crew for the pilot to gain an easier access into the fuselage or descent from it. Hiram, almost hoping he wouldn't be able to gain entrance, but with a feeling of some trepidation felt the door handle move and the door become free.

His heart thumping, he took a last look around and put the duffel bag inside. He pulled himself up into the fuselage through the modified access, though he did not know that the door modification had been to allow the placing inside of quite large containers with a smaller portion of the door through which he had entered as a personal access. He took another look over his shoulder and then pulled the small access door closed behind him.

He listened for a minute, wondering if someone would arrive and challenge him; had he done something stupid? They perhaps wanting to know what he was doing and maybe sending for someone in authority, perhaps even the police. But there was nothing, not a sound. Suddenly it came to him there might be someone in the aircraft's flight cabin and he froze, straining to hear any sound from that area with his hand on the door handle and ready to make a quick exit.

Again he relaxed somewhat and searched in the duffel bag for the torch he'd brought with him from Israel. By its light he examined the interior of the machine. Several wooden crates were lashed to ring bolts screwed into sockets in the aircraft's floor. There were no seats in the passenger area at all and he crept cautiously up to the pilot's cabin.

He listened again, but could only hear the beat of his own heart so, gingerly, he opened the partition door. There were just two seats, both empty and a conglomeration of instruments in front of him and controls around the front area which meant nothing to him.

He closed the cabin door, returned to the rear of the fuselage and examined the wooden crates. They seemed innocuous enough. Some had labels with names he didn't recognize. One did have the name of a

French motor car manufacturer stencilled on it in black paint, together with a string of numbers and a warning that a fine would be imposed by the manufacturer if it was returned damaged. He couldn't help smiling at the incongruity of it all, regardless of his tense nerves.

He turned his attention to the very back of the passenger area and saw a door there. He squeezed past the crates and had just opened the door to look inside, when he heard voices and the sound of the fuselage access door being opened.

Beads of perspiration started from his forehead, his hands felt sticky and he was sure that whoever was opening that door would hear his heart pounding in his chest. He tried not to panic.

He quickly stepped inside the compartment, carefully closed the door behind him and listened. He had switched off the torch and was standing perfectly still in the inky blackness. The voices ceased and he heard the sound of the fuselage door being closed and then, the nerve wracking sound of footsteps. He swallowed with difficulty and the spectre of fear covered him with its cloak as he waited for the moment of discovery. A male voice asked, 'What's behind that door?'

§ CHAPTER 23

The woman stood holding her coffee cup in one hand, her saucer in the other, facing Candor across the table and then, with deliberation, sat down.

'I suppose it is all right for me to sit here Monsieur?' she said.

Candor looked pointedly at other vacant tables, then again at the woman. She returned his stare with equanimity.

'If you must' He said at last, 'but I am waiting for someone to take that very seat'.

The woman ignored the rebuff and placed the cup in the saucer and then carefully onto the table. She pulled at the creases in her slacks, with finger and thumb at the knees to prevent them 'bagging'. She observed him quietly and he returned her gaze with narrowed eyes, thinking it odd that the woman carried nothing with her except the coffee. It seemed strange that she didn't have the usual handbag. He however, said nothing further.

'A very pleasant evening for a long journey' she offered and smiled at him.

Candor was instantly alert. 'If that journey is in good company' he replied.

'Then I was right to sit here. You are the one I was sent to meet Monsieur. I am to fly you in my aircraft for most of the rest of your journey'.

She spoke in a low tone and no-one could have heard even if they had been sat at the next table, not even the young man carrying a duffel bag who was just passing their table as he was leaving.

'You gave me a start when you did sit there without introduction' he said at last, 'I wondered what it was you wanted when all these other tables are empty'

She laughed lightly, 'I am impulsive Monsieur, it is my nature; anyway I must apologise for your having to wait' she said. 'Unfortunately it could not be avoided. One of the crew helping to load the freight into the aircraft, damaged an aileron with his stacker truck. The fool never reported it to me and I only found it on my pre-flight inspection. These things happen, but if I had been notified when it occurred, steps to repair it could have been taken straight away and we could have left at the specified time'.

She shrugged her shoulders and Candor said nothing.

'Still I am here now and when the aircraft has been refuelled and the oil checked, we can get away. You are aware of the stages of your journey Monsieur?' she asked.

'I have a rough idea' Candor replied, not completely mollified by her explanation of the cause of the delay. 'I suppose this imbecile who damaged the plane has been chastised?' he asked.

'Oh yes! To damage an aeroplane and not report it is very serious. I suppose he thought he could get away with no trouble to himself but in fact he has been suspended from his job while a proper investigation takes place. Anyway, enough to know that the plane is now airworthy again.

Now, about your itinerary, you have seen the aircraft I arrived in? It is an old D.C.3 but in first class condition. Ideal for its normal use these days; freight and as I said I have some freight on board for delivery at Paphos in Cyprus'.

Candor raised his eyebrows, about to ask a question.

'Do not worry Monsieur, although the passenger seats have been removed to make way for the freight, you will occupy the co-pilot's seat. You'll be sitting next to me'. She smiled coquettishly, but there was no response from Candor.

'However, the first leg is to Enna in Sicily where it has been arranged for fuel to be available. The authorities there are used to my comings and goings. There will be no trouble with Customs or Immigration or any of the usual irritants so long as they don't see you. If they did it could be expensive for me. There will be no delay and no questions asked. Just land, refuel and take off again. Perhaps five and a half to six hours to Enna from here, depending on the weather.

'The second leg to Knossos in Crete. About the same time duration and the same routine for that leg as before. You will stay in the aircraft each time, no-one must see you. There will be no-one involved in the landing and take off at either Enna or Knossos except those who need to know.

'The fuel and oil will be checked by me at each stop. Just land, refuel and if necessary, re-oil and take off again', she repeated. Candor was impressed by the organization involved but kept his silence.

'The last leg for you on my plane is to Paphos. There my responsibility ends. If we are fortunate and do not run into any bad weather we should be in Paphos in about fifteen hours, taking in to account the refuelling stops. The figure of course is not a definite one; sometimes the wind and weather plays up a little and we have to make adjustments to our course, but that is not your worry'.

'What about your stamina?' Candor sounded a little sceptical. 'Fifteen hours seems a long time to be stuck in the pilot's seat, even in three stages'.

'Do not worry your head about my ability', the woman retorted. My stamina will not be in question. The aircraft has 'auto pilot', it is a great help to me and I have done these journeys many times. Occasionally I take exercise in the main fuselage while the auto-pilot is on, it helps to break the monotony, but the flight, it is routine to me; I shall rest at Paphos while the aircraft is unloaded. There is freight also to be loaded for the return journey.

'You are to continue your journey by ship I believe. That is no concern of mine; is everything clear?'

'Yes! I'm ready when you are' said Candor, beginning to relax a little now the time had come to leave France. 'I have just one question. What do we do about food and drink?'

'That too is taken care of', the woman replied. 'There are packets of food and flasks of hot coffee and soup on board. There is also a crate of cans of soft drinks. There is plenty to eat, but the variety is restricted and unfortunately none of it is hot food except for the soup of course'.

'That seems o.k. to me' said Candor, 'When do we leave?'

'First, you do realize we have to clear Customs here? Is there any problem about that? If there is, there are other ways of getting through if you know the ropes!'

'I would rather not see the Customs or Immigration people. It would prove a little awkward' said Candor, the plastic explosive and the small matter of someone else's passport vivid in his mind.

'Right then, wait a few minutes. I'll go and check and sign for the fuel and then show you a way to avoid the embarrassment of Customs'.

She rose and left the cafe. Candor sat back, relieved that he would be able to evade the formalities of officialdom. He barely had time to go over what she had said about the journey when the woman beckoned him from the cafe exit.

She turned as he approached and he followed her through the main doors and around to the 'hard-standing'.

'When I've finished my pre-flight check, we taxi around to that dispersal over there'. She pointed into the darkness away from the main building where Candor could see another dimly lit area some six or eight hundred metres or so away, though he could not be sure of the distance in the darkness.

'There is a Customs and Immigration post over there. I shall get out of the aircraft and prove my destination by my copy of the 'flight plan'. You will stay hidden in the aeroplane.

'Normally, that is where I would pick up any passengers, after they have been through Customs. It is a million to one chance that they, the customs people will board the aeroplane, I have been through too many times alone.

'If they do, I will delay them at the fuselage door and you must get in the toilet. They will only, at best, have a casual check of the freight against the manifest.

'Now then! If they do find you, you must tell them you stowed away in the plane or some other story. I shall plead ignorance of your existence. I cannot afford to get into trouble smuggling, or aiding the flight of a wanted man. Do you understand? The risk is yours'.

'Quite!' said Candor. He would have no compunction about preventing the pilot from getting caught. He knew that anyone entering the aircraft and finding him would regret their conscientiousness.

They reached the aircraft which was to be his means of carrying out what he thought was retribution for his wife's death, to the enemy's door. He recognized the old aircraft type, knowing it to be a tried and trusted machine with an excellent record of airworthiness.

He watched while the woman pilot went round checking the control surfaces for freedom of movement and damage and the removable panels for security and correct fitting. She removed the 'pitot' head cover which had been fitted by the ground crew on her arrival and went back to him and led the way to the fuselage access door. She had been very thorough Candor thought, but he was anxious to get away from the airfield as soon as possible. He didn't want to waste any more time than necessary to clear the country and leave his misdeeds behind.

'You can put your suitcases anywhere you can find room' she said, opening the door for him, standing on the wooden block. 'This access door makes it easier to gain entrance to the fuselage without opening the freight door'.

He peered inside, then put the luggage in and climbed on board, followed by the pilot; the ground crew man lifted the wooden access block and put it inside the fuselage and closed the access door. He then went and plugged into the aircraft's electrical ground socket the supply cable for the electric supply from the ground accumulator trolley for the starting of the engines.

Candor glanced around at the freight as she checked the door was properly fastened, cutting off what light there was from outside the aircraft.

'Just a moment, I will switch on the 'dim lights' to see better' she said, going forward into the pilot's cabin.

When the lights came on, Candor understood why they were so named. They were dim all right, giving a faint, red tinted glow just enough for him to make out the obstacles in his way as he looked for somewhere to stow the two suitcases. He jammed them between two of the wooden crates, fixing them so that there was no chance of them breaking free during the flight.

The pilot came back from the cabin to check the security of his luggage. 'What about that man whose out there?' Candor asked. 'Won't he have any thoughts about me being here?'

'Don't worry your head about him, we have our own arrangements about these things' she replied and smiled.

Then he noticed a shaded light over a door at the rear of the fuselage.

'What's behind that door?' He asked and nodded in its direction.

§ CHAPTER 24

Patricia Woolley sat cross legged at the table, absent mindedly tapping her spoon on the rush place mat. She wore a grey suit with a light silk neck scarf, a small plain hat, silk stockings and grey shoes with low heels. Oblivious to the other customers in the small Mis'ada, her mind was on the interview which she had just attended in the local office of the Officer Commanding Women's Forces and her features registered her disappointment.

As a married woman she was exempt from military service and her request to volunteer for it had been denied. This had annoyed her; she felt insulted. After all she was a Jew, albeit a newcomer to the faith.

She had chafed and fumed at the restrictions and difficulties she had met when she and Hiram became betrothed. There being no civil marriage in Israel. Or easy divorce for that matter, she had assumed that obstructions to her marriage, even after accepting the Jewish religion as her own, had been deliberately manufactured and not just by Hiram's parents. She had hoped that she would have been eagerly welcomed into marriage with a naturalized male Jew by the authorities but they seemed to her to be reluctant so to do.

Now and to her regret, it rankled that, as an alternative to army training she had been offered service in nursing, teaching or in the social services. She now realized that obtaining her degree in Social Sciences had been a mistake and wished that, like Hiram, she had studied engineering. It seemed to her that male orientated occupations were more acceptable than female ones depending of course on what one wanted to do and she wanted to do what Hiram had done; join the Mossad. There didn't seem to be any way she could do that with her qualifications.

She frowned and pursed her lips, looking around the Mis'ada.

'How can I be accepted by the Mossad if I've had no military experience ?' she thought. 'They're damned unlikely to recruit me if my experience is in nursing or social Services'.

She sighed again and as she looked around her at the other clientele she thought 'I wonder how many of them have had military experience; how many can handle a weapon or, perhaps, defend themselves without a weapon?' she mused.

Then another thought struck her. 'I wonder if some of them carry a gun or perhaps a knife or something, in case there's any trouble going to happen' reminding herself that Hiram had warned her that trouble could occur at any time without warning by some-one willing to sacrifice him or her-self to take others with them.

Suddenly her frown disappeared. What seemed to her like a solution manifested itself.

'That's it! that's it!' she thought, 'private lessons on a range with a gun club. Of course! That's the answer'.

She got to her feet, bumping the table as she did so, spilling some of her untouched coffee into the saucer, but uncaring. Her mind was made up about what her next move must be, she went to the counter and paid her bill, giving a generous tip to the waitress and left.

She headed for the nearest newsagent and purchased all the local newspapers and advertising leaflets and then, excited, drove home as fast as she dare with regard to the regulations. She spilled some of her purchases in her haste to get the key into the lock and exasperated, dropped everything on to the step while she unlocked the door.

A few more minutes and she was ensconced in a deep armchair searching through the papers looking at the advertisements, although some of them were in the Hebrew language with which she was not accustomed. At last she found what she was looking for; a local match shooting club inviting enrolment. Another few minutes later and she had made the telephone call which was eventually to change her life and others.

§ CHAPTER 25

Peter Bracken sat in the driving seat, his hands at the 'ten to two' position on the steering wheel, fingers drumming on the lower underside. The engine was running but the vehicle was stationary. He blipped the throttle occasionally absent-mindedly and Seth Winfild looked at him as he asked,

'What the 'ell are we goin' to do now guv?'

'Search me Pete', was Winfild's response and he meditatively stroked his chin between finger and thumb. They had met perfunctorily, the late Buckland's housekeeper; surely if Buckland had been a misogynist, thought Winfild, he did not know what he was missing. She was a very attractive, though sad looking woman Winfild thought, but she had allowed their request, asked by the police who were present and quite without objection, to have a look inside the premises. She not being sure what their presence there indicated, especially as they were not French, but sounded English which she understood well, but with strange, to her, accents, or at least one, the junior officer had; she decided not to enquire further and they had not stayed long.

'I'd have thought there'd have been something else of interest there beside them golfing magazines the police showed us' he said at last.' And I don't mean just Madame Pentriche. What a cracker eh?

'But how can someone run an illegal arms trade and when he 'croaks' leave not a damned shred of evidence about that activity behind? There's got to be more to this than meets the ruddy eye, I'm thinking'.

'Aye guv, I suppose you're right, but what can we do about it? The trail seems to have gone cold. Unless these plods come up with the car Candor's in, I can't see how we can be expected to find him. They don't volunteer any info'. It's all questions and no answers, but just guesswork for us, it's a right pain and no mistake'.

'Yeah Pete, it is a pain. We're too thin on the ground to go looking for the car ourselves, it's a million to one we'd have no chance of finding it. Until they find it and inform us, we're stuck'. He looked back across Bracken to the imposing house of the late Buckland. 'Didn't do him a deal of good in the end did it?' He asked. 'I wonder what the woman will do there now? I wonder if some other arrangements for this sort of occurrence has been made Surely she can't stay here on her own now can she? Anyway, come on then, let's get back to the cop shop, you never know, they may have got a line on the car'.

Bracken grunted, let in the clutch and engaged first gear. He revved the engine and let out the clutch with a jerk. The tyres screamed in protest and as the car shot up the road, a thin haze of blue smoke gradually dissipated in the damp air and a flock of pigeons, looking for food or grit on the tarmac, took hasty flight to get out of the way.

'Steady on! Steady on, dammit' chided Winfild, 'we don't want to present them with another couple of stiffs'.

Bracken grunted again but eased the speed of the vehicle, his exasperation with the lack of progress in their enquiries somewhat assuaged by his untypical display of pique.

They arrived back at the police station to find the Inspecteur did have some heartening news for them. His order for the inspection of every Renault in the area had been successful in that a battered car of that make had been spotted by a car patrol parked at an Auberge at Boen.

Enquiries made to the somewhat reluctant concierge to comply, had resulted in the search being transferred to a small private airfield at Valeille. The Renault had been seized and was on its way back to Thiers on a transporter for examination by the Forensic people. It had been discovered that the man Candor, identified from a police photograph by the again reluctant concierge at Boen and the helpful receptionist at Valeille, had indeed left on a flight to la Malouesse, south of Aix-en-Provence. The investigation had therefore been placed in the charge of the police at Aix. It had been discovered during the enquiries at the airfield at Valeille that someone else was interested in the journey of Candor; a large man with a foreign accent and according to the woman receptionist, of Jewish countenance, had also made enquiries about the suspected man's journey.

He, the Jewish looking man, had told her he was interested in the movements of the man in the photograph, because he was a friend of the family of the man's wife who was concerned because of her husband's illness and had asked the Jewish looking man to keep his eye on him.

'Perhaps the man who has flown to la Malouesse is not Candor after all' suggested the Inspecteur, 'but the photograph identification seems to prove it must have been him.

'However, the police at Aix will carry on with the investigation now that it is out of our district. We, of course, will have the Renault checked over to find out if it is the one belonging to our murdered officer. We are pretty certain it will prove to be his'.

The two British policemen had listened to all the news with, at first, excitement; then with some disappointment, now it seemed that the wanted man had flown south.

'How far is this other airfield? What did you call it? I've already forgotten the name' queried Seth Winfild.

'Come I will show you on the map' answered the Inspecteur.

They were taken into the Incident room and la Malouesse was pointed out to them on the large wall map there. The two C.I.D. men studied it for a while trying to figure out the distances involved.

'H'm,' said Winfild. 'I suppose we ought to get the go-ahead from London before we travel any further; mind you' he continued, 'we've come two thirds of the way across France now Pete. I can't see the point of packing it in, can you? But I expect it's best to report in first'.

'I expect so guv', said Bracken, 'though I don't suppose they'll be very happy with the progress we've made so far, do you?'.

Peter Bracken was becoming disillusioned with the whole business. He was also wondering what his wife was going to think about his gallivanting around the Continent on a wild goose chase which it seemed to him to be. They'd got no-where so far.

The Inspecteur gladly gave them permission to contact their Superiors in London and the two officers made their report and went to the canteen to drink coffee and await further instructions.

Eventually word came from their headquarters that they were to wait until the police in Aix-en-Provence confirmed that the wanted man had arrived there. If so, they were to catch the next available flight from Valeille to la Malouesse to follow up their enquiries. Funds would be made available by arrangement with the banque de exchange at Thiers. The Home Office had become interested and questions were being asked in the Commons. The integrity and efficiency of the police were under scrutiny.

They were to employ all means possible to obtain a result without embarrassing the French authorities or compromising the British police and thus the Home Office.

If the enquiries by the French police at la Malouesse were to prove negative they were to stay at Thiers and keep in contact with the police there. They were to report back to London when they were in possession of any new information. The orders had come straight from the Commissioner at Scotland Yard.

'Bloody typical' muttered Seth Winfild. 'Get a result any way we can but don't tread on anybody's toes. Be sure it's our heads will roll Pete if this fouls up'.

'I never expected anything different guv' said Bracken. 'If you expect the worse, anything better's a bonus, that's my philosophy'.

'I suspect there'll be few bonuses at the end of this, unfortunately', muttered Winfild. 'Let's go and see that fellow Bonnet. He's a decent sort, he'll let us know what happens at la Malouesse. When we've had a word with him we'll go for a meal. I'm ruddy starving'.

§ CHAPTER 26

The big Mossad agent, Aaron Plaistot looked around at the other five passengers on the small twin engine plane and sighed. He thought they gave the impression they were not real people at all, but automatons. There didn't seem to be any verbal discourse between any of them, they were just sitting there in their seats, obviously just wanting the journey to end and that end couldn't come soon enough apparently.

He wondered what occupations they had which necessitated their journey by plane across half of France and he had surmised, that to them, the flight was no more normal than a drive by car was to him. At Valeille he had noticed that each of them carried similar briefcases, yet none spoke to any other; or to him. They all seemed engrossed in their own business, so much so that they each appeared unaware of the others existence.

When boarding the plane, Aaron had been appreciative of the courtesy of the attractive young lady, a member of the airport staff, who had checked their tickets, wishing each a good flight. The other passengers showed no interest in her, only boarding the aircraft as quickly as possible as if their haste would perhaps shorten the journey, the sooner to bring about their departure and subsequent arrival at their destination.

It also seemed odd to Aaron that they were all male and he wondered why there were no females on board. Surely, he thought there must be some businesswomen who travelled by plane on similar errands as these others. Then he smiled, 'that's typical of my thinking' he told himself, 'always looking for motives and reasons for people's behaviour. I'm always suspicious of people's actions. It must be with me being an investigator. Nothing is simple to me, its typical of my thinking, he repeated; these poor beggars are probably just wondering if they're going to manage to make a few franks tomorrow or, perhaps worried they're going to miss supper if they don't make a connection to wherever it is they're trying to get'.

His gaze turned once again to the darkness outside the window adjacent to the seat he occupied at the rear of the passenger area. He always endeavoured to obtain a seat as near to the tail of an aircraft as possible. Having heard, or read somewhere, that such a position was the safest, should the plane crash. One apparently had thus a better chance of survival.

He heard the note of the engines alter and felt his weight move in his seat. The lights on the ground gave the impression the earth was slowly beginning to rotate about the machine. Looking forward under the aircraft's wing, Aaron could then see the spread of the airfield lights opening out before them.

The instruction to fasten their seat belts and cease smoking caused a small flurry of activity among the passengers and Aaron dumped his cigarette in the ash tray at the side of his seat. A few more minutes elapsed and the aircraft bumped onto the tarmac of the runway, taxied round to the hard standing for visiting aircraft and rolled to a stop in that area so designated. Aaron levered himself out of his seat and as was usual wondered why they never gave enough room for large passengers. He had long since been convinced that transport designers, be they in the car, bus or plane industry, were all midgets.

He looked out of the fuselage windows as he passed, with bent head, along the short aisle to the exit. He could hear the sound of another aircraft's engines now the noise of the plane in which he had arrived had ceased and he glanced idly around as he descended to the ground. He shivered and drew in the collar of his coat somewhat tighter as he stepped down on to the hard standing. The sudden exit from the warmth of the aircraft he was leaving into the cold breeze across the airfield surprized him. It may be supposed to be a tonic, something he had been told by someone he couldn't remember, but it was nevertheless a cold tonic.

In the poor illumination of the airfield pole and perimeter lights he saw an old fashioned Dakota D.C.3 rolling past on its way around the perimeter track to the duty take-off runway and his interest was aroused at the unusual sight. He watched it with a smile as he went into the reception hall to find his contact.

The taxicab driver who had transported Hiram Woolley to the airfield was waiting for him by the reception desk. He turned away as Aaron saw him, signalling his intention and went quickly into the Cafe and sat at one of the vacant tables. Aaron followed, going to the counter for coffee on his way. He took his cup and went to sit at the driver's table, the man appearing agitated, nervously tapping his fingers on the table top.

'Am I bloody glad to see you Aaron at last' he said, his face grim.

'Why, what is the matter Jean? What's gone wrong?' Aaron asked.

'It's that fool who was to meet you at the cafe, who is the matter. He has got on a plane with Candor, for God's sake'.

Aaron almost dropped his coffee cup in surprise.

'What the hell do you mean, he's got on a plane with Candor? Didn't you warn him about the man?'

'Of course I did. I was keeping my eye on him, but he went snooping around the plane when it first came in. He got inside after it had been refuelled and then the pilot, a woman and Candor got in and it left. It took off just after your plane arrived, I couldn't get to him to stop him before the other two got in'.

He rubbed the stubble on his chin and then ran his hand over his sparse hair. 'What are we going to do?' he asked. 'Candor's bound to have found him in there. The fool—the bloody fool. I'd impressed on him not to get involved with the man. Just to observe and see what Candor did'.

'Hang on a moment' said Aaron, regaining a little composure, 'have you reported this yet?'

'No. I was waiting to see what developed when Candor got in the plane and then it taxied out just as your plane landed. I thought I'd better wait and see what you thought about it first'.

'Why are you here anyway?' asked the big man. 'I thought someone else was going to observe this new man'.

'A man called Peitor was to have been the observer, to make sure this Hiram character didn't get into any trouble but he was apparently called away. I received a call on the radio phone in the car to come back here and watch out for him myself. I'd dropped him off here and was on my way back to my Cafe when I got the call.

'When I did get back here, he was nowhere about. I saw the man who I'm sure was Candor, sitting talking to a woman. He certainly fitted the description I'd got. Anyway, I thought he'd be o.k. while I had a look round for our man. I couldn't see him anywhere and came back in here to keep an eye on Candor myself. I sat by that window over there and then spotted the damn young fool messing about round an old aeroplane.

'He got inside the thing, can you believe it? I was just getting up to go and haul him out when the woman and Candor left the cafe together. I followed them so far and I nearly died when they got in the same bloody aeroplane as our man. I couldn't see what I could do except go charging in there myself'.

'No! There was nothing you could have done' agreed Aaron. 'Our job is just to watch and report. Well, if he's tangled with Candor that's his bad luck. I'll have to report and find out what they want me to do next now our man's flown off.

'The trouble is, if Candor gets Hiram to talk, he'll know we're on to him again. It'll make him twice as wary. I believe he thought he'd given us the slip at Boen'.

'Yes. It's a bad business Aaron' agreed the taxi driver. 'I did my best to impress on the young idiot what his priorities were. He could have ruined the whole surveillance for us. How do we know where the fellow's going to turn up next?'

'Oh, we know where he's going now, definitely Israel. Still, it's no good worrying about our surveillance now Jean. You get on about your business and I'll report, o.k.?'

He got up, the coffee almost cold and forgotten. He lit another cigarette from the stub of the one burning his fingers which he then ground out in the ash tray on the table.

'They're not going to like this one bit' he thought, as he went to find a telephone. 'I wonder where he'll dump Hiram's body, over the land or into the sea? I wish I could get my hands on that flight plan. He must be going to Israel, the message in Hassan's car boot indicates that; I dare bet diamonds on it.'

He hesitated, struck by a sudden idea. 'I wonder if it's possible to find out the route that D.C.3's taking' he asked aloud and then looked around a little guiltily, but there was no one interested in his musings.

He went back in to the reception desk to have a word with the woman there. She listened attentively to his story about once being a D.C. 3 pilot and having noticed one taking off, wondered if it was used on scheduled flights.

'Oh non Monsieur'. She laughed. 'It is a private aircraft, sometimes carrying passengers, but mostly freight. The woman pilot is well known here. She regularly uses the facilities of the airfield; she owns the aircraft. Yes! She does fly on quite long trips. This evening I believe she is flying freight to the Eastern Mediterranean area.

'She is 'une femme incroyable' that one'.

She laughed again at Aaron's moue as he said, 'Yes, alas. We mere males will soon be redundant no doubt and then what will become of us eh?'

He thanked her and moved away again to find a phone.

He asked the switchboard to put him through to the Airport Manager's office. A man's voice answered and Aaron asked for information about some freight he'd had delivered to the airfield for transportation to Cyprus. The young man in the Manager's office replied that the transport of freight was not a service provided by the airport, but by contractors who used the facilities available. Unfortunately, the freight office of those contractors was closed until eight thirty the following morning.

'But I need to know whether or not the stuff has left' insisted Aaron. 'It is imperative that the goods reach Cyprus by tomorrow night. They are medical supplies urgently needed there and I want to ensure they left as arranged, on the evening flight'.

'Just one moment Monsieur, I do know an aircraft carrying freight left half an hour ago. You perhaps do not know but that plane is owned by a company run by one Madame Daleille and she flies the machine herself. She often uses our facilities. If you would just bear with me a moment I will check on the destination of that flight with Air Traffic Control. What did you say your name was?'

Aaron was prepared for the question and gave the name of a large pharmaceutical company who had a factory in the area, implying he was the Sales Manager of the firm.

After a few minutes elapsed, the young man asked. 'Are you there Monsieur? The aircraft left at eight p.m. and was due to call at Sicily, Crete and Cyprus according to the flight plan.

'Unfortunately, the copy of the manifest is held in that company's transport Office so I cannot say whether or not your goods are on board. I should think they definitely are. If you could please check with them in the morning? I'm sure they would be able to help about your goods being on board'.

'Very well', grumbled Aaron, trying his best to convince the fellow that he was not completely mollified by the information, 'they had better be on it or, believe me, there'll be some harsh words said. Anyway, thank you for your trouble. Good night'.

He rang off. So, the aircraft was en route for Israel. Cyprus was only a short journey away from the Jewish Homeland and the Mossad had been justified in the precautions they had taken to check on Candor's destination and that was where he was bound.

Aaron rang his contact and reported what had happened. He was instructed to go to the Aerospatiale Airfield at Marseille Provence and return to Israel, He was there to assist in the detection and detention of the assassin Candor when he arrived there.

Aaron breathed a sigh of relief knowing he could now go home again, to see his wife and family. He felt the last few days had been too much of a trial. He had lost a friend and colleague and the fate of his relief assistant was, as yet, unknown. But, in Aaron's mind he believed that the man Hiram, whom sadly he had never seen, was as good as lost. To have done what he had was asking for trouble; there was no way he would be able to defend himself against the skills of the man Candor.

'Well, I must be getting too old for this game', he thought and lit another cigarette. 'Sentimentality is a sin in this business. When you start getting compassionate about someone you don't even know, your armour's beginning to crack. That won't do at all. No! not at all.'

He took a deep pull at the cigarette, letting the smoke drift slowly from the corner of his mouth. He picked up his bag and went to find transport to the large Aerospatiale airport.

He looked up into the blackness of the starlit sky wondering whether the man Hiram Woolley whom he had never seen was still alive up there somewhere or, if his dead body had been ejected from the plane into the sea.

A taxicab driver, touting for passengers answered his hail and drew up at the kerb. He took the cigarette from his mouth and murmured 'Bon voyage, wherever you are'. He opened the taxi's door and got in, throwing the half smoked cigarette into the gutter.

§ CHAPTER 27

Hiram stood stock still in the blackness, trying not to let his knees knock together and his teeth chatter lest they be heard through the material of the door. Horripilation, triggered by the age old instinct, fear, caused the hairs on the back of his head to become erect and his flesh 'goosey' as the cutaneous muscles contracted. He knew he was afraid but could do nothing about it.

He swallowed, trying to combat the feeling of nausea which welled up from his stomach.

'That's just the toilet I was telling you about'. Hiram heard the impatience in the woman's voice.

'Come Monsieur, we must get going. We must be punctual at the given take off time it is very important, if we're late we could miss our slot and that would mean perhaps hours of delay'.

Candor's rejoinder was unintelligible and Hiram relaxed as the footsteps died away. His hands shook as he wiped away beads of perspiration from his face with a handkerchief. He felt the lavatory seat behind his legs and he sat down, rested his head on his hands, elbows on his knees. It was the first time he had felt real, skin crawling fear.

He'd had a very close call he knew and wondered if he could pluck up the courage to open the door of the fuselage and jump out of the aircraft before Candor or the pilot changed their minds and discovered him hiding there, but because of his fear he felt his physical stength was unable to bring about the necessary movement to accomplish the task at that moment.

The matter was taken out of his hands as an engine was turned over by electrical power from the ground trolley accumulator handled by another ground crew man and then fired into life. First an uneven staccato of explosions, then into a regular beat of power. The second engine soon joined in adding its roar to the first and as the engine speed was increased, something by Hiram's ear began to vibrate in unison with the engine noise and he felt by the reaction to movement by his body that the aircraft was in motion.

It was too late. He felt the fear return anew and decided to get out of the toilet compartment and quelling his shaking, he cautiously opened the door. The blackness was partially relieved in the fuselage by several small red lights attached to the deck head and he peered into the gloom. He could make out the shape of the windows by the slightly lighter hue of the night outside.

He waited for a minute, bracing himself against the door frame to maintain his balance as the aircraft turned onto the perimeter track. He decided he could probably hide between the crates and the starboard fuselage side opposite the door side.

He made his way forward after closing the toilet door and stowed himself in the angle between the back of the flight cabin panel itself and the fuselage side. He was concealed from the area behind the cabin door by a large, high wooden crate, which on investigation he found to be in two parts. One secured on top of the other by special pins and brackets to utilize as much of the fuselage space as possible.

There was a window alongside his hiding place and through it he could see the stars in the evening sky beginning to brighten as the darkness intensified. He knew he was now trapped in the aircraft, there was no way he could get out and he berated himself for his allowing the situation to happen. He could only hope and pray that the man Candor would not find him if he made visits to the fuselage cabin; no doubt he and the pilot would have to use the toilet and of course he himself would no doubt need to also at some time. His spirits dropped further, but if he could stay hidden as he was and kept quiet he thought he might stand a chance he would not be discovered.

Candor sat in the co-pilot's seat and was put at ease by the expertise of the woman beside him as she guided the bouncing aircraft along the concrete perimeter track. She held the control column back into her stomach and now and then adjusted the rudder pedals, which he knew operated the wheel brakes; or altered the settings of the two engine throttles to maintain control of the aircraft's direction, occasionally applying a brake pressure to one or other of the two main wheels.

He could see ahead the lights of the Customs area and watched as they drew near for any signs of activity.

The pilot nudged him in the side and as he looked at her, she motioned him to leave the cabin and go back out of sight into the main fuselage compartment. He did as she bade and closed the cabin door. He stood by a window on the port side watching the Customs Post come into view as the aircraft arrived at the 'hard standing'.

The brakes of the machine squealed as it slowed and stopped, the engine's speed dropping back to a tick-over. The pilot's cabin door opened and Madame Daleille passed through, by him without a word and opened the fuselage door. She got out using a lever operated set of special steps and Candor saw her arrive at the Customs Post window.

A face appeared there and the window opened for Madame Daleille to pass some papers through the opening and almost immediately accept them back again; a quick wave of acknowledgement to the person inside and she unhurriedly returned to the aircraft.

She climbed back inside, expertly operated the door with the folding steps and locked it closed. She brushed her gloved hands together in a clapping motion and as she approached Candor she leaned towards him.

'Stay there a few moments out of sight until we are away from here, then come back into the cabin, don't let them see you through the window', she said.

Candor nodded. He heard the engines rev up and the aircraft began to roll forward. He waited until the machine was once more on the perimeter track and then went into the flight cabin and took his seat.

He acknowledged the woman's signal to put on the seat belt and head phones and she said, 'It is a good job these Custom's men aren't always so lax, is it not?' and she smiled.

Candor just nodded, again admiring the way she handled the machine as it arrived at the threshold of the runway. She spoke into the microphone of the head set obtaining final clearance for take off from the tower. She checked the maximum r.p.m. of each engine in turn and carried out a final cockpit check, satisfying herself that everything was as it should be.

A minute later the aircraft was speeding along between the runway width lights and then off into the darkness. When the machine reached cruising altitude she eased the throttles back so that at their new settings the engines would maintain cruising speed with optimum fuel consumption. She carried out a final radio check with the airfield they had just left, received a 'Bon Voyage' from the controller and switched off the radio set. Candor settled into his seat.

Hiram again experienced the onset of mouth drying fear as the assassin stood by the aircraft window at the Customs Post before take off. He could almost have reached out and touched him and it was with great relief to himself that the pilot returned and the aeroplane was once more in motion with Candor in the cabin.

Now they were airborne and he settled down, his head on the duffel bag. He was cold and hoped that the machine would not climb any higher. He considered his position and held out little hope that he would not be discovered before the aircraft reached its destination and wondered where and when that would be.

What would Candor do if he was found? The thought of a quick death and dispatch into the void outside depressed him. He tried to think of other matters and considered the possibility of at least doing something constructive.

He toyed with the idea of opening the fuselage door and if he could find them, throwing out the two cases he knew Candor must have brought on board. That would be something constructive. Candor could not carry out his task without them. Yes! It might be worth dying for.

The thought of death at the hands of the man on the other side of the bulkhead depressed him again. It was a distinctly unattractive proposition. He abandoned the idea of dumping out the two suitcases, the urge to survive was too great. There was no way he could unload them and remain hidden in the aeroplane.

Besides they may have been taken into the flight cabin where it would be impossible for him to get them.

He tried to think of Patricia and wondered how she would feel if she knew his predicament. The thought that she would be devastated if he did not return to her went some way to him strengthening his resolve to do something about his situation. But what could he do? The cold began to numb him and he pulled the neck of the duffel bag open and removed his spare pair of trousers and his raincoat from it. He had a struggle in the confined space, donning the extra clothing, but quickly felt the benefit from them. It had also, for a brief but welcome interval, taken his mind off his troubles. He had not been discovered when the assassin came into the fuselage main area, so possibly he did stand a chance of getting away with it.

He settled down once again. Soon he was sleeping, relieved from the cold and his despair, the constant unchanging throb of the engines had been his lullaby.

⚵ CHAPTER 28

The instructor insisted that ear muffs must be worn at all times when in the firing butts, to deaden the noise of the gunfire. Patricia Woolley wished there was some method of deadening the feeling of repugnance she felt at the sight of the loaded revolver lying on the mat in front of her where she stood in the 'butts'.

It had seemed so harmless when unloaded, especially so when stripped to its component parts. She had, in the last few days instruction, quickly acquired the skill to disassemble and assemble the weapon, to the approval of her instructor.

She knew the names of all the bits and pieces and was also conversant with the quick firing rifle used by the militia. She had been quick to learn and quick to accept the stream of 'do's and don'ts' continually voiced by the instructor in charge. She found there were rules about handling weaponry which had never occurred to her and had to be strictly adhered to. Never leave a loaded revolver or other fire arm lying around; always clear the chamber and magazine; never point a weapon at another person unless you were going to threaten, or to use it; never leave the hammer on a live round when the weapon was in its holster, leave one cartridge chamber empty under the hammer.

These and more she had absorbed into her memory as naturally as assimilating a recipe from a cook book.

Now, she had to handle the weapon which lay in front of her and which was loaded. This was to be the first time to actually fire the thing and she swallowed hard. Little beads of perspiration lay on her upper lip and forehead and she unconsciously wiped the palms of her hands up and down her trouser clad hips.

'Take up'. The instructor repeated the order. Patricia hesitated again; then reached forward tentatively and picked up the cold hard instrument of death.

She glanced along the line of half a dozen other pupils stood at the firing point. They all held their weapon in the right hand, index finger alongside the trigger guard, left hand gripping the right, as she also had been taught to do.

She again faced the distant target in the butts thirty metres away and closed her left hand around her right fist, the revolver pointing at an angle to the ground.

'Remove safety catch and present'.

The pupils, each standing with their feet slightly apart, raised their arms. The weapons held firmly but lightly, in both hands, pointing forwards towards their respective targets, with the right index fingers now lightly caressing the triggers.

'Aim'

Patricia glanced along the top of the barrel, her teeth biting her bottom lip.

'One round, fire!'

Patricia squeezed the trigger and instinctively closed her eyes and turned her head slightly away at the kick of the weapon as it discharged a bullet. A spurt of dust erupted from the bank several metres above and beyond her target, standing in the butts.

'Lower weapons; on safety catches'.

The instructor walked along behind the pupils, praising some, encouraging others and offering advice to another. He came alongside Patricia and stood hands on hips regarding her. She blushed at his stare.

'I'm sorry' she said lamely, 'I didn't quite know what to expect, having never fired one before'.

'O.k., we'll try again. Don't be frightened of it and don't turn away unless you want to injure someone. Keep perfectly still and keep both eyes open as you've been taught. Sight with whichever eye feels comfortable. It seems odd but you'll get used to it'.

Patricia wondered if she ever would, but carried out the routine again, managing the second time to keep still and both her eyes open. She didn't see where the shot scored and was surprised as the instructor said.

'That's much better; you hit the target that time'. He handed her his binoculars and she focused them on the distant target, eventually finding the mark made by the round near the extreme edge of the 'outer' circle.

The encouragement cheered her and by the time the session ended, found the nervousness and repugnance had disappeared. She felt she was beginning to like the sensation of being in control. The kick of the weapon as it fired, no longer jarred, but was absorbed by the muscles of her arms and shoulders and she felt more at ease.

'We'll make a target shot of you yet' the instructor encouraged her, as the weapons were cleaned and oiled at the finish of the lesson.

'Take a note of the serial number and use the same weapon each time. That way you'll become consistent. You might find it hard to believe but each weapon has its own characteristics. When you get used to one gun, you'll feel strange handling a different one, even though they look exactly the same'.

She went home much happier, feeling that she had achieved something which would perhaps, help her in her determination to be accepted as one of the Jewish community, not an alien. She would attend all the sessions and keep practising until the use of weapons became as natural to her as it had to Hiram. It seemed to her that being conversant with weaponry was sadly as necessary for Hiram and his people as any other activity during those dangerous times.

Her thoughts turned to her husband and his induction into the strange and secret world which had taken him, albeit temporarily, away from her. He had been absent only for a short while but already she was missing him. The fact of not knowing how she could communicate with him, or anyone who knew his whereabouts, secretly alarmed her. She felt completely in the dark.

How would she know whether or not he was safe? Where was he now and when would he be home? He had not as yet got in touch with her and she felt disappointed at his apparent lack of consideration and at that time had no idea how she could get in touch with some-one who could tell her anything she needed to know. On her way home she met no-one she knew to converse with, just the occasional 'good afternoon' to the odd passer-by and was unaware of the man reading a newspaper on the opposite side of the street, leaning against the wall, a cigarette dangling from his lips. His instructions were to keep an eye on her whilst her husband was away and to make sure she came to no harm. As she went further up the street, he folded up the newspaper and walked along at a short distance behind her, keeping to his own side of the road. When she reached her home he watched her enter and then turned and waved the paper to someone some distance behind him and shortly after he waved a small black car arrived and stopped. The driver got out and the pedestrian took his place behind the wheel and drove off. The other man walked up to the bus station and sat there, thus giving the appearance of his waiting for a bus. He stayed there until it was apparent that Patricia was not going to leave her home again that night and he left the area in a second car.

She had her evening meal in a state of some anxiety, the euphoria of the achievements at her last shooting lesson was forgotten. Her bed felt cold and uninviting. She tossed and turned for some time, a sense of foreboding preventing her from sleeping. All sorts of thoughts were running through her head and though Hiram had been away from her for a few days and she had slept on those nights; she now could not get to sleep.

After a while she got up to make herself a milk drink, then switched out the light and stood holding the curtain back at the window sipping the hot liquid. In the light of a street lamp she could see a figure leaning on the fence across the road. She wondered what he or she was doing there at that late hour.

A car approached and stopped outside the house and the figure went to the car and got in, but it didn't leave immediately.

Patricia shrugged her shoulders as the car eventually drove away, the mystery of the person's identity, or what that person was doing there, unsolved. She knew though, that it must have been a man, she had never seen a woman that big. He had dwarfed the car as he stood beside it and noted the almost continual glow of a cigarette in his mouth. She sipped some more of the hot drink and then took the mug into the kitchen. She washed it out and placed it on the drainer and went back to bed.

Now fatigued and warm inside she fell asleep not knowing that Aaron Plaistot had also been to check on the house. To make sure that all was well with Hiram Woolley's wife. It had been decided by some-one in authority in the Mossad organisation, to keep Hiram's wife ignorant for the present, of what had happened to her husband, until more was known for sure about his venture. But a watch was to be kept on her and her movements until that knowledge was available.

CHAPTER 29

Seth Winfild and Peter Bracken put their bags down and looked around the reception area of the small airfield terminal building

'Bit of a change from Heathrow Pete' observed Winfild drily.

'Not 'alf guv' agreed Bracken, 'that should make it easier for us to find out what's happened, don't you think?'

'Uh! I'll hold comment on that for a while Pete until we've had a look round. Can you see any of their police anywhere?'

He wandered over to the flights board to check up on arrivals and departures and Bracken looked into the Cafe.

'Over 'ere guv. There's a couple of 'em guzzling coffee', called Bracken.

Winfild joined him and they entered the small refreshments room.'Get the coffee in Pete. I'll have a word with our two friends'.

He walked up to the two officers and took out his identification papers from his wallet.

'Excuse me fellas. Do you speak English?'

The two uniformed men looked at each other and one, a rotund, middle aged individual cleared his throat.

'A little Monsieur' he said, 'what is it that I can do for you?'

'Well. Here are my papers chum. We're supposed to meet a policeman named Birkin; I wondered if you know him?'

'I am officer Birkin Monsieur. So, you are the two English policemen. I am very pleased to meet you'.

He stood up and held out his hand.

When the greetings had been exchanged the French policeman, Birkin, said, 'Unfortunately the trail seems to have gone cold here my friend. Enquiries have been made but no-one remembers seeing your man Candor except for that waitress over there'.

He pointed to the thin, middle aged woman with the streaky grey hair who was busy wiping a table with a damp cloth.

'She remembers the face well enough when I showed her the photograph with which we have all been issued. Apparently he came in here twice during the day. That was the day before yesterday and she has not seen him since. Neither can she recall what happened to him; what time he left after the second visit—nothing.

'One minute he was there drinking coffee, the next she noticed he had left. Of course she was busy, or so she says. 'How can I keep a record of everyone that comes and goes?' she asks and, of course it is something to be able to remember any one person among the many who arrive and depart—is it not?'

'H'm, I suppose so' agreed Winfild. 'Do you mind if I have a word with her? Does she speak English, do you know?'

'We will see my friend'. The officer called to the woman who, at first, ignored his summons.

He repeated the call and the woman threw the cloth down on to the table in protest at his call and wiping her hands down the front of her apron came across to them, complaining volubly in rapid French.

'What do you want now?' she demanded, 'don't you think I have plenty to do without answering any more of your questions? I have already told you everything I know, what's the point of asking them again? I have my work to do'.

'Just a moment Madame' interrupted officer Birkin, 'it is not I who wishes to talk to you. This gentleman is an English policeman who has come all this way just to speak to you, because of the importance of your evidence'. His coaxing flattery fell on stony ground.

'Then it would have been better if he had telephoned you and saved himself the journey. I know nothing more than I have already told you people here. How many more times do I have to repeat myself?'

Her cavilling tone irritated the French officer.

'Madame, you will kindly show a little more consideration and respect for a guest in our country. Do you wish me to have you taken down to headquarters? You will either answer his questions with a good grace here, or you will answer them in a place which will not be so congenial. Now,' here he turned to Winfild who had not understood one word of the woman's tirade or the officer's response, but recognized the attitude of the policeman.'What do you wish to ask her Mon ami?'

'Does she speak English?' asked Winfild.

The officer posed the question to the woman who, pouting, shrugged her shoulders and grunted, 'Un peu'.

'Ask her if she would just speak to me for a few minutes' said Winfild 'I don't want to take up much of her time' and the woman answered him herself.

'Yes. I will talk with you Monsieur. I have said all I have to say to this;—this personne' and she tossed her grey streaked black hair from her brow in a gesture of disdain.

Seth Winfild turned to the French officer.

'Do you mind chum if I have a word with her on my own?'

'No. Of course not, you are welcome to her and I hope you enjoy the experience' replied officer Birkin and turned to his companion, said something in French and the two men went outside, leaving the woman with the two Englishmen.

'Shall we sit down Madame?' proposed Winfild and the trio sat at a table in a corner, chosen by the woman.

'You did see the man in question?' asked Winfild and produced a photograph from his wallet, placing it in front of the woman, then, 'Go and get the lady some coffee will you Pete?' Seth asked his sergeant and Bracken got up again to do his bidding, as the woman picked up the photograph, still with a look of haughtiness on her face. She obviously thought she had scored against the French policeman and now she turned to the English officer.

'You cannot seduce me with a cup of cafe, Monsieur' she said with a sniff.

'Believe me, Madame, that is the last thing on my mind'. Retorted Inspector Winfild, 'I know it is upsetting for you, this constant asking of questions especially when you are busy; first one comes along and questions you and then another wants to go over the same ground again. But for my sake Madame, consider please my position. I am a stranger here, hunting a very dangerous man, who has killed five of your people; your countrymen and one of them a woman. Also at least one Englishman we know of and also he is suspected of the murder of several more. Now we fear he has gone to kill again, this time in Israel, a country living on a potential volcano of trouble. That trouble could boil up into the full scale slaughter of innocent people in several countries; not just Israel, but all the Middle East could become embroiled in the disaster which would follow this evil man's success in his venture and there is no doubt that the trouble arising from his success would not just stay in the Middle East'.

He paused to accept the proffered cup of coffee from Bracken who handed one to the woman and sat down with them. Bracken noticed that already during his absence, his superior must have said something to impress the woman whose demeanour was quite different from when he had left to go to the counter for refreshments.

Winfild continued. 'Perhaps Madame you will reconsider and tell my colleague and I all you know and have seen of this man. I think that on reflection you will agree it is of the utmost importance'.

'So', the woman said, 'Why did not that cretin explain all this to me as you have done? He comes like the, the taureau a le barriere. He shows me a photograph and demands if I know this personne in the picture; he does not say why or what for. I think to myself he is trop zele this one, trop officieux, so I will say nothing except that I did say I have seen the man. To be contraire, you understand—to annoy him. But I tell him nothing else, the cochon,' and she gestured with a hand, a dismissive gesture, towards the door through which the two French officers had left.

Seth Winfild sat back in his chair, disappointment showing on his face. So, she had lied to the officer, to annoy him.

'Well, thank you Madame for your trouble, I am sorry you have been upset about this'.

'But Monsieur', the woman exclaimed. 'I am not fache with you. It was that imbecile. Do you now not want to know what happened?'

'Er—yes Madame. I thought you meant you said you had seen the man only to annoy the officer'.

'Ah! I did want to annoy him, oui. But I did see the man; deux fois, as I told that officer. But oui, oh I saw him'.

Seth Winfild looked at Peter Bracken. He felt a deep relief. He turned again to the woman.

'Just tell us all you know about this business Madame. Just take your time' he said.

'Well, I do not always notice travellers you understand, but sometimes something about a personne will catch my eye. Perhaps, with une femme it may be her dress, her 'tenue'. Her behaviour, the way she walks; with a man perhaps because he is une beau—handsome, elegant, or genereuse.

'This man was peu commun er—exceptionnel. He had the look of suspicion. He sits by the door over there and gives the examination to all, tout le monde. But his eyes Monsieur; you could not forget the eyes'.

She shuddered at the memory. 'I tell you I was leureux—glad; happy, when he left. But before he did he had le conversation with une 'louche individu', a creepy looking fellow. He was only here une moment but when he left the suspicious man followed. He had two valise-suitcases with him. One could see they were tres lourd—heavy? But he took them up and left'.

'How long was he here? Was this in the morning or the afternoon Madame?'

'It was le matin Monsieur. I don't remember the time exact, but yes it was in the er—morning before I had Mon entr'acte pour cafe. That is always at ten of the clock, so it must have been before then. He was only here long enough to drink a cup of le cafe. He did not look comfortable. Almost as soon as he sat down with his drink the creepy fellow came and spoke to him, but only for une moment, then he left and the other man followed'.

'And when did you see him the second time Madame?'

'Ah! Well, you see that here we have the arrangement that we two serveuse stay in the matin until eleven of the clock. Then go away and come back later, at five of the clock in l'soir—er evening until half after the nine o clock. The following day we change and work from eleven of the clock until five of the clock and then nine and a half of the clock to eleven of the clock. It makes sure that each pair of the serveuse work le same number of hours each month and meet le same number of peoples. It shares out the work-load?'

'Yes Madame. So, you came back at five o'clock in the afternoon. What happened then regarding the wanted man?'

'Ah! Yes. I can tell you that when he came back in with his baggage I was tres mal-heureux. My friend, the other serveuse was fearful as well as I. She would not serve him but kept out of his way when he came to the counter.

'I tell her to not look at him but, although it was une bouleversement—er the upsetting that he should come back, I was not too afraid of the man. We have le pressoir et if I push le bouton le security people will come aussitot and take him away'.

'I bet they'd certainly have their hands full' thought Winfild, knowing Candor's reputation.

'But Monsieur, there is something that I have to tell you which could get someone whom I have le great respect for into trouble. First you must promise not to tell that grose cochon what I have to say'.

She looked at him waiting for an answer.

'Well Madame, unless it is absolutely necessary to do so I will not inform any-one of what you say, especially to the French police. That is really all I can promise'.

He wondered why she had such a vitriolic hatred of that particular French officer but decided he would probably never find out.

'I trust you then Monsieur. So; there is une femme here who is une aviateur. She flies her own aeroplane, not for pleasure, but for profit you understand. She flew in to le airfield from somewhere that evening, I don't know where, but I believe she should have been here earlier—in le matin. But anyway, she came in for cafe and we have une badiner, le joke, a laugh together, you know. Then she took her cafe and sat with l'homme we are talking about. She said something to him, I don't know what and then they went out together. Il prit ses bagages avec lui er—He took his baggage with him'.

'Were all the tables full Madame?' asked Peter Bracken, before Seth Winfild could ask the same question.

'No! Monsieur. That was what was etrange. I was confondu—puzzled by this. That she should sit with this homme. You see I'm sure she did not know him.

Yet they talked together and went out together. I thought pour une moment, then I went to la toilette. The one for the serveuse; le window there can be opened et I looked out.

'The man was putting his baggage inside le aeroplane of la femme and they got in together. Soon c'est qui marche er—going away. They did not come back. That is it. I wonder about it pour a time but then I forget about them. It is no business of mine.

"But now, this man, this assassin. I have to tell you. He must have le punition pour what he has done, yes?'

'Oh yes Madame. He must be caught and punished for his crimes and what you have told us will help us in our efforts to bring him to justice. We are very grateful to you. You have our thanks Madame. There is just one question more Madame if you will; can you tell me what time the plane left?'

'It would be about eight of the clock in le soir er-evening. There was a plane had just arrived and some of the passengers came in for rafraichissement. My time became occupied and I put l'incident out of my mind'.

'Thank you Madame', said Winfild, 'I hope you are not troubled again. Now I ask you to excuse me. I have many things to do'.

Seth Winfild and Peter Bracken got to their feet and watched as the waitress left them to carry on with her duties.

'There you are Pete' said the Inspector, 'just shows you what a bit of civility can do'.

'Not forgetting an ounce or two of bull guv' corrected his Sergeant. 'Still, it got the right result guv. I bet the French officer would be a bit peeved if you told him what she'd said. I wonder why she had it in for him guv?'

'I don't know Pete. He hadn't won any popularity stakes there. Still, it's a bit of a bloody nuisance the beggar getting away like that'.

'Too true guv. What do we do now?'

'I'm thinking Pete, I'm thinking' Winfild replied. He picked up the cold cup of coffee and handed it to his colleague, 'first go and get some hot stuff instead of this and while you're about it, see what sandwiches they've got'.

Bracken obediently went away and Seth took out his pocket book and pencil. He scratched his ear and began making notes on what he had heard and which he intended to report to London back at the last police station.

The Sergeant returned with some hot coffee and a few packs of sandwiches. They sat, drinking and munching at the refreshments, both of their heads busy with thoughts about the situation as it now stood.

After a few minutes Bracken asked,' Do you reckon they have 'in' flight and 'out' flight passenger lists in this place guv?'

'I reckon so Pete. Why, what's on your mind?' asked Winfild, taking another bite of the bread and ham.

'Well. I just thought we could have a look who else has been coming and going while Candor was here. That Inspector at Thiers said another guy had been asking questions about Candor's whereabouts so, I thought it might be interesting to see if we could spot who it was from the 'in' flight passenger list of planes from Valeille'.

'Good thinking Pete. You could be right on there you know. Come on, let's go and see if we can find out'.

Inspector Winfild drank the rest of his coffee, picked up the remainder of his packed sandwiches and stuffed them in his pocket for attention later. Bracken, still chewing, followed him out to the reception hall.

A few minutes later, having made their identity known to the Airport Manager, they were allowed to peruse the passenger lists of the people who had arrived and who had left, on the evening of Candor's disappearance.

A plane from Valeille which had arrived some five minutes or so before the woman pilot, Madame Daleille, had taken off had contained eight passengers. One name stood out from the other's in Seth's opinion.

'There you are Pete; that must be him, its obvious isn't it. Aaron Plaistot. You couldn't have a more Jewish Christian name—er, I mean first name. He'd hardly be a Christian with a name like that would he? What do you think then?'

'Sounds true guv; should we go and ask that old bird you were gruelling earlier if she remembers him? He was a big Jewish looking guy, the Inspector said. She just might remember him. She might be able to tell us something'.

'Right Pete, let's go'.

The waitress who now was quite eager to give what information she could to the two British C.I.D. men, confirmed that a large Jewish looking man had indeed been in the refreshment room for coffee.

She did not know the name, but he had talked with someone she had seen many times, a taxi driver who quite often used the facilities of the restaurant and often touted for custom near by outside. She had seen the big man on that night once or twice within an hour or so and then he too had disappeared. She believed the two men had not left together, the taxi driver hadn't stayed long, not more than ten minutes or so on that occasion.

The large Jewish man had been around quite a while after that. Yes, she had confirmed, the taxi driver might turn up at the restaurant at any time, but he had not been there that day yet.

Seth Winfild asked her to point the man out to them if he should come while they were there and she agreed. She was most pleasant and helpful with the two English policemen now.

'There seems to have been a bit of a conspiracy here Pete, I reckon, what with people arriving from elsewhere and plotting with others from here. I wonder what interest the big man has in our bloke. When you put two and two together, things begin to gel. I think we can safely say that Candor is on his way to Israel, that's my belief from what I can make of the situation.

'That woman's plane is certainly big enough to get there comfortably though they'll no doubt have to stop somewhere for fuel. I wouldn't think an old D.C.3 would get all the way on one tank full, though I know nothing at all about planes; still, he'll get there all right. He's almost certainly got explosives with him or he'd have risked a normal flight straight there from an International Airport and of course there are a few more checks made at an International Airport, aren't there? Such as passports and stuff; luggage searched sometimes too. He wouldn't have wanted that, would he?.

'Then, a guy who is keeping tabs on him is most certainly a Jew; which again leads me to think that the Israeli Secret Service the Mossad, is already interested in Candor. This big Jewish fella is almost sure to be working with the Mossad and he's been talking to a taxi driver here. He also could be an Israeli agent couldn't he? We know ourselves in the police, that they've got people everywhere. They're a pretty shrewd lot from what I know of them—which isn't much I must confess but I admire them for it.

'I dare bet my pension, if I live to get it, that our chum the taxi driver is a contact of the big guy. He's been watching for Candor to come and kept an eye on him until this Aaron fella got here. Mind you, it seems to me, if I've got the timing right, the big guy missed Candor and has now gone off himself, probably back to Israel to join the welcoming committee.

'The beggar's are two steps ahead of us again Pete. We always seem to be the back markers in this race. Always adding up when someone else has put the sum on the board. Well, I'm getting fed up with this situation.

'We know that Candor's off to Israel so we'll contact London and find out what they want us to do now. If the Mossad get him we can say goodbye to this job, we'll be back directing traffic in Piccadilly if we don't watch out'.

'Ay guv, and it's a bloody cold job in the Winter!' Sergeant Bracken was rapidly losing interest in what they were trying to do.

The two men decided to go to the police station to use the facilities there to again contact their Superiors in England. They were just leaving the reception hall when a call caused them to pause.

'Monsieur, Monsieur' the waitress with whom they had been talking earlier ran up and grasped Winfild's arm. 'He is here Monsieur. The taxi driver with whom you wanted to talk; you asked me to let you know if he came back while you were here. Well, he has just come in for rafraichissement'.

'Ah, thank you very much Madame, I'm obliged to you'.

Winfild and Bracken followed her back inside the refreshment room and the waitress gestured with a look and a movement of her head. 'There Monsieur, he is over there; the table by the window'.

'Ah I see, thank you again Madame, you have been most kind and helpful. Come on Pete, let's introduce ourselves shall we?'

They walked over to the table where the taxi driver sat. 'Are you for hire Monsieur?' asked Winfild in English, 'I'm told you are a taxi driver'.

'Certainement; are you in the hurry Monsieur? I have just bought le cafe'.

'No. No particular hurry. May we sit here too?'

'Of course Monsieur'.

'Thanks' said Winfild and the two officers sat themselves at the table. The taxi driver looked at them over his coffee; then, 'Where is it you wish to go Monsieur?' he asked.

'To the nearest police station Monsieur' replied Winfild watching for a reaction from the man. But he just took another sip at the coffee and said with a laugh,

'L'accommodation is better in an hotel I am thinking Monsieur'.

'No doubt you are right! Still, we have to see someone at the police station. We have an arrangement to make'.

'All right Monsieur. Shall we go then?'

The three men got up and left, the driver leading the way to his car. They got in the car, the two English officers in the rear seat and eventually they arrived at an unpretentious building about ten minutes drive away and the driver said, 'here we are Monsieur, the Commissariat'.

'I see' said Winfild; 'look, how far is it to the nearest International Airport?'

'The Aerospaciale at Marseille-Provence is about forty to forty five minutes away Monsieur'.

'I see, thank you. Do you live here Monsieur?'

'Oh non! As a matter of fact I live near l'Aerospaciale you ask about. I have a little Bistro there. Only a small concern you understand. But it keeps my wife happy and occupied. It is important that, eh Monsieur?' and the man laughed and lit a cigarette, quite content to keep talking while the meter was running.

'Ah well; so we may call in for refreshment if we have to go to the Airport, Monsieur', said Winfild. 'We are not just too sure what we may have to do yet'.

'Here is my card then, it has l'address' said the taxi driver taking a little card box from his pocket and extracting a small square of plastic from it. He handed it to Winfild. 'You will be made very welcome there Monsieur'.

'Thank you' said Winfild and took out his wallet, put the card inside and passed over a bank note for the fare, back to the driver.

'By the way, do you perhaps know a friend of ours? He was here only the other day, name of Plaistot, Aaron Plaistot'

There was an instant guarded look on the face of the driver, the cigarette drooping from his mouth flipped up as the man's jaw muscles tightened and his lips pursed. He took the cigarette from his mouth and looked at it; holding it like one would a pen, tapping it with his forefinger.

'I do not know the name Monsieur' he said, frowning, as if trying to remember. But Seth noticed a slight change in his voice; a hardness of tone.

'I meet so many people in this business. I may have seen him. It would be difficult to say without knowing what he looked like'.

'Oh! You wouldn't forget him if you had seen him Monsieur' said Winfild, 'he is a great giant of a man—Jewish, always smoking. He was at la Malouesse the day before yesterday; came down from Valeille, before us'.

While Winfild had been talking the taxi driver's mind had been racing, considering his position. He knew he had to be careful. Although the two men were English they could possibly be with the police. He mentally cursed himself for giving them the address of the Bistro. That had been stupid he could see now with hindsight. Still, how could he have guessed their true identification? They had seemed so innocent, just two travellers. He could not know they were on to Plaistot. Anyway, the man was safely away. He had left for Israel on a flight the day before. Better to just string along and play the innocent.

'Ah! A big man. Oh yes!' the taxi driver laughed. 'I saw him at the Airfield Restaurant at la Malouesse. He asked me if I was for hire, as you did. Unfortunately, I had to wait for someone, to take them to Marseilles. He was quite a card, your friend. He enjoys the joke and the cigarette, yes?'

'Oh yes' agreed the Inspector, 'he can be quite a character. Well, thank you Monsieur. As I say, if we go to the Aerospaciale we may call for a coffee at your Bistro. Good Bye'.

The two police officers watched the taxi drive off, joining the stream of traffic.

'Definitely cagey guv' offered Bracken.

'Yeah! He knows Plaistot all right. Still I'm going to keep quiet about it for now. Why should we cause him any aggro'? If Candor's off to Israel like we think, it's no doubt that Plaistot has already gone too. Even if we let on about the taxi driver to the French we can't prove anything. Also, if the guy's Bistro is some sort of staging post for the undercover guys of the Israelis' and the plods start asking questions, they'll only move somewhere else. I'd rather they were left where they are.

'Besides, our people might be interested in knowing about it without the French having knowledge of it as well'.

The two men entered the building to make their request for help in contacting their Superiors in London. They had more information to impart but were no nearer apprehending Candor than they were when they arrived in France. Seth Winfild felt convinced they were further away than ever of getting hold of the man before someone else did and he wasn't very happy about it.

He advised his Superiors in London of the results of his enquiries and also the name and address of the taxi driver's bistro and the conversation with him regarding the Israeli Aaron Plaistot who Winfild said he believed the man was in the Israeli secret service. He was told to wait for further orders. When these were transmitted to him later he had to inform Sergeant Peter Bracken of that officer's command to return home. Seth Winfild was to fly to Israel where arrangements would be made for him to assist the Israeli police in the apprehension of the criminal Miles Scholland, alias Candor.

Seth's assumption that Bracken would be disappointed at being relieved of his duty was not confirmed by the man's attitude. Instead, he seemed to Seth to be positively happy at the prospect of returning home. Seth was right. Peter Bracken hoped he hadn't given away to his superior his sense of euphoria at being ordered home, but he felt they had been on a hiding to nothing in their attempts to find Scholland, especially as the French police had not co-operated as fully as he would have liked. There was no regret in his mind as he packed his bag for the flight home, just relief. He must also cable his wife before he got on the plane to let her know he was coming home.

§ CHAPTER 30

The sudden cessation of the drone of the two engines roused Hiram from his doze. Collecting his wits after the long haul since they became airborne was something of a struggle. The utter mind-numbing boredom of lying on the floor of the fuselage with absolutely nothing to do but think and try to keep warm, had several times roused in him a feeling of recklessness. He had been hard pressed to prevent himself getting up and doing something which he knew would jeopardize his safety.

The snag being, he was at a complete loss as to what he could possibly do which wouldn't do just that. Only to be there was soul destroying and frustrating. He daren't get up and walk about for exercise in case Candor or the woman came through from the cabin. Something which each of them had already done; Candor twice; both of them to use the lavatory in the toilet compartment at the rear in which Hiram had first hidden.

Fortunately for him, the woman had used it almost immediately after Candor's second visit, which had enabled Hiram to do the same with a greatly lessened risk of discovery.

Nevertheless, he had been extremely frightened in case either of them came into the main fuselage area while he was in the toilet compartment. On that occasion he had been most relieved and grateful to get back to his refuge place unseen. Also there was no quick way to get back to his corner, sqeezing past the crates to do so and of course he realized he had to be quiet too in case he was heard scuffling about, though he believed the engines would hopefully dround out any sound he might make.

He knew from repeated consultations of his wrist watch they had been airborne for over five hours and tried to estimate in his mind where they could be. Now it was obvious from the changed note of the engines that something was going to happen; perhaps they were going to land somewhere.

Occasionally now, the engines would change tone or be throttled up or down. Then he had the disquieting feeling in his stomach that he was floating, as the engine noise momentarily disappeared, followed by a different sensation. This time of heaviness and he heard the bang of the oleo's compressing as the undercarriage hit solid ground.

He felt the violent movements of the taxying aircraft's yawing as it braked and slowed. Then the alternate revving of the two engines as the machine turned this way and that.

Suddenly there was complete silence and the loss of the sensation of movement. He knew they had arrived at the terminal of some airfield, but hadn't a clue where or which. He felt again the onset of fear. Was this to be the end of the journey for him?

The flight cabin door creaked as it opened and he heard the voices of the woman and the man as they walked down the sloping floor of the fuselage. The pilot was remonstrating with Candor.

'But, you must stay on board. It will only take half an hour or so. I know it is dark but you must take your fresh air inside the plane. If you are spotted here it could cost us a great deal of money and my future activities, you understand? They do not know you are here; that you are on board, we do not want any complications believe me'.

'Well, leave the door open then. I feel as though I've breathed the same air more than once'.

'That I will do, but keep away from the cabin and the windows. You'd better stay back from the main door too. I can't understand why you want fresh air anyway, the aircraft has ventilation ducts for fresh air whilst flying. Perhaps you'd switched them off inadvertantly'.

'Maybe so, you'll have to check when we get off the ground again; o.k. I'll stay out of the way, but I'm not getting in that toilet; that's for sure'.

The woman tutted her tongue at him as though he was a fractious child and opened the fuselage access door as Candor moved back towards the flight cabin.

Hiram could hear the man moving about and then heard the rattle of metal on metal outside the plane. A low revving engine was started somewhere near to where he lay and then he could detect the sickly smell of aviation fuel as someone began filling the wing tanks.

He suddenly had a dreadful thought. As he was lying adjacent to a window it would be possible for the person filling the tanks to peer inside and perhaps get a sight of him. He did his best to wriggle the collar of his dark raincoat over his head without making a noise which Candor might hear.

Suddenly the dim lights were extinguished and he realized Candor must have had the same worry about being spotted inside the plane. Now it was impossible to see inside the fuselage without the aid of a torch. Hiram relaxed a little more but wondered if anyone outside thought it odd that the dim lights had gone out with no-one to switch them off. Candor had obviously thought that risk worth taking. Hiram wondered what the pilot would have to say about it when she got back in.

The refuelling seemed to Hiram to take an age and it was with some sense of relief when the pumping vehicle's engine ceased its throbbing. It was only minutes after that he heard the whine of the vehicle as it was driven away. Then the pilot climbed on board and shut the access door.

'Stay in the fuselage until we get clear. The bowser man noticed the dim lights were extinguished and I pretended to curse the fuse for blowing and he seemed satisfied; we were lucky there', she chided Candor and then the cabin door closed and the dim lights came on again.

There was the sudden chatter of another engine outside and Hiram realized it must be the ground electric generator which would enable the pilot to restart the engines without running down the aircraft accumulators. He wondered indeed if it was possible to start the engines from the aircraft batteries. In any case the aircraft shuddered, as first one and then the second engine burst into life.

Almost immediately the taxying began but Hiram did not completely relax until he heard the opening and closing of the cabin door which indicated that Candor had joined the pilot. Soon the bouncing and rocking of the aircraft ceased and he realized they were airborne again, the engines' noise showing they were once more on full throttle until they reached towards there cruising height.

He knew that to have attempted to make a run for it when they were grounded at wherever it was would have been suicide. There was no way he could have got out of the fuselage without Candor seeing him. Even then he would have had to evade whoever was outside. Also, where would he go? He had no idea where they were, except that they had been airborne for a little over five hours.

He consulted his watch again. It was almost one forty a.m. and he knew they had left at eight p.m. Where would they have flown in that length of time, knocking off about twenty five minutes for the refuelling stop?

He tried to remember some of the geography from his lessons when a school child and suspected, that as no doubt the aeroplane was on its way to his homeland, Israel and keeping clear of the land so to do, they would first of all be flying in a slight South Easterly direction. He considered therefore, that the first landfall would probably be either the 'toe' of Italy or the Island of Sicily.

The plane was old so, he guessed, the air speed would be in the region of one hundred and ten knots which meant flying a distance of about five hundred and fifty to six hundred miles. Yes, he thought, that definitely ruled out the first land mass of Sardinia. He was therefore in no doubt that the landing had been at the extreme Southern tip of Italy or on Sicily.

He also considered the remark made by the pilot; stating that it would cost a lot of money if Candor was seen. Therefore he reasoned, the people concerned in the refuelling were, like the pilot, not strictly law abiding. Otherwise a sight of Candor would have meant questions by people in Authority and prevention of the take off while there was an investigation; not a bribe to forget what they had seen.

He knew it was all conjecture and determined that the next time he had an opportunity to use the lavatory he would try and see if he could check on their flight direction by a study of the star pattern.

He settled himself down again, wondering if his scant knowledge of astronomy would suffice to resolve such a problem. He lay listening to the drone of the engines and wishing he was at home with Patricia; or at least not imprisoned in the damned aeroplane with a man he considered to be a lunatic. Even if that lunatic was unaware of his existence, but hoping that situation would remain.

Soon the unwavering beat of the engines, together with the coolness of the interior and the time of night, all combined to lull him into a fitful sleep.

Later he awoke with a start, almost immediately realizing where he was, but utterly confused as to what had awakened him. Then he heard a voice a woman's voice, then the deeper tone of a man's voice in a more argumentative manner. Both the pilot and Candor were in the fuselage cabin talking in a cross-voiced way, both trying to make their opinion heard, each to the other.

The voices ceased for a minute and then he had to strain to hear above the noise of the engines. He could make out mutterings from the pilot and then other stressed words from the man and he wondered what the devil was going on. It was obvious the plane was being controlled by the auto-pilot, their both being together in the aircraft's freight area demanded that to be so.

'Will that do?' he heard the woman ask, you're sure you will be able to manage the door now? Anyway I would like to have some more thought about it before I agree to you jumping out in the dark'.

'It will do for me. I'm sure I'll be able to manage all right, I don't see why you can't understand that it's the best solution to my problem. Candor's voice was unmistakably confident.

'Of course! I understand why you want to do it this way instead of getting a boat for the rest of your journey'. The woman sounded somewhat disappointed at having agreed to what they had just been arguing about.

Hiram strained his body into a position where he could just peer through the tiny gap between the two crates hiding him from the couple and the bits of their bodies he could occasionally see.

Above the sustained note of the two engines he could hear their voices, faint as they were; but found it difficult to hear everything because of that sustained engine noise.

At last Hiram got a view of part of the bodies of the pair who were standing by what appeared to be a folded black plastic sheet and was in fact an engine cover. 'We shall need to put these covers on and then try to disguise the plane by other means.' Hiram heard her say and couldn't think what the idea was. What had she meant about jumping out in the dark?

'My God' thought Hiram, 'they're talking about him parachuting into the country at night, aren't they?'.

He was both astounded and relieved. Yet, at the same time, he felt that he himself would be left to try and get the pilot to land so that he could get out and warn his compatriots as to what Candor had done. The arguing couple obviously did not know he was present but at the moment he was not too worried about that. He tried to make out the sounds of their talking but could not hear every word. That they had decided at last for the passenger to off load himself and his goods as he himself lay imprisoned behind the wooden crates seemed to him an answer of a sort to his own troubles but he must find some way for the pilot to agree to allow his own exit from the plane. It was obvious that the plane would have to be over Israeli air space for Candor to jump and his hatred of the man whom he feared welled up in him at the thought that he could do nothing about it. But then he thought there must be a way to make the plane land in Israel at the Ben Gurion airport at Lydda, probably; if he could only force the pilot to do that.

The frustration caused by his enforced witnessing of the sound of their arguments and the inability to hear every word, grieved him greatly and he began to try and think of a method which would allow him to do that; his fists clenched in anger at his enforced inability to act.

He forced his thoughts to turn to Patricia and he yearned for her; for the comfort of their own embraces and the gentle giving and the acceptance of their love for each other. He could not understand how the man Candor could have pursuaded the woman to give in to his argument for her to, as she said, fly over Israeli territory as they had been together for such a short time and surely his charm couldn't have made her agree to his wishes, against the possibility of danger to herself. What sort of a woman was she to acquiesce with him in such an escapade? She must have weighed the danger against the remuneration she would receive for her daring? He knew he never would know and prayed for the flight to end soon.

The arguments which had so confused him ceased. The man said something in a harsh voice at which the woman laughed, a hard brittle sound in the monotonous muffled tone of the engines. 'Come on' she said, 'we came out here for exercise like I always do on these flights, not for you to talk me into breaking the International laws of aviation. I need also to check the auto pilot hasn't led us astray'. He heard the flight compartment door slam closed and that ordeal was ended, not only did he now know how Candor intended to enter his country. But also he still remained in the aircraft in their ignorance.

§ CHAPTER 31

Seth Winfild looked around him at the throng of people as he humped his suitcases towards the queue at the Customs 'Green' channel. He was to be met by someone from the police but could not see anyone in police uniform who gave the impression they were looking for a particular individual. Perhaps they did not care much for the insinuation of a foreign policeman into their own affairs.

After he had passed through the immigration check where he filled in the obligatory Form A L 17, he was also surprised to read a notice to the effect that he would have to pay an exit tax fee when he eventually left the country, the amount dependent on the airport from which he would probably leave. He paused in the entrance hall looking for somewhere to deposit his luggage if he wasn't met and felt a hand on his arm. He turned and a serious looking youngish man, dressed in slacks and shirt with a tie, but no jacket, said in good, but accented English,

'You are Inspector Winfild I take it. Sorry I'm late. I could perhaps have got you through that lot without too much trouble if I'd been on time. My name's Zeb Stretton. Welcome to Israel'.

As he talked he produced a plastic wallet and showed his identification to the new arrival.

'Thanks. I'm Seth Winfild. I was looking for a uniform'. He too showed his warrant card and passport.

'O.k. right. There are plenty of those about and army types too, you'll find. I suppose I'm what you would call C.I.D.

They shook hands and the Israeli took him to where he'd left his car, helpfully carrying one of the two suitcases Winfild had brought with him.

As they drove from the 'Ben Gurion' Airport at Lydda towards Tel Aviv, Stretton explained the situation as far as he knew it.

'We know the man Candor left on Thursday evening from a small airfield in Southern France and we believe, arrived in Israel early on Saturday morning. From information we've had for a few days now, it's almost definite that he's heading for Jerusalem. Apparently he has ideas about blowing up the Knesset, but our under cover agents are keeping a round the clock watch for the guy there.

'All the police are on their toes, but we're obviously trying to keep things as quiet as possible. We don't want any panic and we're being attentive and observant without being rash'.

'Aye. You'll have to keep on your toes all right. The beggar's a slippery customer and no fool. He's led us and the French a merry dance. Unfortunately we, the C.I.D. didn't get in on the act early enough. The top brass wanted to get hold of him before anyone else did but that's a lost cause now. They're what you might call 'dischuffed' somewhat. It's been rollickings all round. I did have a sergeant with me whilst in France but he's had to return home and I must say I think he was somewhat pleased to get back'.

'I can understand' said Stretton, 'I don't suppose there's much difference between any of the police forces when everything's boiled down, especially in the Western countries. They're all trying their best to keep the peace and at the same time as we're often told, keep within the budget'.

'If you don't mind my saying so, you seem to have a bit of an American accent' observed Winfild. 'Where did you learn your English? It's perfect; better than mine!'

Stretton laughed. 'I was Canadian, but we left Canada when I was a young lad. Both my parents are dead now. Dad was a German Jew, got out before the Second World War; just. Went to England where he wanted to join up in one of the forces but wasn't considered fit enough, then to Canada, where I was born. Then in '67 we came here!'

'I see' said Winfild, I suppose that sort of story is general among the people here eh?'

'Yeah. As a matter of fact, more than half of the population are native to our country, but you don't have to go far back, say a couple of generations or so to find they too were immigrants. People from every place on the globe almost, came here.

'Now their offspring are called Sabras, native born. Roughly five out of six of the population are Jews. The rest are mostly Arabs and they are, in the main, Muslims. There's a few Christians, Druze and Bedouin, even 'boat people'!'

'Aye. I see, quite a mixture. Now you've got this bloke Candor trying to rock the boat again and causing you a load of grief. I always thought you'd got enough on your plate without him shoving his oar in. I can't quite see why one of your undercover agents didn't see him off before he got here'.

'Yeah, but we want to find out, if we can, who's behind it all. If we can get hold of the guy alive we might be able to get the 'big man' behind him. Otherwise, they'll probably send someone else to do the job. We know about this guy, we might just miss the next if we can't eradicate the source.

'We believe that a lot of the smaller aggravation, if you can call it that, from border raids is set up by outsiders trying to stir things up for their benefit, not the Palestinians. We did have a couple of men watching him on his way here, but one was taken unawares and murdered by him. Before we could spare someone to take over, Candor had moved and then left France by plane, as you know'.

'Yes! We know of one man of yours who was asking questions about Candor. A big guy named Plaistot wasn't it? We saw his name on a flight list from Valeille to la

Malouesse', offered Winfild, taking care not to mention the taxi driver, but noted a slight look of surprise on Stretton's face as he admitted, 'Well, yes he was one, but he's not police, he's Mossad-Intelligence'.

'Hmm! How did Candor get in? Surely the plane didn't land here, did it? He'd be taking too much of a risk doing that, surely"

'That's a bit of a story on its own' said Stretton.'The plane did land but Candor had already arrived by then. One of our intelligence people, a young guy, was on the plane unknown to Candor or the pilot. He was hidden behind some crates the plane was supposed to be delivering to Cyprus'.

'By God; that takes some nerve' Winfild said admiringly.

'Well. In fact he was a bit fortunate not to get spotted, but he got trapped on the plane by accident. He was nosing around the aircraft, got himself in and before he could get out again, Candor and the dame pilot got in and it left.

'Mind you; you have to give him credit for not panicking. Some would have done and got themselves bumped off. Anyway, this is what happened'.

Stretton, still a little put out by Winfild's disclosure of his knowledge about Plaistot, went on to explain how Candor and the agent arrived in Israel, the day before.

As Hiram broke the seal on his second and last soft drink can, the contents effervesced through the hole wasting some of the valuable liquid. He felt dehydrated and hungry. Not knowing how long the journey would take he had sensibly husbanded the remaining sandwiches purchased at la Malouesse and wisely put them in the duffel bag.

He had just finished the last crumb, carefully putting the plastic wrapper back in the bag and he decided to break into the remaining can.

He wasn't sure whether the effervescing was due to the motion of the aircraft, or the altitude at which they were flying. Fortunately for Hiram, who had no access to an oxygen supply, as had the pilot in the flight cabin, the journey had so far been conducted no higher than two or three thousand feet. Whatever the reason, some of the soft drink soaked into Hiram's trousers and more spilt on to the fuselage floor. He managed to wipe up the fluid on the floor with his handkerchief before it had the chance to run under the crates; he daren't take the risk of the stuff being seen oozing out on the inner side.

He muttered a curse as he surveyed the remains of the tin's contents, wondering if he dare take a sip from it and deplete even further the small amount left.

He looked at his watch and reckoned they had been flying for a few minutes over five hours on this second leg. He had been surprised when he woke up to see that it was daylight and though his thirst had by no means been quenched by the sips from his soft drink supply, he wondered if he dare risk a trip to the toilet.

While he was thinking about it and was about to raise himself to look out of the window, the engine note altered and he could tell by the change in the aircraft's attitude they were about to land once more.

After the episode in the middle of the night when he had been a silent witness to what he felt was another example of Candor's ability to manipulate someone else to his own interests, his fear of the man had been expunged. Now he only felt a violent simmering anger against the man. How could the woman have agreed to do his bidding at her own risk of losing her licence and perhaps her livelihood, which she would if her actions were ever discovered?

He'd had visions of taking the full, soft drink can, opening the cabin door and beating the man senseless with it; taking charge of the aeroplane and forcing the woman to fly them all to Israel and justice. Only the knowledge that they needed to refuel prevented him from trying out the attempt. Now, it appeared the aircraft was going to land for that reason and he prepared himself, fully alert, for a chance to get the better of the assassin.

A few minutes later the aircraft had landed and parked; the flight cabin door opened and the pair came out into the fuselage.

'Well, I still think it is a crazy idea' the woman said and Hiram listened intently, trying not to miss a word of Candor's reply.

'No! not by any stretch of the imagination is it crazy, it 's expedient. You say we shall have the fuel to get all the way this time, so why waste time and attract danger by extending the journey when it is not necessary? That's why I brought the chute. I've carted it all the way from England. Jordan told me the final phase was by plane so I brought it, just in case I could make use of it. I know the people I have to meet and where. I'll just be a day earlier, that's all.

'It's a big risk for me though' said the woman; 'I'm still as I said, not too happy about it. It means staying here all day,at some risk I might add and then when we get airborne and get to where you want to go, there's the risk of me being forced down inside their air space. Anyway, I'll see to the refuelling and then we can talk some more'.

Hiram heard the access door open and close and the sound of it being locked and wondered where Candor was. He could hear no movement inside the aircraft, just an occasional creak from the structure. He strained for the slightest sound that might tell him Candor was still in the fuselage but could hear nothing. He felt now that he knew everything and heard all the talk about Candor's parachuting out of the plane. He didn't have the engine noise drowning out most of their earlier arguments.

He got up slowly, gingerly and looked around the crates. The interior of the aircraft was empty apart from the freight. He risked a glance through the window above where he had hidden during the flight but could see nothing but mountains and scrub. Taking a chance he crept across to the other side of the fuselage and had a careful look from one of the windows there.

Candor and the pilot were stood by the tailplane in earnest conversation and a fuel bowser was approaching along a dusty track. There seemed to be no activity at all from any ground crew that he could see. He took advantage of the inactivity, especially that of Candor and the woman, who both had had their exercise whilst arguing in the night, to take some exercise himself. He slowly did a few stretching movements and knees ups, thinking about what Candor had said concerning the chute. Obviously the man had meant parachute and seemed determined to use it, if he could persuade the woman to fly all the way; which meant they couldn't be too far off the end of their journey. Obviously not more than five hours away.

The pilot had said it meant staying where they were all day, in which case Candor must hope to get there before daylight. Hiram thought it risky to be parachuting into a strange country by night and grudgingly admitted that Candor had nerve. Still, he knew such activity had been done by service men and women many times during the Second World War and sometimes with uncertainty about their safe arrival on the ground. Would there be friends or foe waiting to welcome them?

But how could he prevent the man leaving the aircraft? Once Candor was out, he himself would no doubt be flying off again somewhere else and none the wiser. Candor could disappear and Hiram's people would have no knowledge of it. He believed they didn't know where he, Hiram, was and had probably accepted his disappearance never to see him again.

He had to have a plan! What could he do to make the woman land in his country for him to leave and warn his colleagues?

The bowser drew up alongside the trailing edge of the port wing and the woman pilot left Candor to go and talk to the bowser driver. Hiram moved back to his hiding place taking the precautions he had on the previous refuelling occasion, not to be observed.

As he lay there thinking, the sounds of the fuel tanks replenishment eventually ceased and the noise of the bowser's engine gradually diminished and became imperceptible as it was driven away. He waited for the opening of the fuselage access door and the entry into the aircraft of the man and woman who, at the moment, held his immediate future in their hands.

At last the pair came in. He heard the rattle of a key in a lock and the woman said, 'these will have to do, I only have enough to cover the cockpit and the engines. We'll put the control locks on too and throw a few shrubs on her'.

Puzzled, Hiram heard the grunt of assent from Candor and the sounds once again of the door opening and closing and being locked. He lay in apprehension and not a little nervous tension as the noise of activity became apparent on the outside of the aircraft. He could hear someone walking on the mainplane, dragging sounds, curses from Candor and protestations from the woman. Eventually the labour ceased for a time and then he heard faint scratching sounds as if someone was combing the surfaces of the machine.

He lay perplexed. The sounds stopped again for a while then began again; scratching noises, then silence once more. He waited for a continuation of the noises but there was nothing. Then a new sound, a motor vehicle again. He heard a door slam and the vehicle's engine noise recede until there was only the sound of his own light breathing. By his watch he saw that an hour and a quarter had passed since the aircraft had parked after landing and he was desperate to use a toilet. He waited a further five minutes and after they had dragged by, in desperation he got up and looked out of the window.

The whole airplane on that side was covered with brush and thin leafy branches. He changed position and looked forward over the engine; that was covered in some grey/ green material.

Now there were no sounds at all but his own; his heart and his breathing seemed to him to ring in the stillness. He padded across to the port side and carried out an investigation through the windows on that side. No more activity, the same scene met his eyes; the aircraft as far as he could see by his restricted vision was covered in brushwood, which explained the scratching noises. Of Candor and the woman there was no sign.

Obviously they had, as far as was possible, camouflaged the aeroplane from being identified from the air, or from the ground at a distance and gone off in the second vehicle. 'Probably fetched by the bowser driver', thought Hiram. It seemed to him they had decided to stay grounded for the day after all, to be able to carry out Candor's plan to parachute from the plane early, before daylight the following morning. So the pilot had been persuaded to agree with the assassin.

He relaxed; he went into the toilet compartment and after using the lavatory was in a quandary whether or not to operate the flush, thinking at first, that the contents would be discharged on to the ground if he did so, thus leaving evidence for the pair to find. With relief he realized it was after all, a chemical toilet and he carried out the necessary neutralizing routine which was promulgated on an instruction sheet stuck on the lid of the can by the side of the bowl. He wondered how he had got away without doing so when he'd used it during the flight, then supposed the woman, who had used the facility next after himself must have blamed the omission on Candor.

He washed in the tepid water from the tank-supplied, wash basin; using only a minimal amount, as that was discharged onto the ground. He believed, however, that it would be quickly evaporated away. He considered drinking some of the supply, but daren't risk it, thirsty as he was.

It suddenly dawned on him that the pilot and Candor must have a drinking supply somewhere and with some haste began to search for it. He eventually found it in the flight cabin and drank one of the cans of non-alcoholic beverage from the crate there. Realizing the brand was identical to that he himself had bought at la Malouesse, he took another one and substituted for it the empty can from his ruck sack.

He soon discovered the packs of sandwiches and other foods and helped himself to a little from each of some of them. Hunger satisfied and thirst slaked, he made sure everything was as, he hoped, the pair would think they had left it and went back into the passenger area.

As he walked up and down the confined space with bent head, necessitated by the lack of headroom, he thought about what he should do when the aircraft took off again. He decided that Candor should not be hindered by any attempt by himself to deter him from parachuting from the plane. The fact that the aircraft had been left unattended by the pair meant they had definiely decided to carry out Candor's plan for him to enter Israel by descent using the parachute he had brought with him, as he had earlier surmised would happen. It also meant the aircraft must at that moment be parked illegally in some remote uninhabited place somewhere, hence the camouflage.

Hiram, therefore, could not expect any help from locals. He couldn't get out of the plane anyway, before the couple returned, without forcing the door and he had no means of doing that. So! He had to wait until Candor jumped, then persuade, cajole or force the woman to land in the territory she would then be flying over, Israel. How could he do that?

The answer came to him suddenly and he wondered why he hadn't thought of it when he was helping himself to the food and drink which had been kept in the flight cabin, supplied by his unwitting hosts.

He opened the flight cabin door again and looked up at the 'Very' pistol clipped above the co-pilot's windscreen; also adjacent to it, half a dozen of each colour of red and green cartridges. A look at the port window by the co-pilot's seat also confirmed the thought he'd had about the pistol's use. There in the window was a hinged circular piece of Perspex covering a hole provided specifically for the firing of the pistol.

The flare pistol then, was the means whereby he could force the pilot to land where he wanted. He took it from it's clamp to check it was easy to remove quickly then replaced it and returned to the passenger and freight compartment, closing the flight cabin door behind him. He could do nothing until the pair returned and the aircraft took off on the last leg of the journey to his home. The sooner the better, he thought.

He might yet be able to gain an advantage on Candor and see him brought to the justice he deserved for his crimes, but there was nothing he could do yet until Candor left the plane.

Later, feeling bored out of his mind as he had times before, he lay in his hiding place. It was pitch black outside and he heard, both with relief and apprehension, the sound of an approaching vehicle. The slamming of doors and then the labour as the aircraft was cleared of its coverings.

He heard again the sound of a small engine, deciding it must be a ground generator. The access door was opened and he heard Candor say, 'Thank God that's over. Let's get these covers stowed away and get the hell out of this place, I hope never to have to see it again'.

Soon the necessary preparations to leave had been made, the engines burst into life and the aircraft was turned into wind for the take off.

Hiram lay considering his plan to take charge of the plane once Candor had jumped from it. He knew he would have to be quick as the aircraft would turn away from the land as soon as Candor left. He had no doubt in his own mind about the success of his plan. He believed that the pilot would have no choice but to do as he wished. The drone of the engines soothed his nerves and he became more relaxed as he knew he would not now have to tackle the man Candor by himself, although he was also no longer in fear of him.

He knew too that Candor had to risk his neck by jumping in the dark and even if successful he still had to complete the journey to Jerusalem or wherever it was he was making for. By then he, Hiram, would have alerted the security forces that Candor was in the country.

He felt secure and for the first time since he got on the plane, happy. He would again soon be seeing Patricia, his darling wife; probably it was just a few hours to that joyous moment. He lay, eyes closed, thinking of her and again slipped into slumber.

He woke with a start. For a second or two he panicked, wondering if he had missed his chance. There was a roaring noise from the rear of the plane and the dim lights were on; it was also very cold. He cautiously raised himself and changed his position to one where he could see around the crates to try and identify the cause of the noise.

Candor was standing by the open door; he had a large pack on his back and was adjusting the straps fastening one of the suitcases to his chest. The other suitcase lay open and empty on the floor.

As Hiram stared, almost unbelieving at the sight, the dim lights went out and then came on again. Candor stood and braced himself with a hand each side of the opening, unknowing of Hiram's interest and then the lights went out again.

Hiram realized the man was gone. His silhouette no longer blocked out the night sky at the opening. Within seconds the engine noise changed and the aircraft's attitude altered.

Hiram suddenly remembered what he was supposed to be doing and he got out as quick as he could from behind the crates. He took a deep breath, opened the flight cabin door and pushed himself in and grabbed for the Very pistol and cartridges as he dropped into the co-pilot's seat. He loaded one of the cartridges into the pistol and turned to look at the woman. She had turned uncomprehending at his entry thinking that Candor had changed his mind about jumping and ready to chide him for not closing the fuselage door.

Now she stared in utter disbelief and concern at the young wild eyed man who sat within touching distance of her. Her eyes were afraid and her mouth opened, but no sound was uttered. Then, gathering her wits, 'Who the devil are you? What are you doing here?' she demanded in French.

'Never mind about that Madame, you are in serious trouble. You are to land at Lydda. Open a frequency to the airport there and advise them you are coming in'.

'Don't be a fool, I cannot land there, its not possible for me to do that!'

'Believe me Madame, you can only land there. If you do not hail the controller at Lydda airport I shall dump the fuel', here Hiram put his hand on the fuel dumping levers on the floor between the two seats which ejected all the fuel in the main tanks, 'and then I shall fire this flare into the instrument panel. Believe me, I shall do this. You will be flying blind and you will have only fuel enough to get you into the middle of the sea'.

His voice sounded high and slightly hysterical.

'But you can't, we'll both be killed if you do that'.

'Yes Madame. I am willing to die if you do not obey; are you? I shall count to ten. If you do not get in touch with the airfield by the time I reach ten, I shall do as I said. One, two, three—'

As he reached the count of five the woman capitulated, much to Hiram's relief and operated the switches on the radio set.

Almost immediately, a voice in English, then repeated in French, demanded their identification.

The woman spoke into the old fashioned, hand held microphone and gave the aircraft's call sign, 'Lima Hotel Uniform Five Six Zero'. She requested a course to the airfield at Lydda and permission to land there.

Hiram reached for and snatched the microphone from her. He pressed the 'talk' button. 'This is D.C.3

aircraft, call sign Lima Hotel Uniform Five Six Zero calling Lydda airfield. Request urgent. Course to Lydda required and please advise police to meet on landing'.

He repeated the message.

The woman's look was vitriolic. 'Cochon!' She spat out the insult.

'I am sorry Madame. I'm afraid it will probably mean gaol for you'

'Oh yes! It is not I who am hijacking the aircraft. It is you who will have to answer questions. I will say you forced me here. I was to land at Paphos in Cyprus, but you took over and made me fly here'.

'I'm afraid that will not work Madame' said Hiram, thinking quickly. 'You have been under observation since before you met Candor at la Malouesse. I was placed on board specifically to observe what routine you would carry out and how Candor was to effect an entry into my country. We have known of his intentions since he left England. You have no choice but to co-operate'.

The woman suddenly looked downcast at his reply; it looked to her as though she had lost everything by giving in to Candor's entreaties, whichever way she turned; either the loss of the plane and probable death, or a life of imprisonment. The earnest young man holding the Very pistol looked quite capable of carrying out his threat. Was he then a member of the Mossad and aware of the intentions of her passenger who had just left the aircraft? He seemed though young, to be determined to have her obey. Dare she take a chance?

Her thoughts were interrupted by the flight controller at Lydda giving permission to land and a course to get them there. He confirmed Hiram's request that the police would meet the plane on landing and that the Israeli Air force had knowledge of their flight and a couple of jet fighters were already airborne.

Hiram acknowledged the transmission and thanked the controller. He looked at the woman to see she seemed not to have heard. Her shoulders had drooped and her attitude showed the complete loss of her former self assurance. She was completely overwhelmed by the turn of events.

Suddenly, he felt sorry for her. After all, he thought, she was only making use of her journey for the delivery of freight, to take a passenger also. Probably lured by the money offered and unknowing of Candor's intentions and past crimes. He could not believe that a woman with that knowledge could have succumbed to Candor's arguments in the way that she had.

'Madame, the course! Change to the course he gave'. Hiram nudged her shoulder.

She turned her head; looking blankly at him and he could see tears had welled up in her eyes. She shook as if suddenly chilled and she looked away from him again, to the compass. She carried out the manoeuvre to bring them to the course given, but said nothing. A tear rolled down her cheek and Hiram felt uncomfortable.

'Look, Madame', he said, 'I am sorry things have turned out badly for you, but that was the risk you took. You have broken the regulations of several countries to bring an assassin to my own. He has already killed several

301

people and is trying to do something which will cause the deaths of many more. Surely you cannot complain if your scheme, a gamble for reward, has failed'.

The woman did not answer, her misery was all too apparent. The tremors of her body became more pronounced and she began to shake violently, her whole body shuddering and writhing.

Hiram became greatly concerned. He realized the woman was losing control, both of herself and the aircraft, which began to yaw and pitch.

'My God! She's not going to be able to land like this' he thought.

'Madame' he said aloud 'are you all right?'

She turned to him, releasing the control column and made as if to get out of the seat. He could see that all her self control had gone. She seemed unaware of him and she was moaning as if in pain, her features distorted. Hiram shuddered. The aircraft began to veer to port and Hiram suddenly realized the enormity of their predicament.

He slapped the woman hard across the cheek but she seemed not to feel his blow except to plump back into the seat, her head bowed, with her face in her hands and her elbows on her lap. She wept openly and bitterly.

The aircraft had by this time, made an increased turn to port and the instrument showing the 'artificial horizon' indicated that the plane was losing height, as was confirmed by the altimeter; also the engine note had risen.

Hiram grabbed the co-pilot's control column and moved it into a more central position. He scanned the instruments and identified each. By slight experimental movements of the control column he managed to stabilize the aircraft's attitude. He gently eased back slightly on the column and watched the gradual movement of the indicator on the artificial horizon instrument move below the reference line across the centre of the glass face. He kept it in that position, watching the altimeter confirming their slow but positive increase in altitude. When they reached two thousand feet he tentatively moved a switch marked 'Auto' /'Manual' to 'Auto' and felt the control column become independent of his attention. He breathed a sigh of relief and felt his pulse begin to slow to something like normal. He wiped away the cold sweat from his forehead as he saw the instruments now seemed to be stabilized.

He looked again at the woman who had not changed her position; she was looking down into her lap.

The radio suddenly crackled and the voice he had heard previously announced, 'You are off course. Please turn to the course given'.

Hiram found the microphone again and pressed the talk button. 'We've got an emergency here. The pilot has been taken ill. I have set the auto-pilot; request your instructions as to procedure'.

He repeated the message. There was a short delay then the voice asked, 'What's your altitude, airspeed and fuel content? Also the course indicated on your instrument?'

Hiram gave the information after a searching identification and examination of all the instruments involved in the checks, repeating the statement.

'Information received and understood. Indicated course correct. Will pilot be able to regain control?' asked the voice.

'I'll try and find out' said Hiram.

He put down the microphone and reached for and took the woman's left hand in his right. He squeezed it gently and said, 'Look Madame; we are in a difficult position. Do you not understand?'

He put down the Very pistol he had been holding in his left hand on to the floor between his feet. He reached across and with the same hand turned her unresisting head so that he could look at her. She had ceased to weep but just stared at him as if she was looking through him to something far away.

'Madame; Madame, listen please'.

She seemed at last to become aware of him again and he put his left hand on to hers, held in his right. He massaged it gently, soothingly.

'You are the only one who can get us out of this situation we are in you know'.

Her forehead wrinkled as if she was trying to remember him; her gaze became intent. He could not but notice the inroads into her make up the tears had made. She pulled her hand away and straightened herself in her seat.

'I shall die in there' she said at last and looked ahead at the sky through the windscreen where the soft light of the morning sky was beginning to hide the myriad stars.

'Die? In where?' asked Hiram.

'In their prison. But it will be preferable to life in there'.

The radio voice crackled again.

'Will pilot be able to regain control? If so, readjust to course given'. The question and directive were repeated.

Hiram took the microphone. 'Pilot recovering, please await further transmission', he said. He turned again to the woman, feeling uncomfortable and embarrassed, as if somehow he was responsible for her predicament.

'Look! I feel bad about this' he said. 'There must be a way out for you'.

She looked at him, a sudden determination showed in her eyes. 'There is only one way. I am not going to your prison'.

She leaned forward suddenly and switched off the auto-pilot. Moving the control column to the left and backwards toward her stomach, at the same time she pushed the engine throttles forward. Almost instantaneously the aircraft rolled to port and came round in a tight banking turn, the engines roaring. She straightened it out on the new course she had chosen.

'Go ahead and fire the pistol, it will solve both our problems' she said.

'No! there is a way' shouted Hiram, 'a way for both of us'.

'All right then. What is this way out?' she asked in a mocking manner, but throttling back the engines.

'Listen! You land the plane at Lydda. Slow down and stop as quickly as you can and I will jump out. You can then open up and take off again straight away; this is an old kite, the runways there are made for Jumbo's, you'll have plenty of room to take off without turning round and going back to the start of the runway'.

'Yes! And get shot down by your Air Force'.

Hiram thought for a moment; he had forgotten about the jet fighters in the confusion.

'Look. Couldn't you fly at a very low altitude, they wouldn't dare have a go at you from above their own territory would they if you were near the ground? Besides, once you are over the sea you'll be out of their air space in a jiffy. At least it's worth a try, it's a chance. They might not fire at all, at least they wouldn't fire at you, probably ahead of you to try and make you turn, but they wouldn't shoot you down I'm certain of that. I know it is not a policy of our Nation to shoot aircraft down without trying to get them to land and they would need permission from some-one really senior to do that and they haven't had the time to get it'.

He could see the woman pondering over the problem and knew that every minute took them further away from the airfield at Lydda.

'And what do you tell them? That you could have stopped me, but you decided to let me get away? This is nonsense, we are either going to Cyprus or into the sea. The choice is yours'.

'I would tell them that when you were slowing down on the runway I went back out of the flight cabin to get my duffel bag and unknown to me you had a pistol hidden away. That you braked and almost stopped the plane and caught me unawares in the passenger area, where you made me give up the Very pistol and jump out on to the runway. Then of course, you took off and beat it out to the coast and out of the air limits. After all it's only about twenty kilometres to the coast from Lydda. Just a short flight away from safety; safety for the two of us'.

The woman looked at him again for a moment. The doubts were in her mind, but what he had said sounded feasible. The choice; death for both of them if he carried out his threat to dump the fuel and damage the instruments, or a gamble on a race of a few minutes duration to escape the jet fighters patrolling somewhere in the vicinity. For a while she hovered in indecision, then, to Hiram's relief, she said, 'Well I think it might work. Why die when there is the chance to survive? Although I believe you have the better part of the deal. Still this will give me a little hope. Ask them for the course'.

She once more brought the aircraft on to the course for Lydda supplied by the controller there and Hiram relaxed, glad now that she had accepted the manoeuvre would perhaps solve the problem for both of them.

Eventually the old D.C.3 bounced down on the runway and rapidly lost momentum, the brakes squealing in protest. A couple of police security cars and a collection of airfield 'emergency landing' vehicles raced from a parking area adjacent to the runway threshold after the slowing aeroplane.

The drivers were surprised to see a figure jump from the aircraft, tumbling over on to the concrete before it had stopped and then the plane accelerate away, both engines roaring on full power. It lifted up off the runway and banked away, gradually becoming a speck in the sky.

Hiram, bruised and winded from the fall, stood looking up after it as the vehicles drew up beside him. A very short time after the D.C 3 disappeared from view there was a roar over head and a couple of Israeli jet fighters screamed across the airfield at low altitude in pursuit of the intruder.

As the security police pinioned Hiram's arms and escorted him back to one of the cars, he turned once more, peering into the sky in the direction in which the aircraft had disappeared. He listened thinking he'd heard a distant light explosion or firing but then dismissed the thought. Probably just his imagination he decided and bent to enter the police vehicle.

'So then you see' Stretton went on, 'he got out of the seat a bit too soon. When he went into the freight area the dame slowed down the plane to a crawl, got a revolver from some hidden place in the pilot's cabin and got the drop on him. She made him give up the Very pistol and jump out of the crate. He might have broken his neck.

'At any rate she beat it off into the 'wide blue yonder' as the Yanks say. Fortunately for her the two jet fighters had been ordered not to shoot her down and she ignored their orders to turn back and they let off a couple of shots to try and make her change her mind but to no avail and she was soon out of our air space. Apparently it's all down to politics; we haven't got to upset anybody and the registration number of the plane had been checked as being belonging to a French woman. Our country don't want to upset the French; you yourself know we have agents over there with their permission. As at the time there was some doubt about the legality of the occurrence and Hiram's being an unpaid passenger, she got the benefit of the doubt; young Hiram not having been able to give his story before she was 'up and away'; I doubt she'll be welcome here in the future though. I expect she'll want to give us a wide berth anyway. As I said, it's all politics; we don't want to upset them and though they may make a protest about her behaviour, they'll not harp on about it too much '.

'Lucky devil, your man though all right', said Seth Winfild, 'but she had some guts, that woman. She took the chance to get away and made it otherwise she might have been fish food, or if she'd landed like your agent wanted she could have spent quite a while in prison. Yes! She also was lucky all right. Your guy had guts to do what he did though without getting caught while in the kite and when he jumped out'.

'Yes you're right, but anyway here we are. I'll take you in and introduce you to the boss. Then we'll find your 'digs' and get you a meal is that o.k.?'

§ CHAPTER 32

Candor briskly rubbed the sore place on his arm and checked to see it was not broken. In the pre-dawn blackness he couldn't tell whether or not it was badly bruised but it certainly felt like it, the pain he was getting from it, he thought.

It caused him some difficulty rolling up the parachute and he would have liked to set fire to it but considered that too dangerous, he might be spotted. At last, stumbling about in the rocky area where he had come down, he managed to find a deep enough gap between some boulders in which to hide the mass of silk and support lines and cover it with some smaller rocks.

Still not completely satisfied that it wouldn't be discovered he decided to wait a little longer so that he might have a better chance to make sure when the dawn light arrived. An hour or so later and he was moving in a North Easterly direction to Ashkelon away from the Gaza Strip, making a detour around the Kibbutz at Yad Mordechai, named after the Jewish hero Mordechai Anilewitz. Candor was careful also not to approach the settlement at Negba, Yad Mordechai's sister Kibbutz to the East.

In the early morning gloom he met no-one who could report seeing a stranger in the area. For this he was heartily grateful, unwelcome attention being the last thing he needed.

The sixteen kilometre, difficult walk in the rough terrain to the North of the Kibbutzim took him more than three hours and when he approached Askelon, one of the world's oldest cities, he was more than ready for a rest and a meal. The suitcase weighed heavy in his hand and as he had progressed, he had changed its load from one hand to the other and back again, after that one again became numb from the weight, each one taking its share in the strain. He only stopped twice to rest as he was eager to progress to his destination. The smaller rocks sometimes hidden by the scrub, had been a nuisance, jarring his ankles and bruising his feet, sometimes cursing them as he progressed.

He had no regrets about the jump from the old D.C.3 instead of the easier, but much longer and therefore much more dangerous, journey from Cyprus by sea and having no knowledge of Hiram Wooley's presence in the plane, thought that it would probably now be at its original destination, off loading its cargo.

As he neared the road junction leading to the outskirts of the city, leaving the rough tracts behind, he spruced himself up as well as he could, though his soiled clothing belied the impression he was trying to create. He was at last relieved to see a battered taxicab coming along the road from Kiryat Gat as he stood at the crossroads.

He hailed the vehicle and the driver, a moustached Arab, cigarette drooping from his lips, pulled up unable to believe his luck at the chance of a fare that far out of the city. By the use of a smattering of French and Arabic, the latter learnt during his earlier sojourn at the time of his service in the Royal Marines, supplementing his English, Candor managed to explain his desire to the driver, to reach the docks at Ashdod.

After some bargaining and the overcoming of the driver's professed reluctance to go so far, by the offer of a bonus, Candor settled into the back seat of the taxi. He was glad of the respite from the long hike from the Northern tip of the Gaza Strip and it gave him the opportunity to think more clearly about what he had to do without the worry he'd had about being spotted and reported to the authourities by some suspicious and zealous observer, whilst walking.

Soon he was taking a late but welcome breakfast in a cafe in the dock area of Ashdod, a city founded only thirty years before. He finished eating, drank the last of the coffee and made enquiries, not without some difficulty, about the location of the address he'd been given in Buckland's instructions regarding his contact in the area.

A further half an hour's search found the home of the man who was to assist him in his project.

Hussein Muhkram was a large muscular individual, an undercover agent of the P.L.O.

His searching black eyes set in swarthy features gave no hint of surprise at Candor's early appearance, though he hadn't been expected for quite some time. The drooping ends of Hussein's moustache, partially covering the thick red lips, allied to the deep clefts each side of his mouth gave him a somewhat sinister, sneering expression, emphasized by his heavily lined brow.

Candor spent an hour at the man's abode and when he emerged he was not of the same appearance as when he entered. His hair was completely grey and covered in part with the white crown cap, typical of the Palestinian Arab, in contrast to the swarthy look gained by the staining of his skin, His clothes were old and oversize and scruffy sandals almost covered his stained feet. A huge false grey moustache hid his top lip and he had the stooped and weary look of an older man.

He wore a grubby pullover, partly hiding the slack waisted trousers tied for security with a length of thick string, underneath a jacket with frayed cuffs. He looked very poor and of little consequence. He believed that no-one would give him a second look, or question his presence.

There was no hint of the cotton belt next to the skin of his waist. The belt, divided into several pouches carried not only a large sum in various currencies but also contained a large quantity of plastic, chemical explosive of the latest type, odourless and high in destructive power. One separate pouch contained a number of pencil detonators.

He had also fitted the soft contact lenses which changed the fierce blue of his eyes to a more liquid brown; a device he had used before during his earlier activities in the cities of Britain.

Hussein Muhkram wore a similar belt with pouches of explosive and a pair of small revolvers with ammunition. He also carried a small radio transmitter and a receiver. The former powered by three A.A size alkaline 1.5 volt batteries, was fitted into the case of the ubiquitous personal tape player complete with earphones. The latter similarly powered was hidden inside a battered and scruffy camera case.

The pair boarded an omnibus full of vociferous humanity bound for Tel Aviv. There they changed, somewhat relieved, to a not so crowded second, en route for Jerusalem. They alighted at the central bus station and from there walked the one and a quarter kilometres to the Knesset where they joined the throng of Saturday sightseers by the Whol Rose Garden.

Candor had expressed his desire to familiarize himself with the area. The lapse of so many years had dimmed his vision but he was surprised to see that his memory had not completely betrayed him. Little had changed, but like always before, there was a medium sized crowd of varying nationalities wandering about, many carrying cameras and he found the constant flashing of the photographer's cameras, a nuisance. He kept shading his eyes not wanting himself to appear on their snaps, perhaps at some risk to himself; above all he wished to remain anonymous.

They did not stay there long. Muhkram was decidedly edgy about the chance of being stopped and searched by the uniformed patrols though, to Candor, the possibility of being recognised among the crowds seemed remote. He would have liked to have joined the tourists on a visit to view the inside of the Knesset but had not the necessary papers to match his new identity.

Candor did not bother about the danger of his being recognised, even at times, pushing his way to the front of people to search out anything which might assist him to carry out his plans.

He wished to refresh his memory about the area surrounding the Knesset so that he might find a convenient position to set off an explosion. The range of the small low powered transmitter was very limited he knew and the closer the distance between the transmitter and receiver the more chance there was of success.

He knew that a back-up transmitter was available but it was bulky and would have aroused suspicion. Even so, it would need to be hidden from view and within range of the building if it had to be used, though that range would be increased.

Candor, scowling, eyed Britain's gift, the seven branched Menorah, standing in its circular, fenced compound, the symbol of all he had come to hate. He did not realize that his features, even disguised as they were, betrayed that hatred. An elderly white woman tourist at his elbow, happening to glance at his expression, edged away from him, pulling at her husband's arm, horrified at what she could see there.

The occurrence, observed by Hussein Muhkram, did nothing to ease his nervousness and he pushed his way in beside Candor whispering urgently in his ear. The pair made their way back through the crowd, but as they were leaving Candor noticed a large pantechnicon which seemed to be carrying out an exchange of furniture at a side entrance of the Parliament building, which increased his interest.

He pulled at Muhkram's sleeve and halted the man's endeavour to leave the vicinity as fast as possible. They observed the procedure for a few minutes, trying not to let their interest in the to'ing and fro'ing of the workmen be noticed by anyone who might question their behaviour.

The van driver and his mate seemed to be exchanging chairs, watched by a couple of uniformed and armed I.D.F. men. At least, as they took each one from the building, they replaced it with one from the vehicle. The operation being photographed by some interested onlookers; anything seemed to take the interest of some people thought Candor, whose own interest was for a completely different reason.

The business intrigued Candor however, who asked Hussein what he thought the exchange meant. He replied that it happened every now and then, though he wasn't sure of the time period between changes. Apparently, the heavy wooden chairs became soiled from much use and a local firm had the contract for the cleaning and refurbishing of them. It was, apparently quite a big job and because some sort of seating was necessary all the time, the firm kept a batch of chairs, similar to the originals, which had been a gift from America, in stock as temporary replacements while the job was done.

He mentioned that the workmen would not be Jews as the day was Saturday, the Jewish Sabbath, but Candor seemed not to have heard him. He was preoccupied with his thoughts, an idea, the germ of which had been sown while listening to Hussein's explanation, was carefully elaborated and trimmed in his mind as they walked on.

When they arrived at the house where Candor was introduced to Hussein's kinsman, he had completed and perfected the stratagem which he believed couldn't fail. He asked some more questions of Hussein and established that the premises of the firm, whose name and address he had memorized from the lettering on the side of the furniture van, was not very far away from Hussein's house.

He then outlined to them the idea he had developed whilst out visiting the Knesset and because of what he had seen happening there. They admitted the idea he had, appeared to them to be sound and congratulated him, admiring his perspicacious and bold thinking. It also enhanced their enthusiasm for the project in hand, knowing the risk to themselves was minimised; they would not even have to enter the building and they could choose any time they liked to set off the explosion inside the place, from outside.

It depended of course on their ability to carry out the work which Candor had detailed and which would have to be carried out correctly and secretly. They decided to go and see the location of the firm and check the possibility of obtaining some of the chairs. The taking of them would have to be after the work of renovation had been carried out. This would however give them time to produce the necessary number of miniature receivers they would require.

As the explosive would have to be split into the requisite number of parts and there was no possibility of wiring the detonators together, each would have to be triggered individually, but the lot simultaneously; but Candor did not believe that would be difficult to achieve.

Hussein was convinced he could get the radio receivers obtained without too much trouble. They would each have to be tiny enough to fit into a small cylinder, not much bigger in diameter than a cigar tube and definitely not more that twenty or so millimetres, he thought, from what he could remember of the chairs. Candor agreed and specified the use of two batteries, each of one point five volts to power each receiver. It was decided to investigate the possibility of utilizing the receivers from model aircraft which were readily available for a price and hopefully small enough for the size mentioned.

While his cousin led Candor to find the firm of carpenters, Hussein set off to see about the receivers, their availability, price and perhaps possible modification to fit the proposed holes in the chair legs. Adam Buckland had told Candor of Muhkram's many contacts and now the man was proving Buckland to be correct in his high opinion of this particular Palestinian.

At the carpenters workshop, which they soon found, they made a thorough, detailed examination of the building and its accesses. Candor could not see how they could be prevented from gaining an entrance to 'borrow' the chairs they needed. While he had another look round the place, Hussein's cousin made some enquiries inside, pretending to try to obtain employment there as a labourer.

He was taken into the workshop proper where he could not but notice the stacks of chairs which Hussein and Candor had seen earlier that day. He thus managed to get a better estimation of the size of the various parts and was surprised to note how solid, heavy and large they were.

He eventually returned to Candor to report. He had been taken on as a labourer which could prove to be a great help in getting into the place when the time came. Also if they needed to take one chair at a time and had for some reason to retain it during working hours he might be able to disguise the fact that there was one chair missing. He saw there were indeed a large number of them; the van used to transport them had of necessity been vast in its capacity.

The two men returned to their base and found Muhkram waiting for them. He had obtained a small container of the type he hoped to use for the radio receivers and enquired of Candor if he thought it suitable. His cousin was convinced it could easily be accommodated in one of the massive legs of each of the chairs they would utilize. Candor however would not commit himself so readily and it was decided to obtain a piece of wood similar to one of the chairs front legs and experiment with that before confirming the size of the containers.

Satisfied that such a piece of wood could be obtained the following day, Sunday; they settled down to plan how the work was to be carried out and how many chairs they would need, each man giving his suggestions as to how the operation could be performed and in the end an agreement was reached. Each man concurring with Candor's view of the situation.

One of each chair's legs to be bored, would have to accept a part of the explosive, a receiver and a detonator. The number of chairs required would be determined by the time taken to bore the legs, fit the three components into the holes and then disguise the work done. The whole job was dependent on the receipt of the radio receivers in their containers. Candor had more than enough money to finance the undertaking, money would not be a problem.

It had been a busy day and Candor was glad to retire. He was content and pleased that the question of how to get the explosive into the Parliament building had been solved. The witnessing of the exchanging of the chairs had been a stroke of luck and his ingenuity in making use of that occurrence meant that the successful conclusion of the operation was now assured. It only remained to get hold of the chairs one at a time, doctor them and return them to the workshop. He lay back in the bed thinking, but was soon fast asleep.

The following morning Hussein's cousin Tariq went away to obtain the test piece of wood. At the same time

Hussein left to purchase the necessary tools and was back home first, bringing with him a large hand brace; varying diameter wood drill bits, gouging chisels and a large tin of plastic wood. A small tin of oak varnish completed the purchases, paid for by Candor and obtained at the local D.I.Y. store which was open for business seven days a week.

The afternoon saw the successful completion of the boring of the wood pattern. Some fine chiselling had ensured the empty receiver container, obtained by Hussein the previous day, could be fitted tightly as the last component after the detonator and to which it was wired.

Candor had decided to sacrifice one of the detonators to test the working of the model, once a completed receiver was fitted instead of the empty container. He felt it was necessary to check the maximum range of the radio receiver and transmitter. The original receiver brought with them disguised in the camera case, now being redundant, he had to be sure the small ones would be sufficient for their task.

Not wishing to attract attention by the sound of the exploding detonator, he knew a journey into more uninhabited country would be required. That could not take place however until they had a receiver of the type they believed they needed.

There was one snag which caused Candor some thought. The batteries to be used in the receiver being small in capacitance and it being necessary to switch each one 'on' as it was fitted into its chair leg, meant that the time taken to complete the work, added to the time the chairs stayed in the store afterwards before being returned to the Knesset, must be as short a duration as possible.

Tariq's first duty on starting work at the carpenter's shop was to find out and report back, how long the renovation of the chairs would take. To get a better estimate of the time required to fit the components, Candor decided to 'borrow' one of the chairs as soon as possible. He resolved to do so on the evening of the following day, Tariq's first in employment at the workshop.

Chief Superintendent Arthur Oakey received a telephone call from Janet Brookfield, the Commander's secretary asking him to attend the Commander's office as soon as possible. As he was almost always busy with regard to his senior position in his office in the Yard he was somewhat perplexed that the secretary hinted that the Commander was not in a very good mood and was at a loss to see what he himself had done to warrant the Commander's displeasure. He decided he must put aside his present occupation with crime statistics and go at once to find out what it was the Commander was in such a mood about.

He arrived fairly quickly at the secretary's office and she explained to him that she believed her boss's present discomforture was because the Chief Superintendent hadn't reported to him any news about their Inspector's progress with the Candor affair. Forewarned being forearmed, he did a swift about turn and raced back to his own office to retrieve the file on Candor. Having obtained the document he arrived back at the secretary's office, though late, a little more positive in his belief that he would be able to hold his own against his superior's questions. He gave a nod and a wink to Janet who smiled and knocked on the Commander's door. There was a grumpy sounding 'Come in' and Arthur Oakey entered, keeping a watchful eye out for the position of the Pomeranian which, as it happened, was lying in its basket adjacent to the Commander's chair, its normal position.

'Well Arthur, what's happening about our man over in Israel, that's where he is, isn't it? See what's his name?' He did sound a little piqued, thought the Chief Supeintendent.

'Well, yes sir; Inspector Winfild is our man over there, he did arrive in Jerusalem eventually. His being there is to advise the Mossad and their police, of course what he knows about this criminal Candor. I have the file here sir. Would you like to see it?'

'Er—no Arthur, just give me the gist of what's going on. I haven't the time to wade through that lot. Just remind me about what's happened since you last came here'. He looked over his glasses at the Chief Superintendent. 'It seems to be a long time since you appraised me about that sequence of events'. It sounded to the subordinate as something of a reprimand, or at least a reproach for his not keeping the Commander up to speed about the amount of information which he should have imparted and he decided to watch his step. Also he noticed the Commander's eye occasionally glanced towards the whisky cupboard door; his own towards the Pomeranian which didn't appear to be too comfortable at the moment; at least it kept a watch on the Chief Superintendent. He thought it always gave the impression it was about to spring on whoever should enter the office and after the incident concerning his own trouser leg he was always watchful in case it decided to have another go. He picked up the file on Candor, which he had put down on to the Commander's desk and began to summarize the contents.

'Well sir, our man Inspector Winfild, is now liaiseing with the Israeli people, having parted company with his Sergeant, Peter Bracken who is now back with us, sir. Apparently one of their men was stowed away in the aircraft which Candor flew in, unknown to him or the pilot and apparently Candor parachuted out of the plane over, they believe, er—the Gaza strip. Of course the Israelis and our man are keeping watch in Jerusalem because it seems another of their agents, when in France, was informed by a French policeman, who it is thought was also working for the Mossad, although we can't be sure of his being a double agent; and that Candor's quarry was to be the Knesset. It seems a difficult place to blow up with all the security they have around it, I would have thought, but we knowing Candor and what he can do, cannot rule out an attempt being made by him; nor can the Israelis. Their Mossad are apparently pulling out all the stops on this. They think an attempt may be made at the next sitting of the Knesset and they and our man are watching out for anything unusual'.

'You think they've got everything sown up then Arthur? We can't keep our man hanging around over there if there's no point in him being there, can we?'

'Well sir, we want to be sure that our man can pass on all he knows about Candor and it may help in their prepartions for capturing the villain. Also of course we want to get some of the kudos when he is caught and see if we can get him extradited back here to pay for his crimes in this country. I believe that it is imperative that our man stays there until Candor is caught to keep our 'irons in the fire' as it were, to keep our interests to the forefront. Don't you think that is important sir?'

'Well, yes Arthur. All I'm saying is that when the arrest of Candor is made, that we try to get our man back here. I don't like our people wandering all over the place, we've got enough work for them to do here. However I take your point. He's obviously some use to them but when, as I say, Candor is arrested, our man must not be allowed to dilly dally over their. Get him back here as soon as is able' and he started to get up out of his seat.

Arthur Oakey knew what was coming next and he was right. The cupboard door was opened and the two glasses were brought out and the Commander poured a generous quantity of the whisky into each. Arthur Oakey often thought that the whisky must be supplied to the Commander at cut price considering the amount which was consumed by him and visitors to his office.

'Right Arthur' he said, 'We'll just drink a toast to our friends over in Israel and with our man's help, no doubt things will go right for a change'.

Arthur Oakey took the glass, not without some misgivings, but realized that he was not getting a reprimand after all. At least the Commander seemed a bit more equitable and friendly than when he had first arrived. He put the glass to his lips and swallowed the spirit in gulps as fast as he could manage without choking and made his farewell to his superior and departed, his face quite reddened due to the effect of the whisky and already feeling somewhat light-headed. The Commander's secretary looked up as he came through her office and asked him if he was all right. He just shook his head and went through the door without speaking. Janet guessed what had happened again and smiled to herself at his parting.

When Tariq came home that Monday evening, he reported that the chairs were already being worked on, as all of them had to be finished by the end of the fortnight for replacement in the Knesset on the Saturday morning. Apparently a meeting of the Knesset was to take place on the Monday following and it was traditional that all furniture, fittings, decorations etc. were complete and in place.

He had been employed removing the old varnish from some of the chairs himself that day. As each chair was reworked it was put aside to be recovered with quick drying varnish and eight of the chairs were already renovated and four of those re-varnished.

All the chairs would be ready on the Saturday before the Parliament sitting. The work had always been done by that same firm and they always managed the completion of the renovation in the time allowed without any problem.

The three men went to the workshop that night as soon as it was dark. Tariq had arranged with another relative, who was also employed there as a labourer and who knew the security routine well, to meet them. He showed the easiest way to gain entry as he had used the same method himself in the past to obtain various items for his own use and had never been suspect.

Candor was, at first, reluctant to involve another person but Hussein put his mind at ease. The code of co-operation between the members of a family of Palestinians, especially when fighting for a cause, whether it be true or false, was not to be broken, no matter how distant the relationship might be. The reason for their visit however and its significance, was not divulged, just that they needed to gain entry.

Tariq's rickety Citroen van was soon conveying them and one of the chairs back to his home without any cause for trouble. Fortunately in that district at that time of night there was little vehicular movement. The skill with which Tariq carried out the work on the newly varnished chair surprised Candor. They had decided that the fitting of the explosive, detonator and receiver would be best made in one of the front legs.

'After all', Candor remarked, 'someone leaning back on a chair with a seriously weakened back leg would find himself on the floor with the break revealing its sabotage and dangerous potential to all!'

When the work was completed and the small rubber boot from the bottom of the leg replaced, it was impossible to tell that the chair had been tampered with. All that remained was to obtain the radio receiver and carry out the work correctly, not with just an empty container. The work had taken less than an hour and Candor decided that they would use seven chairs and work on the lot after one raid on the firm's carpenter's shop.

It would mean that one of them would have to stay behind or walk as the old van of Tariq's would not accommodate all three of them and the seven chairs. Also, an advantage would be that all the work could be carried out on the night prior to the chairs being returned to their rightful place in the Knesset, giving the best chance for the receiver batteries remaining in a charged condition until the following Monday. Rechargeable batteries would be used after a fresh recharging of them, it was decided.

The sample chair was returned that same night. The following day, Tuesday, Hussein obtained three of the radio receivers in their containers from the maker. Candor and Hussein then journeyed south eastwards for some eight kilometres on the road to the Mar Saba Monastery before Candor was satisfied that the experiment they were to carry out could not be witnessed, or that they could be surprised by some curious travellers.

One of the detonators was wired some distance away from one of the receivers which was placed behind a rock to protect it from the chance of damage from the report of the detonator when it exploded.

Candor walked about a half a kilometre away from the receiver in the difficult terrain and then turned and walked slowly towards it. He kept the transmitter button pressed and turned the strength knob to 'full power' with the short aerial pointing in the direction of the receiver as he walked.

Eventually there was a crack like a pistol shot as the detonator exploded and Candor then paced out the distance from that position to the receiver. As he bent to recover the vital piece of apparatus he realized he should have carried out the test with the receiver completely hidden behind the rocks or, better still, buried among them; thus to simulate the penetration of a building by the transmitter's signal.

He mentally upbraided himself for his error, but decided not to waste another detonator. He would assume half the distance he had measured would perhaps be a more realistic figure, as a maximum transmitting distance, when the receiver was inside the building.

Somewhat disappointed, but still confident he would succeed to set off the explosion he had worked so hard for, the two men returned to Tariq's house in Jerusalem; they had been unobserved. All that was necessary was to wait until the Friday evening that week end.

By that particular Friday night everything was ready and the two Palestinians went to the factory and obtained seven of the chairs including the one already prepared but minus its receiver which still had to be fitted. This had been marked by Tariq, when it had been returned, with a tiny slip of wood no larger than a matchstick pushed into the rubber boot of one of its other legs.

The work duly completed by the middle of the night, every-one giving a hand when necessary, all the explosive, detonators and receivers in place with the batteries fully charged and the rubber boots replaced, the innocent looking furniture was returned to the factory premises. A sharp look-out had been kept so that they should not be discovered in their nefarious activity by some innocent, curious observer.

Candor had been the look-out man, travelling on foot to the carpentry shop at the furniture firm's premises. The others followed on in the Citroen van with its load of chairs, after an interval sufficient to allow Candor's arrival to check all was clear first. The return was completed without incident and the three arrived back at Tariq's house, jubilant; everything having gone according to plan.

The following morning Candor and Muhkram left Tariq and went to view the return of the chairs to the Knesset, something Candor could not wait to see. There, Candor watched with satisfaction the renovated furniture being unloaded and the firm's recovery of the temporary seating. He was jubilant as the last of the original chairs disappeared through the entrance into the building, taking with them the means of avenging himself on the Israelis.

The conclusion of his crusade was at hand. He had only to wait until Monday when the Knesset were to sit in debate; then the repercussions of the explosion he would set off would be felt, not only through the Middle East, but the whole world.

With the destruction of the Knesset, both building and Parliament, the Palestinians and their allies would rise up and overthrow their leaderless oppressors. The Jews would be under siege again from the alerting and awakening of their neighbours. This time they would to be defeated and thrown out of Palestine.

The avenging of the death of his beloved wife Candida would then be achieved, he kept telling himself.

He turned to Hussein and laughed, a grim sound in the morning air, his piercing blue eyes vivid in his brown stained face. Hussein looked at him and grabbed his arm, his face drawn.

'Come! We must leave here at once', he demanded in a low insistent voice, Candor's laugh having been noticed by some of the watching people.

'Why? Don't you realize this is the moment I have planned for? All my work finishes here on Monday. Seven chairs for a seven armed Menorah'.

He laughed again. 'A nice touch don't you think?'

'Come' insisted Hussein, 'your eyes. Where are the lenses?'

'Lenses?' then realization of his mistake overriding his euphoria, 'My God. I forgot to put them in. Yes! We must go' he affirmed.

It was unusual for Candor to show concern but he too realized the danger if he was identified. He looked about him with questioning glances but could see nothing to arouse his suspicions that he may have been noticed by any-one who mattered. He followed his accomplice Hussein away from the area and back to the man's home.

∮ CHAPTER 33

Hiram Woolley was white faced. He had to find a phone and quickly; it was no use trying to report what he had just seen to the I.D.F. soldiers on patrol in the area, yet he could see no-one he recognized as being a member of his own organization. He had to be quick or by the time he could alert someone to assist him Candor would be gone. He was sure that was the man he had seen on the other side of the crowd.

He and Patricia had been enjoying his leave. His relief from duty for a few days had been spent visiting relatives and after their devotions had been made at the Synagogue that morning, they had decided to have a walk among other visitors, in the Whol Rose Garden.

It had been some time since he had been in Jerusalem and wondered that, perhaps, his interest in being there was not just the urge to go visiting relations. Possibly he had been subconsciously drawn to where he knew Candor was going to do his utmost to cause trouble, leave or no leave. He had felt restless all morning and he had a strange urge to go to the Knesset. Patricia, unaware of where he was leading her, had happily accompanied him on his way, glad that she had him back with her once again, though he had been reluctant to relay all his dangerous adventure to her, holding back the risks he had taken and of which she still remained unaware.

They saw a small group of people attracted to a strange occurrence; the unloading and exchanging of a large number of chairs at a side entrance of the Knesset building under the keen eyes of a couple of armed soldiers.

'Damn' he said. 'Have you seen a phone near here Pat?'

'No Hiram. What on earth has happened? Tell me why you suddenly want to make a phone call and who to?' she insisted. Then his words frightened her.

'I've just seen Candor. We've got to find a phone. I've got to let the others know he's here'.

'Look' said Aaron Plaistot, 'this is our pigeon. How you fella's got on to it I don't know. But seeing that you do know and want to do something about it, we'll do the undercover work and your lot can stand by to help grab him when we spot him'.

'Oh fine, fine. I'm sure the boys will agree to that. What do you people think we're here for?' complained Zeb Stretton. 'This is a police matter too. The guy's here illegally and though he hasn't committed a crime yet, in our country, we want him as much as you do'.

'Oh yes! Don't forget he 'topped' one of our men, the bastard and we want him for that and to find out what he's cooking up here'. Retorted Aaron.

'Just a minute you two' interrupted Stretton's superior, Isaac Rowsely who, up until then had been quietly listening to the argument. This isn't going to get us anywhere. We should combine forces on this and work together. After all we just want to bring the fellow to the courts to see justice done, personal vendettas are not on, besides which, the man has, as Zeb here says, up until now committed no crimes here we know of yet, except to enter the country illegally. That would mean, as a normal procedure, to hold the man while enquiries were made to his country of origin to see if he was wanted for any crime there; and if we have the proper relations with that country, he would be deported there, unless of course he was to claim political asylum. That's a different kettle of fish all together'.

'But', interrupted Seth Winfild who had been listening to the talk with some frustration, 'haven't you got a law about the prevention of terrorism? For God's sake, that's what the whole episode has been about, hasn't it? The guy's a 'psycho', a mean bastard who kills anybody who gets in his way.

'We're sure he's got explosives and he hasn't brought them all this way for a fire work show. He's going to blow something and somebody to Kingdom come if he gets the chance and talking about enquiries to his country of origin; what do you think I'm here for?

'We want him as much as you do. God knows how many he's topped in Britain. The French tried to catch him because they want him for the murder of several of their citizens, one a woman. What more evidence do you want against him? While you sit here arguing about who's to have the privilege of getting hold of him, he's probably just waiting for the right moment to pull the pin.

'What was he doing near the Knesset anyway? I thought you'd got people there waiting for him to show up?'

'I'm on your side friend', agreed Plaistot, 'we know what the guy's capable of. We can't forget the fact that my chum Mradmoor warned us what the man was after either and for all we know everything could be set up already by him. While we're talking about whose going to have him, he could be, as our British friend here says, just waiting to pull the pin.

'Woolley spotted him and reported to us, the Mossad. He's a terrorist so that means he's our pigeon as I said before, so let's go and find the bastard'.

Irritated by what he thought were petty irrelevancies Plaistot got up in a huff, knocking over his chair. He reached down and picked it up thumping it back in place under the table before going to a large map of

Jerusalem on the wall. The other men followed him there.

Plaistot, though working in a different area of policing was of equal rank to the most senior policeman at the meeting. Though a field man at heart and could not happily stay anchored to a desk, he still possessed the authority, backed by Parliament, to run things his way and he was certain that now was the right time and his, the right way.

He stabbed a huge forefinger at the red square on the map representing the Knesset building.

'How's he going to get explosives in there, or maybe, how's he got them in there and where are they?' he muttered the questions half to himself as much as to the others.

'He can't get explosives in there and hasn't a chance of doing so'. This from another policeman.

Stretton spoke up. 'There's no way into that place if you're carrying anything. You need a pass or passport and the whole place is guarded at every access point'.

'What about staff?'

'The same applies. All the staff are known, all have identification and any bag or whatever they take in is searched. It's the same with the members. Even they can't get in without their passes'.

'O.k. perhaps Candor can't get in himself, but if you study hard enough you can always find ways of doing things. When's the next sitting?' Asked Plaistot, the cigarette bobbing up and down on his bottom lip as he spoke.

'I checked' said Stretton, 'it's Monday afternoon'.

'Hmm, that means, if he's going to do anything at that sitting, he's got to do it quickly' observed Winfild, 'unless of course he's already done it like I said?'

They all turned to look at him.

'Yes, but how? How could he already have done it?' another police officer asked.

'Well, it's apparent he can't get it done between now and Monday afternoon, whatever it is. So, unless he's prepared to wait for the next sitting, he's already carried out his preparations. After all, he's been here a fortnight now. He won't want to hang about much longer will he? For obvious reasons'.

'But, if it's explosives, how did he get them in?' insisted the man again.

'God knows. But what I do know is, the place wants going over with a fine tooth comb' said Plaistot.

'Again I think our friend here is right. I reckon he's just waiting to set it off. How he's done it I don't know as I've said before. The security men usually search the place before every sitting, but this time it's going to be the most thorough ever. By the way', here he turned to Winfild, 'what's your name again?'

'Seth Winfild'.

'Right! I'm sorry I forgot. You'd better keep me company. We'll go and have a word with Woolley; have you met him yet?'

'No I'd like to. He had quite an experience on that plane'

'Yeah, lucky devil. He's only a young man, a novice, but means well. He was only on probation of course but he handled himself o.k. when it came to the crunch.

He shouldn't have been in the damned aeroplane in the first place, but I think he's learned his lesson. He'll be bit more careful in future perhaps'.

Here he turned to the others believing that what he thought needed to be done, was going to be done. 'Right! Make arrangements for close surveillance of the place; plain clothes though, we don't want to scare him off; he's got to come to us, we'd have no chance trying to find out where he's hiding out, so just make sure everybody is clued up and knows what they've got to do, o.k.?'

The meeting broke up, not without some feelings of resentment and umbrage by the more senior officers, at Plaistot's seemingly self imposed leadership. Plaistot and Winfild left together to find Hiram Woolley, whilst those senior police officers went to brief their subordinates.

The Chief Superintendent, Arthur Oakey, had a grim, worried look on his face as he waited to be invited into the Commander's office. Janet, that Superior's secretary, had telephoned him to say that he was wanted urgently by his boss and he believed he knew what it would be about. It certainly wasn't good news he knew, he himself had been greatly disappointed at their failure to apprehend the man Candor and now it was obvious that the man had reached Israel, his believed rendezvous with others who were going to help him in his endeavours. Commander Allfield's secretary popped her head around the door into the annex where the Chief Superintendent sat waiting and said that he was now to enter the Commander's office.

'Come in Arthur' his superior said as he tentatively knocked on the door, 'what have we got in report about this Candor individual? It seems we've had no favourable messages since we apparently gave up in France. What else has happened? It would be nice to know what's going on, nobody seems to want me to know anything!'

'Well sir you are right',said Arthur Oakey, having checked on the whereabouts of the Pomeranian, but couldn't see it which increased his unease, 'we've had nothing passed on in our favour yet about Candor and yes, it is believed he has managed against all our efforts and of course the French, to get where he wanted to get, namely Israel. Also we believe he's going to go to Jerusalem. The authorities there have had some word from their Mossad that the man may have arrived in Jerusalem already. There's been an interesting story put out by some-one in Israel about Candor being monitored on a flight by one of their intelligence men, who hid inside the same aeroplane as the assassin and made the pilot let him off after Candor parachuted out, in one of their airports, Lydda I believe. The tale takes a lot of believing to my mind, how this chap could stay clear of the pilot and Candor seems a bit far fetched to me, but apparently Candor did parachute from the plane while it was still dark and this Mossad man made the pilot land to let him out. Can you believe it?'

'I don't know about believing it Arthur, but if Candor's got there and they, the Mossad, know about it. How the devil did they know? They've certainly stole a march on us, haven't they? The upper people here are not pleased about how we performed our role in this Arthur. Is one of our men still over there with them?'

'Yes sir. Inspector Winfild is acting with the Mossad on our behalf. I have been in touch with him and impressed on him how we need to get first hand reports about what's happening back to us on a regular basis.' He still hadn't spotted the dog though he had made a thorough eye search of the office whilst giving his information.

'Right Arthur'. Here the Commander went to the cupboard holding his whisky and took out two glasses to the disappointment of the Chief Superintendent and the bottle was upended, spilling its contents into both. 'To the confusion of the criminals Arthur' he said, handing over a glass with a large measure of the spirit to Arthur Oakey. He lifted his glass and clinked it against the Chief Superintendent's and drank half the contents of his own glass whilst Arthur had a sip at his. The wary eye of the Commander never left the Chief Super's face as he watched him swallow most of the glass' contents in small sips and then finished his own.

'Right Arthur, don't keep me in the dark. Any reports you get let me have a copy straight away. I've somehow got to keep the upper hierarchy off my back, perhaps confuse them in some way until we have a bit of success with this operation. That's all for now'.

The Chief Superintendent put down his almost empty glass and turned and left the Commander's office, wondering if he might have some better news for his Superior soon. He hoped so and also hoped that the whisky bottle hadn't been refilled before he had to enter that office again. As he passed throught the secretary's office he managed, in a stage whisper, to ask Janet where the Commander's dog was and was told that the Commander's wife, Isobel, had taken the dog to the vet's for some check or other. The Chief Superintendent was disappointed hoping that the animal had possibly been lost, or perhaps something worse, never to again get the chance of its getting its teeth a hold of his trouser leg. But he supposed it couldn't always be good news.

§ CHAPTER 34

'Yes! It was definitely him' said Hiram Woolley after being introduced to Seth Winfild,' I'd swear to it, I'll not forget him ever again. His disguise didn't fool me, he doesn't look much like his photograph, but I couldn't mistake those eyes. Besides his build is also as I remember it. I've given the artist all the information and the picture he produced is pretty good, especially when it's allied to the photograph. I should think any of our men should spot him all right'.

'Good', said Aaron. 'Now we'll go to where you saw him and try and figure out what he was doing there; what he was looking for, o.k.?'

The three men got out of their car near the Bezalel Academy of Art. Aaron was determined to walk the eight hundred or so metres to the Wohl Rose Garden and to the Knesset. They crossed the Sderot Ben Zvi road to the Ruppin road and approached the building from the South side. Every male face they saw was scrutinized and every yard examined, until they came to the spot where Hiram Woolley said he had seen Candor.

They walked to the exact position where he had stood and looked around. There was nothing to indicate what Candor had been watching or looking for and there were still quite a number of people about.

'You say this is where he stood; the exact spot? Questioned Aaron.

'Yes! Exactly there. He was watching the workmen moving furniture; a load of chairs'.

Aaron turned in a flash. 'You mean there were workmen going into the building? Why didn't you say so before?'

'They were only moving some chairs in and out. I didn't think there was any significance to it at the time and didn't even remember until this minute'.

'What do you mean, moving chairs in and out? What was happening exactly? His tone was stern.

'I don't know. Er—well, they seemed to be taking some chairs in and some chairs out. Exchanging them, it seemed to me. Why? I don't know'.

'Right we'll find out why. Come on'.

Enquiries were made about the chair exchange and the name and address of the firm involved was obtained. After the matter of the exchange had been reported to the police headquarters all the chairs were examined by them but they seemed innocent enough.

'Why would he be interested in this lot of chairs being moved in?' Aaron asked Hiram.

'No idea. He seemed to be talking to someone by his side and kept looking at the work being carried out and then they left. I only saw them for a couple of minutes. They moved away and I tried to follow but lost them'.

'Hmm' growled Aaron, 'it sounds very bloody fishy to me'.

Aaron requested permission to remove one of the chairs for a more thorough examination and permission was granted on condition that it was returned immediately afterwards.

The three men went with it to the police laboratory where one of the civilian carpenters who worked for the laboratory took it to pieces, stripping it down to its individual parts. The bits and pieces were examined thoroughly but gave no clue as to why Candor and his accomplice had been interested in its exchange earlier that day.

The three were baffled and leaving the carpenter to reassemble the article of furniture, made off to the premises of the firm who had been responsible for the renovation of the whole batch.

Their conversation with the manager told them no more than they already knew. They accepted his assurance that the real reason for their visit would remain undisclosed. Ostensibly they were partners in a furniture retail outlet looking for possible suppliers and as such they would be allowed to talk to the workers, asking them questions about their jobs, pretending interest about their abilities and their training.

They examined some of the products and made enquiries about the staff which was of mixed race and religion. Almost all of the Jews were absent as it was their Sabbath.

As a matter of routine, to make sure nothing was left to chance, they again chatted with some of the workers about their jobs, skills and past experience in the furniture industry, trying to glean any information they could. They had no reason to doubt the legitimacy of the business and its employees when they were through, except for one worker who gave Plaistot some cause for concern. A Palestinian who had been set on as a labourer a fortnight before and who hadn't come to work that morning as he was expected to do. A half day was worked on Saturdays, but only when they were busy.

Aaron obtained the man's name and address and decided to check both before accepting that the firm was in the clear. They went to the man's address, or what he had supplied the firm with as his address; the place did not exist.

The searched the area to make sure but other residents in the area knew nothing of the man or the house they were interested in.

The three hurried back to the factory but, since they left, it had closed for the week end as was its practice at Saturday lunch time. It would not re-open until Monday morning at eight o'clock.

Aaron cursed loudly but knew that even if the place had still been open, they could probably have obtained no more information on the absent workman. It was doubtful if the manager or any of his staff had checked on the man's background. After all, they knew that as a labourer he would not have to produce indentures of apprenticeship or papers of any kind proving a skill he did not need, but now there could be conjecture about his intentions seeing that he had given the firm false evidence of his identity.

Aaron and Seth left Hiram and returned to base to try and figure out what significance the chairs could have in the mystery. Hiram went to the hotel in which he and Patricia were staying. Patricia was none too pleased with Hiram for having left her that morning after phoning in his story about seeing Candor. He had been absent since then, leaving her to her own devices. She became interested as he explained what had happened and about Aaron's belief that the answer to Candor's visit to the Knesset lay somehow with the chairs.

Monday morning found Aaron, Seth and Hiram attending an early emergency meeting of police and I.D.F. officers to discuss and arrange the defence of the Knesset and the safety of its members at the start of the Sitting of Parliament due to begin at eleven a.m. that day.

The meeting had begun early at seven a.m. and by nine thirty a.m. every officer and subordinate knew their position in the city in which they had to be and their role in the day's proceedings. By ten a.m. all those positions had been filled, Seth remaining at base to help correlate information from the 'field'.

Aaron and Hiram were making a round of the Mossad agents under Aaron's supervision to check all were armed and alert for any signs of suspicious activity and to receive any reports they may have. They received no sightings of any-one behaving in the least suspicious.

Eventually the pair arrived in Zion Square, Aaron still trying to figure out what the chair exchange could have meant to Candor. He knew there must be a link between the terrorist, the chairs and the missing workman, who had again been absent from work that morning. Aaron had checked with the firm earlier to find out and had not been surprised when informed of the man's absence. He was still worried and felt frustrated. Ever since he had taken up the chase in Thiers, France; Candor had been that one step in front.

He threw the cigarette butt down with a curse, spitting out a tiny piece of tobacco from between his lips into his handkerchief. He wiped his mouth, replaced the gaudy square of cloth and absent mindedly took out a cigarette packet, extracted one and lit it without thinking. He blew the smoke from the corner of his mouth without removing the cigarette. This time however, he thought that they may possibly be just that one step ahead of the assassin for a change.

Hiram touched his elbow.

'They're coming up from the Post Office. It's them all right'.

Aaron leaned forward to look in the direction his excited partner had said. At first he could not identify anyone as being like Hiram had described on the Saturday. Then he noticed the two figures, dressed rather shabbily, with the white head cover typical of some Palestinian men.

The two Mossad agents turned and took a few steps towards the Anna Ticho House and waited for the two men to arrive in the square.

'Damn', said Aaron, 'if he catches sight of me, he'll remember me from the cafe where I first got a close look at him. You watch for him Hiram and follow him when he turns up and for God's sake don't lose him. I'll try and keep close behind you'.

'Right! Are you going to call up reinforcements?' Hiram asked, his heart beating faster, the adrenalin charging his arteries. Before he could get an answer the two 'Palestinians' arrived at the junction and watched for a gap in the traffic before crossing the Jaffa road towards the pedestrian restricted Ben Yehuda Mall.

Hiram did the same, careful not to lose the two men in the crowd of peopled milling around the various cafes, or just wandering about in no fixed direction. He was aware of Aaron following on behind, but someone he was not aware of, was the woman who had been seated at one of the tables under a cafe's striped canvas awning which protcted its customers from the sun's rays.

Patricia had just put her coffee cup down in the saucer when she saw Hiram wandering past a few yards away and he seemed to be behaving in an odd and furtive manner. She got up to call to him when she saw someone else she knew but to whom she had never been introduced. The big man Aaron 'something' she thought; 'Yes! Hiram told me about him'. He too was behaving oddly. She assumed he was following Hiram and that her husband was aware of the fact.

She thought their behaviour was tantalizing; they not noticing her and determined to see what was happening herself and followed the big man. He was the easiest to keep sight of among all the wandering people who seemed to her to have no fixed destination in mind.

The two 'Palestinians' left the Mall, turning left on to King George Street. Hiram and Aaron, the latter having been busy radioing to the other agents what was happening, but telling them to stay at their posts, hurried on to catch up to within a closer distance of the two supposed Palestinians.

Hiram realized that about three hundred to four hundred metres further down the street there was a right turn which led almost directly to the Knesset, less than a kilometre away. His pulse began to race and he had a quick glance behind to ensure Aaron was near. He still didn't see his wife amid the pedestrians and who was almost directly behind his colleague.

He turned the corner and saw the two men; one he believed to be Palestinian and the other Candor, dressed in disguise, both about a hundred metres in front of him. They were stood together, one apparently handing something to the second man. To Hiram it was difficult to see what at that distance, but it did appear to be a radio and tape player of the small portable type used by many young people, popularly known as a 'Walkman'.

The one whom he was sure was Candor, stepped to the pavement edge and did something with the small box as though trying to get a better reception signal, turning the thing in his hands and holding it away from his body.

'What the hell's he playing at?' Aaron's voice grated in his ear as he came up behind him.

'He seems to be having trouble receiving a station signal on the Walkman he's got' answered Hiram.

'Uh, we're sure it is him I suppose?' grunted Aaron Plaistot, blowing a cloud of smoke over Hiram's shoulder.

'Of course I'm sure. Shall we nab him?'

'Not yet' growled the big agent. 'Let's just see what he's up to'.

They watched the two men for a few seconds and then Hiram grabbed the big man's arm.

'Just a minute' he almost shouted, 'what's he doing searching for a radio station and he hasn't even got the head phones on. The other guys wearing those and the lead can't be plugged in. Look at the distance between them'.

'What do you mean?' questioned Aaron, then realization dawned.

'My God you're right. It's not a bloody receiver at all, it's a transmitter'.

The last part of Aaron's outburst was almost lost to Hiram as the big man darted past him, jumping into the roadway to avoid the pedestrians and narrowly missed being mown down by a furious motorist on the legitimate motorway who swerved aside to avoid him; he running towards the two men.

He shouted to them to stay were they were, reaching for the revolver in the shoulder holster under his jacket and trying to give a radio message at the same time.

The pedestrians between the two pairs looked towards the running agents in amazement and alarm, wondering what the commotion was about as the big man and his companion, both waving revolvers, came charging down the roadway.

Not far behind them, a young woman, well dressed and high heeled, followed; but still not seen by Hiram who was too busy trying to keep up with his companion.

The agent's quarry, taken by surprise at the big man's shout, turned immediately and fled towards the Hechal Slomo and Great Synagogue where they turned into Ramban Street to the Rehavia, but which again led towards the Knesset.

It suddenly dawned on Hiram that the two terrorists were having difficulty transmitting a signal powerful enough to fire whatever explosion they had set up, due to the distance they were away from the receiver or perhaps because of the buildings between that and the transmitter. The nearer they could get to the Knesset before they were stopped, the greater the chance of their success he thought.

Aaron discarded the radio at the feet of a surprised, somewhat angry, Jewish matron who had been standing open mouthed watching the strange, huge apparition bearing down on her in hot pursuit of the two shabbily dressed men who had almost knocked her over a few seconds before.

In an attempt to intimidate the two and bring about their surrender, Aaron fired a shot over the heads of the startled onlookers which caused more panic amongst them, opening up a path for the two running agents. The fleeing pair immediately split up, one turning towards the German Colony area. Aaron slowed, pointed after him and shouted to Hiram, 'Get him!'

But as they both arrived at the corner he staggered and clutched his chest as, simultaneously, there was a crack of a shot. Blood oozed out between his fingers and he slumped down on to the pavement edge.

'Get Candor', he managed to shout at Hiram, the words more of a groan than a command. But his associate felt as though they were a shout, even above the cries of the frightened bystanders and reluctantly he left him to continue the pursuit.

He couldn't be sure who had fired the shot, whether it had come from the side street leading to the Van Leer Foundation which one of the terrorists had taken or whether Candor had been the culprit. He didn't see his wife, having at last caught up with the action, squat down to look at the big agent who was slipping into unconsciousness.

'Get an ambulance' she shouted at one young couple, frozen into frightened immobility, the girl holding a hand over her mouth while the young man, wide eyed, stared at the agents life blood ebbing away from the wound in his chest.

Patricia jumped to her feet and poked him in the stomach. 'Get an ambulance' She screamed at him and he turned away running towards a telephone box.

Patricia then saw the fallen agent's revolver lying half covered by the wounded man's leg and she scooped it up and dashed off after Hiram.

Candor cursed as he saw the young agent in pursuit. He had seen Hussein Muhkram stop around the corner of the side street and take the revolver out of his jacket pocket. When he heard the shot, he realized that one of the agents would have been hit, Hussein didn't miss at that range; but he knew also that he wouldn't hang around to see the result.

He, himself was unarmed; he had refused the gun offered by Muhkram but now regretted having done so. He couldn't understand why the transmitter hadn't done its job. He had left it switched on since he'd heard the big man's shout and become aware of the pursuit by the two men.

He was now only about three quarters of a kilometre from the Knesset, but as yet had heard no sound of an explosion. He had to do something though, about the other man who was chasing him waving a pistol, so he stepped quickly around the next corner on the left and waited.

Hiram came to a halt at the junction, swallowed and took a deep breath to calm himself. He stepped around the angle of the building, the revolver held forward in both hands. He immediately received a blow under the left kneecap from Candor's kick and screamed in agony as the patella was torn out of position. Another blow delivered a split second after the kick, by the edge of

Candor's hand to his wrists, dislodged the weapon from his grasp as he fell to the ground in considerable pain.

Candor reached down and took up the revolver from beside the fallen man, taking a grip on the butt as he began to straighten up to fire, his intention obvious.

'No!' The word was screamed out by the young woman who had just appeared from around the corner.

Candor, pointed the gun at the agent's head. There was the deafening report of a pistol and a bullet whizzed past Candor's ear; he spun round to face the intrusion as a second shot followed the first and a low velocity, large calibre bullet slammed into his right shoulder, paralyzed the arm causing him to lose his grip on the revolver which fell to the floor. Almost immediately another bullet from the woman's weapon hit him on the shin shattering the bone and he collapsed to the ground unable to prevent his cry of agony at the intense pain of the two wounds.

Patricia stood there, feet slightly apart, the revolver gripped in her right hand which was clasped by her left, her finger on the trigger, ready to fire again. Candor looked up at the woman who had just shot him and gasped in surprise as he began to slip into unconsciousness from the pain and loss of blood. He couldn't believe what he was seeing. The young woman saw that he was not now dangerous and stepped forward to pick up the other revolver and shouted to the people who were appearing, wondering what was happening, to stay back.

'Candy,' he muttered and again, 'Candy why?' and reached out a bloody left hand to her, then lost consciousness altogether.

Patricia heard him say the name, puzzled at what she was hearing, but turned to her husband who was still lying on the pavement clutching at his knee and moaning, his face grey. She did her best to make him comfortable by which time two members of the I.D.F. had arrived. They disarmed Patricia of the two revolvers she was keeping by her side and one radioed for an ambulance for the two wounded men. Patricia left her husband for a few minutes to go and look at the man she had shot; trying to ignore the blood, she gazed at his swarthy features with the grey and black moustache and for a few seconds he opened his eyes, looking at her. He murmured something which sounded again like 'why Candy? but she could not make out for sure if she had heard correctly what he said and then one of the I.D.F. men took her arm and moved her away.

Something about the man had seemed familiar, but it was his eyes which fascinated her when he had just looked at her. It seemed she had seen those eyes before, but could not remember where; and the name he had called, she had definitely heard that name before, it was her father's pet name for her mother.

She went back to her husband. 'Are you all right Hiram? The ambulance will be here in a moment or two. Hiram, he called me Candy; that was my mother's pet name which my father used for her. Why did he call me Candy Hiram?' She started to shake and suddenly burst into tears, beginning to feel the shock after all that had happened and not being able to pin it down to a cogent idea. The idea that perhaps she had behaved incorrectly although not to have done what she did would have meant the loss of her beloved Hiram.

'Don't cry Pat. You did a great thing; you saved my life and he deserved what he got. He was a terrorist, a killer and would certainly have killed me if you hadn't stopped him'. This only served to increase Patricia's sobbing and the tears flowed freely from her. Hiram reached and took her hand in his but she was not easily consoled. She stole another glance across at the prone figure on the edge of the pavement, then perplexed, the tears destroying her make-up, she asked again, 'Why did he call me Candy Hiram?'

§ CHAPTER 35

'What's going to happen to them now?' asked one of the Mossad agents about Aaron and Hiram at the next meeting to discuss the events of the previous Monday.

'Oh, they'll both be spending quite a time in hospital. They've got the bullet out of Aaron's chest and although he's not too well they say he'll be fine in a few weeks. Hiram's had an operation as well on his knee cap. He was lucky he didn't get shot'.

'Yeah, and what about that Candor bloke; what did you say his proper name is?'

'Well that British copper Seth Winfild, says it's Miles Scholland, and I bet you don't know what? that's Hiram's wife's maiden name; Scholland', he said conspiratorially.

'Yeah, I heard something about there being some sort of a connection with Hiram's wife but it's being toned down. They don't want to make a big thing out of it, for the wife's sake'.

'Yes, and what about this Candor guy, any idea what's happening to him?'

'Oh he's covered in bandages and some of these new fangled splints and you know what? He's only come up with the notion that he and a friend were minding their own business when they got chased by another couple of fellas who were waving guns about. He reckons he doesn't know how Aaron got shot, neither him nor his friend were armed, they were, just as I say, minding there own business.

'Anyhow, that idea isn't going to make much headway. They gave him a good wash in the hospital and all the staining came off; he's definitely a Westerner, not Palestinian. Also they found a transmitter behind a wall where the shooting took place and it's got Candor's prints all over it, so he wasn't minding his own business. He was up to no good all right, how he expected to get away with that story no-one knows'.

'Yes' said the other man 'he's got no passport either, at least they didn't find one on him and he won't tell where he was living and who with, or how he got here. He's definitely in the country without going through the proper channels, so he's an illegal immigrant. That British policeman reckons he's wanted back in England for crimes committed there; several murders I believe and apparently the French want to get their hands on him also for several murders of their citizens. I reckon England will get him though. They've got an extradition agreement with us, so I think the French will be unlucky'.

'I suppose everybody will have to wait for the criminal to get well before they can bring him to court, won't they?'

'I believe they're going to hold a special hearing and there decide what's going to happen to him. Some say he'll be extradited whether he's well or not. I think they just want to get rid of him, he's a big embarrassment to this country apparently and I suppose, to his own, although I expect they'll want to have him back as soon as possible'.

Despite the aid of the two sticks Hiram shuffled with difficulty through the spring loaded door of the private ward, holding it back with his elbow and shoulder, trying not to let the rubber tipped sticks slip on the tiles as he did so. He didn't want to finish up in a heap on the floor again as had once happened, not helping his injury in the process.

Eventually accomplishing the feat, he readjusted the crutches under each arm and swinging the injured leg clear of the floor he 'dot and carried' himself over to the bed containing the supine figure of his associate, Aaron Plaistot.

The wan features of the big Mossad agent relaxed into a smile at the sight of his limping subordinate. He was weak from his recent escapade, narrowly averting death and he had just been moved from the Intensive Care Unit into the single bed cubicle. A couple of glass containers stood on the floor at the side of the bed, both partly filled. One collected fluid via a tube, retained by a suture to the skin, from his chest cavity. The other similarly collected urine from his bladder via the urethra.

Another tube, inserted into a vein in the back of one hand, fed him with a saline drip.

He looked very ill.

'Hello Hiram' he managed to say and waved his unencumbered hand limply in the direction of an easy chair by the bed.

'Take a seat lad'.

'I'll sit here thanks' said Hiram. He hooked the upright wooden chair at the side of the patient's cupboard by the top of one of its legs with a crutch handle wrapped round it and drew it to where he could sit and see comfortably the man in the bed.

He sat down carefully, thrusting the injured, plastered leg out stiffly in front of him. 'I'd never get back up out of an easy chair' He said at last.

His face had a worried look, but Aaron, even through his discomfort, could tell it wasn't just from the pain of the wounded leg. He had other troubles which he, Aaron, could only guess at but nevertheless had an opinion about and which he kept to himself.

'How are you Hiram?' he asked.

'Not too bad thanks. At least I can get about, after a fashion. What about you? It was good to hear they'd discharged you from the I.C.U. That must be a good sign, musn't it!'

'Yeah, sure'. Aaron carefully shifted his weight on the bed. 'I'm dying for a smoke Hiram, he managed to gasp. You wouldn't have any cigarettes would you?'

'No, I don't smoke you know. Besides, it wouldn't do your wound any good Aaron. Best to wait for a bit, don't you think?'

'That's what they keep telling me. It's not easy, lying here with nothing to do and wanting a bloody smoke'.

There was silence for a minute, then, 'How's Patricia Hiram?' He asked, concern showing in his voice.

Hiram shook his head sadly. His face reflected his misery and distress. He didn't answer for a moment, his thoughts far away.

'I don't know what to do for the best, every time she comes to see me she cries all the while she's here. It's been a big shock to her to find out it was her father who was doing all those terrible things. She can't cope with it and she of course regrets shooting him now she knows who he really is. She seems to blame me for that, as if I shouldn't have been there, though she hasn't said as much. She wants to go home for a bit to her Aunt's in England, she says; I don't know what the outcome will be, its perhaps best that she does that. Have a quiet holiday, I think the publicity she got didn't do her any good'.

'Anyway' said Aaron, 'that's nonsense about you being to blame, you didn't know who he really was'. The effort of talking and the strain of moving, even of his head added to his discomfort.

'I should have known that Candor was only a pseudonym. I should have checked'. Hiram shook his head dejectedly.'I don't know what I would have done if I had known who he really was'.

'Even I didn't realize the connection' Aaron said, 'I knew his real name was Scholland, but the name was never used, I never heard any-one mention it. It was always 'Candor'. I didn't know Patricia's maiden name you see, it never crossed my mind to ask. I mean why should it? Anyway, you can't blame yourself'. He stopped talking and got his breath back. 'His true identity was revealed to me by that English policeman; Seth Winfild. You were on leave at the time so you never got to know. He was never referred to as anything else but Candor. Apparently he had been in one of the British Services at one time, That's where he gained all those killing skills; they taught him; the Forces, Royal Marines I believe'.

'That doesn't excuse me not finding out. 'Never assume anything' I was once taught. 'Check and recheck'. I could have prevented her from being there. She would never have seen him and'—he didn't complete the sentence and shifted uneasily in the chair.

'Look Hiram, it's not going to do either of you any good to keep thinking about it. Somehow you've got to get it out of your minds. Now the bastard's been extradited it's in somebody else's hands, it's their problem, the British. It doesn't change the fact that he was a killer, an evil man who caused a lot of people a lot of grief. Never forget those facts and another thing Patricia has got to remember; you can't choose your parents. Apparently it was her mother's death, a mistake by the Israeli defence force, us, you might say; our responsibility which caused his change of character but that doesn't really excuse his behaviour in any way'.

Aaron closed his eyes, the effort of talking had wearied him, draining his strength; he breathed in quick short breaths, almost as if he was asthmatic. His face, drawn and pale, reminded Hiram how ill the man was, how near to death he had been and how lucky he was to have been Hospitalized as soon as he was, which to a great extent was due to Hiram's wife following them and being on hand at the time he was shot.

'I'm sorry Aaron. I shouldn't be troubling you with my worries, you've got plenty of your own. You get some rest'.

He got to his feet with some difficulty and looked down at the figure which now seemed so vulnerable. 'Thanks for the talk. I'll see you again after I've been to England with Patricia, if we go. They're going to give me sick leave if I want it, to go with her'.

'Yes lad, come and see me again after your leave'. The voice was strained, almost a whisper.

Hiram limped away, the rubber tips of his crutches squeaking on the polished parquet floor. He again successfully negotiated the spring loaded door and looked back to the man on the bed before inexpertly, but carefully, making his way along the corridor to his own cubicle.

The two small cases, ready packed with his few belongings and bundled into his cases by his day nurse, stood by the neatly made bed and he glanced at his watch; he had only a few more minutes to wait for his father to arrive to drive him home to his house where, if necessary his mother would nurse him if Patricia couldn't.

He dropped awkwardly down on to the hard wooden chair, a sad, wretched figure. Hiram had become genuinely fond of his superior, especially after hearing about Aaron's concern for the well being of Patricia; keeping a check on her safety while he, her young husband's whereabouts had been in some doubt after being seen boarding the old D.C.3 at la Malouesse. This had been reported to him by one of Aaron's other colleagues.

He fidgeted and sighed, wondering if his and Patricia's life would ever get back to the caring, loving relationship it had been, now that she knew her father's history. He moved and sat on the bed edge, trying to put his doubts about their future out of his head as he had a thousand times before. Trying to achieve some peace of mind, some comfort, by forcing himself to think of other things.

The recent events had left its mark on him; he was despondent and easily irritated. He had difficulty turning his mind to anything but that which he so wanted to forget. If he could only remember things as they had been, the happiness he and Pat had known, yet try as he might, he once again found himself being tortured by the reality of what had happened.

Sometimes he felt that nothing mattered any more; nothing was as important as that which had almost devastated his life. The advice of family and friends, so freely propounded, fell on deaf ears, any reaction usually caustic. How was he and Patricia going to put this behind them? To get to how they had been, before Candor's true identity had become known to them, especially Patricia, how could she cope now? How could she begin to understand the reasons for her father's actions? She had been but a small child when her father's change in character had begun, when her mother had died. How could she relate to her father now?

Absent mindedly, he pulled repetitively at the elastic bracelet of his wrist watch and he forced himself to think of his companion, Aaron Plaistot and how the man had outwitted the terrorist, Candor. Hiram could not think of that man as father-in-law; the term seemed so absurd considering the truth of the man's activities.

Unknown to anyone, Aaron, apparently at the suggestion of the English policeman, Seth Winfild, had ordered the removal of all the restored chairs from the Knesset. They had been exchanged again for the temporary set during the very early hours of that Monday morning. The only civilian to know of the plan was the manager of the firm whose employees had worked on the permanent set.

The factory had been opened after midnight and the usual temporary replacements brought out of store and loaded into a large military van. The exchange had taken place under guard; not even they knowing what was happening. Just making sure that none could observe the occurrence should anyone be in the vicinity at that late hour.

The van, backed up to the service doors, had the gap between it and the doors cloaked off with a large tarpaulin. Only the driver and two members of the I.D.F. who did the work, besides Aaron, the firm's manager and the Chief of Security of the Knesset and of course Seth Winfild who'd suggested it, knew of the exchange. The suspect furniture, transported to a warehouse in Ramallah, was eventually to be dismantled, item by item.

Only after the events of that black Monday, when Aaron was in the Intensive Care Unit of the same hospital as himself, was Hiram informed of the exchange by Seth Winfild, before the Englishman returned to London. Hiram had been a little sneaped at first but soon admitted to himself the necessity of the precautions Aaron had taken and his reticence about the matter.

His mind wandered again, away from the subject of the chairs, back to that of his wife's unhappy despondency. 'Damn the chairs. Damn Candor. Damn everything'. He almost shouted the expletives and stood up, not without difficulty, from the bed. As he did so he saw the figure of his father appear at the glass door of his private room. He turned away so that the tears in his eyes should not be seen. He took out a tissue from his trouser pocket and blew his nose, then reached for the two crutches leaning on the bed side.

'Hello son. Ready to go?'

'Hello dad. Yes, let's get away from here. I don't suppose Patricia's in the car, is she?'

'No son she doesn't seem fit enough to go anywhere yet. It will take time and lots of it I'm thinking before she can make sense of what's happened. I feel so sorry for the girl'.

Hiram just grunted, he'd not expected her to come to the hospital now he was being discharged, but was nonetheless, disappointed.

He leaned on the crutches and made his way to the door. His father carrying the cases, put one down and opened the door for him and he passed through. Hiram looked down the corridor towards the room of Aaron Plaistot, then turned and made off towards the exit, the rubber tips of the crutches squeaking on the polished parquet floor again.

Suddenly, hearing a shout he looked up and there was Patricia running towards him. He stopped and she threw her arms around him, 'Oh Hiram darling, I'm so sorry. Please forgive me' and she burst into tears. Hiram suddenly extremely happy but afraid of falling over, wrapped one arm with a crutch around her shoulders. Was it possible that things were going to be all right after all, he wondered.

⸸ EPILOGUE

It was Monday evening. The small Jewish boy had recently celebrated his twelfth birthday. One of his presents was a radio controlled model aircraft which was powered by a small I.C. engine. His father had instructed him in the operation of the expensive gift and gained as much pleasure from it as the boy, upon whom he kept a watchful eye.

This particular evening they had taken the model away from the built up area of their home town, Ramallah. All employment for the day was finished and the open ground near a large, Government warehouse was ideal for flying the model, the father thought, especially as there was a fairly flat piece of ground for the model to land on.

The pair prepared the plane for its first flight, filling the fuel tank with the special alcohol fuel and setting the controls of the hand held transmitter. New batteries had been clipped into their little compartment and the plane was ready. The father had purchased a special gadget for spinning the propeller to start the engine without using a finger to do so, a method not without some danger to the digit.

The father spun the starter and the plane's engine coughed into life. He placed the model on the ground, pointing it into wind and allowed it to move off, bouncing across the parched, stunted grass. He moved the elevator control on the transmitter and as the little aircraft lifted from the clinging herbage, it accelerated away, rapidly gaining speed and altitude.

The father gave the instrument to the boy and he took it carefully, proud to be entrusted with its operation. He gingerly moved the little control levers, first one, then another, all the time under the supervising eye of his parent. After a time the boy became a little more adventurous, increasing the speed or the altitude of the model, as instructed by his father. Then carefully making it roll as he had seen the full size prototype behave in films or on the television.

Suddenly, with the aircraft in level flight there was no response to the movement of the levers on the transmitter and the boy passed the controller to his parent, who had become somewhat concerned.

The plane ignored all signals sent by the controller and was moving further and further away; the worried pair running in pursuit, the father moving the control levers in rapid, random jerks. All to no avail, the plane was becoming smaller and smaller in perspective, heading to the old warehouse, about half a kilometre away. When it reached the building, it had gained enough height to pass over it. The frantic father, losing ground in the chase, tried changing the transmitter frequency and moved the cyclic stick on the instrument to operate the aileron control to turn the aircraft.

At the second frequency change the man and boy were stunned into immobility by a colossal detonation. The ground seemed to move beneath their feet as the building in front of them swelled outwards, the walls cracked and the roof lifted into the air releasing a blast of flame. The walls then leaned towards the startled pair, collapsed with a roar and the whole warehouse was hidden in a billowing cloud of dust and smoke.

The man clasped the boy to himself, shielding him from the falling debris, unable to comprehend what had happened. As the light breeze slowly cleared the area, all that could be seen was a huge mound of stone and dust and the odd remaining flames of some combustible material. Of the model aircraft there was no sign.

The small white overall coated figure, with the name badge clipped to the breast of the overall and a stethoscope placed around the neck, carrying a tray with a cloth covering some article on it, walked slowly but purposely along the corridor towards the man in police uniform seated outside one of the private rooms in the hospital. It was well after midnight and the officer was having difficulty in staying awake, but nevertheless turned on hearing the steps of the figure coming down the corridor.

The man, fairly small in stature, swarthy, blue eyed with brown hair, with the small tray in his right hand, approached the door of the room behind which was the bed in which Miles Scholland lay in a fitful sleep. The officer didn't get up, but wearily signalled for the man's identification. The white coated figure just pushed the name badge with his left hand at the sleepy officer who just waved his hand at him in acceptance of his identity. He opened the door and quietly went in, over towards the stand which carried the drip container. It didn't take more than a few seconds to empty the syringe's contents into the container and he then turned and walked out. 'He's sleeping, I'll not waken him just now. I'll come again later'. The officer yawned and tried to find a more comfortable position on the seat he was sitting on. He had great difficulty keeping awake, the boredom of his job as guard of the patient/prisoner was mind numbing.

The man in the white overall coat passed back up the corridor with no haste and the officer lost interest in the interruption.

Later the following morning, at about six o'clock a nurse arrived at the room to check on the inmate. After a quick look at the man in the bed she slammed the emergency crash button and there was a sudden change in the quietness of the area. Three people came tearing down the corridor with a resuscitation trolley and burst into the room ignoring the startled guard who held the door open to see what was happening. The threesome's efforts were however in vain, Miles Scholland was quite dead.

At the enquiry it was established that the terrorist Candor alias Miles Scholland, had died of a heart attack. However a piece of paper had been found on the side table with two words written on it and about which no-one knew was their significance. They said. 'For Adam'.

'What's all this about the man Candor being dead?' The Commander asked. He looked annoyed, thought the Chief Superintendent who was not surprised.

'Well sir' his subordinate explained, 'after he was sent back to us, he was in rather a bad way, medically and was therefore hospitalized so that he could recover and be fit enough for trial for all his misdeeds'.

'I know that' said the Commander, 'but how did he die? What was the reason, wasn't he under guard in his cubicle?'

'Well yes sir his cubicle did have a guard outside with instructions to only let in medical people, but at an early hour of the morning along came this bogus doctor; at least we think he must have been bogus, but he had a correct identity tag and he had some medication for the patient. He was allowed by the guard to enter the cubicle and after a short period, he left and Candor was, in the morning, found by a nurse, one who had been put in charge of him that is, er,—found to be dead of a heart attack. The body was subjected to a post-mortem and was found to contain a large quantity of some drug, cocaine I think, or was it morphine? Whatever; it was that which was believed to have caused the heart attack which killed him'.

'Very unsatisfactory, Arthur. What about this guard, was he interrogated? How did he let some-one in who was bogus?'

'Well sir, the 'bogus' doctor had the correct identity badge on him, the guard swears it was a pukka er—genuine badge and he had no reason to query it or prevent the 'doctor' from seeing to the patient'

'Hm'. Muttered the Commander' This sort of thing doesn't give the general public, or our superiors much confidence in our ability to carry out our responsibilities, Arthur'. He went to the cupboard, to the distress of the Chief Superintendent and opened it, brought out two glasses and the whisky bottle. 'Ah well, Arthur, he was a ne'er-do-well, a criminal and a murderer, perhaps we've done the world a service by allowing this to happen and we'll drink to that. What the repercussions will be is anybody's guess. We'll just have to man the ramparts and keep our heads down for a while'.

He poured out a large quantity of the spirit into each glass and passed one to the Chief Superintendent. 'Confusion and consternation to the criminal Arthur' he said clinking his glass with his subordinate's. 'Down the hatch Arthur and your good health. I don't think in this case we need to worry about our pensions'.

THE END

Lightning Source UK Ltd.
Milton Keynes UK
UKOW030756121012

200474UK00001B/3/P